Also by Michael P Brawn

Pangur Ban
Flaming Margarita
TENSE
Wollemi Dreaming
Killara

THE WOLLEMI

MICHAEL P BRAWN

Published 2019

Second Edition 2021

Third Edition 2023

First Printing 2019

ISBN 978-0-6480912-4-0

Published by Ashbourne Publishing

ashbourne.publishing1@gmail.com

DEDICATION

This book is dedicated once again to my lovely wife, confidant, partner, and guide, as well as my editor and chief critic, Louise. She helped and supported me throughout the writing of this book.

Without your supportive comments and advice, this book would never have been completed.

CONTENTS

INTRODUCTION

Although the basic concept for this story came to me many years earlier, while travelling through the Wollemi National Park, I came to write this book mainly whilst staying in Settlers Road, Wisemans Ferry, on the very edge of the wilderness. The novel is not exactly sci-fi or strictly as fantasy, although there is an overlap. To me, it is a bit like a peculiarly Australian attempt at magical realism. This second edition was triggered by some very frank feedback from my friend Mihajlo Starcevic; no pain, no gain, I guess.

Anyway, this is the basic idea: If the Wollemi Forest can hide the Wollemi pines for over two hundred million years, and keep them safe, then what else might be out there?

RUPTURE

When the call came, Harry Soames did not pick up immediately. A sixth sense told him, *'This is your last moment of calm'*, and when he did pick up, he wished he hadn't. The voice on the other end of the line was calm, unhurried. He knew the man's voice — German accent.

"It's time."

"You're sure? It's not just a flareup?"

"It's happening. I am seeing it with my own eyes. A girl's gone missing."

"Can we be sure the threat is real? We know so little for sure."

"It's happening, that's for sure. Reports from all over. The veil is weakening."

Soames felt his guts begin to twist in the pit of his stomach. Was this truly, as the protocol seemed to suggest, the sum of all fears?

"We must find some way of protecting the veil, threat or no threat."

"OK."

"If it is a threat, then the survival of humanity itself might be at risk. If not, then it's the survival of the Wollemi." Homes felt sick. "How many sightings? What have you actually witnessed?"

"Only one changeling here so far. More around the world, I'm told, and here and there, the veil is failing. I've been monitoring it."

"We may still have time. Get ready your end. We will need your boys, old friend. No one knows the forest like Jack, and Jerry has his unique skills too. I will call our people together tomorrow here at the CDC."

"Understood. No problem. I will call the boys."

"This is the moment we've been dreading Max." The line crackled a little. *Probably sunspot activity.*

"It's been more than twenty-five years, Harry. We always knew this moment would come. Seems it's finally arrived."

Involuntarily, Harry Soames let out a long sigh.

"Talk tomorrow." The line went dead.

There was one more duty to perform, one more trigger to pull. This was it, though. Once he made his call, right or wrong, wheels would be set in motion. Actions would be taken that could not be undone. Venerable National Agencies would dust off long-made plans. Things would start to happen.

Harry paused, martialling his thoughts. At last, he made his decision. It was time to initiate an old protocol, *the* protocol. The only one that mattered now. Harry Soames sat at his desk and logged into the Centre for Disease Control's secure network. It was with a growing sense of unreality, dissociation perhaps, that he triggered the protocol and sent the pre-programmed message.

He sat back, waiting for the phone to ring. Who would be first, he wondered, the Department of Defence or the White House? The White House had it by a whisker. Soames picked up the phone. At the same moment, the call waiting symbol lit up on his screen. It was Defence.

'You snooze, you lose.' Harry thought to himself.

"Harry Soames speaking."

There followed a short, highly charged conversation with a relatively junior presidential aide. The White House had assumed it was a false alarm. No such luck.

"Yes, this is the Centre for Disease Control."

"Yes, I am Harry Soames".

"Yes, I am Director of Intelligence at the CDC."

"No, this is not a drill."

"No, this is not a false alarm."

"Yes, I can make a call at 7:00 am tomorrow."

Again, the phone went dead. A moment later, it rang again. It was Defence. The conversation this time was a little less shrill. They were just calling to make a couple of things abundantly clear.

Firstly, they knew it was not a drill. Second, this was a CDC responsibility, not the military, unless there was a military threat. Third, they expected to be kept fully informed of everything at all times.

They hung up. Harry took a few moments to consider his next move. He picked up the phone and called the one person he hoped, he believed, had the very particular and indeed unique set of skills he needed. A young woman answered. Irish accent beneath an American overlay.

"Hello?"

"Hi, Kaitlin, it's Harry. Can you be in my office tomorrow morning? Early please." Kaitlin paused. There was an unsettling tone to Harry's voice, fear, resignation, or perhaps both.

"Err, Ok, no problem. Can you tell me what this is about?"

"No. Not over the phone. But I'll explain all tomorrow."

"Ok. See you tomorrow."

The phone went dead once more.

Harry Soames leaned back in his seat. Most of the staff had already left for the day. The building was quiet. Through the glass wall of his office, Harry studied the decorative frieze on the lobby wall down below. "The Swarm". *Apposite*, he thought to himself.

Soames remained at his desk, chewing his nails. No one knew of his secret fear, a self-doubt that, at times, he found almost crippling and which he had always been at pains to conceal. Soames was troubled by a recurring dread that he would, inevitably, at some point, be called upon by fate to act in the face of some existential threat and that, in the face of this threat, he would find himself petrified, frozen to the spot. Unable to act, or worse, he would turn tail and run, abandoning self-respect, cringing and abject. That prospect was something Harry Soames could not face. That was his deepest fear. He would do anything to avoid it.

Try as he might, he could not pinpoint its onset. He had enjoyed an untroubled childhood. As a boy, he'd spent his summers white-water rafting on the Salmon River. The so-called 'River of No Return'. Boyhood in the wilderness was idyllic. Harry would take his small hiking tent and disappear into the forest for days at a time. One time, he was gone three weeks before his frantic parents found him wandering along the banks of the river. Demands that he explain himself, where he had been, and what he'd been doing remained unanswered. He seemed unable to illuminate his reasons, even to himself. The path of Harry Soames' life appeared at times to have had a mind of its own, culminating in this moment at his desk in the CDC, having just triggered what was, in effect, an alien invasion alert. Except they weren't alien, and they weren't invading. *Were they?*

No amount of soul-searching or introspection could explain the life choices that had guided and directed him to that point. Perhaps some invisible hand was guiding him. And that, in itself, to someone as considered and rational as Harry Soames, was perhaps the biggest mystery of all. But here he was, and his call to action had come.

KAITLIN O'NEILL

Kaitlin O'Neill found a place for the phone on her cluttered kitchen table. She had reached her sixth cup and second pot of strong Irish breakfast tea when Director Soames had called. The scent of hot buttered toast hung in the air. Not being a great cook (or indeed any sort of cook, really), tea and toast were the staples of her diet.

After she hung up, she stared at the phone. It didn't sound good. Kaitlin felt uneasy. Something was pricking the outermost edges of intuition. Whatever this was, it wasn't good. Last time Harry Soames had refused to explain something over the phone, she'd been sent to Alaska for an entire winter. Kaitlin picked up the phone and called her mother. Knowing even as she did so that she would probably regret it. It was a sort of ritual. Whenever Kaitlin's meddlesome sixth sense began to jangle its warning of danger ahead, she'd call her mum.

'Still of childbearing age', as her mother never missed an opportunity to point out, and 'descendent of kings', Kaitlin was at best ambivalent about her mother's guidance. *She's right sometimes, though*, she had to admit.

"Hello, O'Neill household." Katlin's mother had on her special Telephone voice.

"Hi Mum, only me."

"Have you called to tell me you've finally found a boyfriend?" Standard opening question.

"No, Mum", standard answer, "I'm only thirty. There's plenty of time."

"Not that much time, madam."

"I have to focus on my work, Mum."

"What about the boys at the office? Surely one of them would do?"

"I would quite like a boyfriend, mum. Someone to talk to of an evening."

"Well then, get your head out of your books and take a look around the office."

"The guys in the office are a little too bookish even for me, Mum, and nerdy too."

"Well, why have you called then?"

"I'm heading off again. I probably won't be able to call you for a while."

"Where to this time? It'll be Ebola again, for sure."

"Don't know yet. I find out tomorrow."

"Well, find a fella while you're at it, hen. I can't wait forever for grandchildren."

"I'm not likely to find a man in the middle of an outbreak of plague or whatever."

"Ah, you will. Some tall skinny doctor with dreadlocks, I know what you like." The indefatigable hopes of a desperate mother, perhaps.

"I won't, Ma. I won't be looking. I'll be working."

"Stop wasting time, Kaitlin. I haven't forever. Sure, you've a strong sort of a face rather than a pretty one, and some boys like a red-head." Kaitlin pulled off the largish, round, gold-rimmed glasses she had worn since childhood and rubbed her eyes, stifling a peevish retort. She imagined her perfect man as physically strong, independent, and capable. He would be good with his hands, the sort of guy who could fix stuff around the house. He would be intelligent but not weirdly so like the guys at the office, and he would be a little bit taller than she was, but he didn't have to be particularly tall, and he only had to be ok looking. She wasn't after a pretty boy.

"I'll keep a weather eye out, Mum. You'll be the first to know."

"Ok, pet. Well, take care."

"Yes, Mum."

"I mean it, Kaitlin. Take good care. I've an uncomfortable feeling."

"Bye, Mum."

Kaitlin waited for the click as her mother hung up. The jangling warning at the back of her mind had not been quieted by her mother's comment.

She had to pack. Kaitlin thought of herself as a no-nonsense, out-doorsy sort of a person and habitually wore stout, sensible shoes as though to prove it. Actually, braving the great outdoors was, if you're being picky, somewhat aspirational. Guys would have to wait. She had her girlfriends and her work. That would do for now.

Kaitlin kept a small travel bag packed in case of such eventualities. It was time to pull it out from the back of the wardrobe. She'd have to fling in a few things in the morning, but there was no rush. She set an alarm for 5:00 am and went back to what she had been doing before the Director called.

After graduating first in her class, Kaitlin, like so many thousands of young Irish men and women before her, had accepted the call of America with alacrity. Her phone rang a second time. It was her mother.

"Now, listen while I tell you. I don't know why you insist on gali-vanting around the world to all the most dangerous places where an old-fashioned look from a fruit fly can kill you stone dead, but I don't like it. I don't like it, Kaitlin. I've a very bad feeling about it."

"Mum, we've been through this. I had no work when I left univer-sity. When the offer of a research grant and a green card came out of the blue, I had to jump at it."

"You didn't have to, and I wish you hadn't".

"They were offering me the opportunity to study and research at the Centre for Disease Control, Mum, in Atlanta."

"I know, pet, but I'm worried about you."

"I'm not researching epidemic diseases, Mum. After Kosovo and Rwanda, mass hysteria got on the agenda of the CDC."

"I know, but…"

"I'm an academic Mum. I'm tracing the history of mass hysteria, from its earliest origins and in all its forms."

"Well, what were you doing in Alaska for an entire winter then? That didn't sound very academic to me."

"Mum, my job is to identify patterns, recurring themes, causes, and outcomes. I'm not standing around in personal protective gear, Ma. The Centre just wants to avoid an outbreak of irrational behaviour in the good 'ole US of A."

"Fat chance of that, love."

There followed a short toing and froing of reassurances before Kaitlin once more hung up the phone. She leaned back in her chair, sipping from a cooling mug of tea. Her mum had a point, though. This was never her childhood dream.

Staring at the phone lying innocently on the kitchen table, Kaitlin wondered, *How on Earth did I end up here?* She swigged down the cold remains of her tea, shuddered, and poured another cup.

On her first day at the CDC, Kaitlin had been allocated a particularly earnest 'Induction Buddy'. She was, he had said, at the forefront, the vanguard, indeed the very bleeding edge, of mass psychic and psychotic research. "It's the future!" her Buddy had beamed.

Coming from a country historically beset by troubles, Kaitlin had been damned sure Rwanda, Kosovo, and American Presidential elections were a great deal more complex than the Salem Witch Trials. Her Induction Buddy was an idiot.

Kaitlin put her phone on to charge and returned to reviewing the Odd News from around the globe. What for some might be an idle or capricious activity was, for Kaitlin, a matter of the utmost seriousness. There was a message in it. She felt certain. Not a sort of 'Men in Black', 'Aliens from outer space' message. Something more homegrown but equally world-changing

Occasional squalls of rain pattered the window. Grey light seeped in from a cloudy sky. The air smelled damp. Atlanta in February was crap. That was Kaitlin's settled point of view on the matter.

Today was a bonanza day in terms of the quirky and bizarre. Despite herself, Kaitlin began to cheer up. Yet another one of those weird 'previously-unknown-to-science' critters had washed up on a beach somewhere. Kaitlin's current pet theory was that they were all evidence of the workings of the Akashic Field. 'Scientists were baffled'. There was nothing Kaitlin enjoyed more than baffled scientists and their disproved or collapsing theories.

Kaitlin, who kept rough track of these occurrences, decided the count must be around five unidentifiable creatures in just over seven months. The pace of new manifestations was increasing. At this rate, the whole place would soon be plastered with dead mythical animals. *What will happen when the live ones show up?* The teasing thought just seemed to pop into her head.

Furthermore, and this was really very pleasing, yet another so-called 'universal constant' wasn't, or possibly mightn't be. That is, wasn't any more, or perhaps never had been. She wasn't certain which. No matter. There was something very agreeable about the slow unravelling of the sacred numbers of modern physics. So far, Alpha and the speed of light were under attack, Planck's constant was looking a little ordinary, and even the persistent and inviolable charge of the electron was becoming a bit of a worry.

Marmalade, slowly dripping from her thickly buttered toast, pooled on her keyboard, finally, perhaps, reaching a point where something would have to be done. For Kaitlin, not being what one might call 'domesticated', this would inevitably mean replacement rather than cleaning. Indeed, it was her mother's fear that she would never find a husband prepared to clean up after her. A fear she would often express, typically in the company of phrases such as "you'll never get an offer" or "no man would go down on his knees to ask for you". To be fair, these rough terms of endearment were never intended as the cruel barbs Kaitlin perceived them to be. Nevertheless, they were internalised, of course, becoming a kind of psychological trigger. When watching romantic comedies with her girlfriends, Kaitlin would inevitably shout, "Oh, for God's sake, will you get up off your knees, man. You're making yourself look ridiculous!" whenever a man proposed. As you might expect, her girlfriends found watching these movies with her a somewhat trying experience.

It was no good. The foreboding would not go away. The sense of approaching danger had found root and continued to grow in the quiet backwaters of her mind. It was going to be a sleepless night.

By the time Harry Soames arrived at his office next morning, the place was already buzzing. Word had gotten around. The general sense of unease was palpable. This was not COVID-19 or Ebola, something easily understood. This was something... other.

At precisely 6:00 am, there came a gentle tap on Harry Soames' office door. For some reason, rather than calling out, Soames walked to the door and opened it himself. Outside stood a Marines Lieutenant Colonel in military fatigues. Soames recognised him from occasional previous meetings.

"Tom, isn't it? Tom Olsen, NASA liaison?" The CDC's Special NASA Liaison Officer smiled, his oddly youthful face expressing boundless energy.

"Yes indeed. Good to see you again, Director."

"We met a few months ago at a conference, right?"

"Yes, sir. It was about patterns of social order amongst indigenous peoples, as I recall."

"You're in intelligence, right? Tell me, is there much call for expertise in indigenous peoples, animistic religions, and cultures within military intelligence these days, Tom?" Harry Soames examined the man opposite him with care. *Why was he here? Why now?*

"Not really. It's a symbolic post at best. And Alien diseases are not high on the CDC's agenda these days either."

"That could change, of course, if a Mars colony ever gets going." Soames ushered him into his office in silence.

"You prefer fatigues, Tom?"

"Guess so. I can't seem to get away from the haircut either."

Tom Olsen was a man a few years shy of middle age, sporting the typical jarhead haircut of a Marine and a youthful and carefree face.

"Do you always carry the feather?" Soames eyed the long grey feather Tom was fiddling with. Curiously out of place in the circumstances.

"It's the symbol of my people, a whooping crane flight feather."

Tom paused, taking a moment to listen to a niggling voice at the very edge of consciousness. Although he was pleased to be engaged in a meaningful project once again, Tom fancied he could hear the teasing voice of intuition nagging at the edges of thought. This 'mission', whatever it would turn out to be, was not good news. He somehow 'knew' it could all end badly, very badly indeed. Tom fiddled contemplatively. Ok, he had no choice; he would trust the process, pay close attention to the flow of events and act when the moment was right. Until then, he would listen and learn. Tom took the proffered chair and sat.

"Probably best not to place my faith in a Mars colony just yet." Tom smiled, "Believe it or not, I was in high demand a while back when we were either supporting or fighting every weird and wonderful resistance movement in the third world."

"So, Colonel," Harry Soames offered the man his best avuncular smile, "Your role as NASA liaison is finally paying off then."

Tom shifted in his seat.

"Yes, Sir, it would seem so." he began, "I've been allocated to you as your field liaison officer for the duration."

"The duration of what?"

"NASA is not sure what this is all about. An old alert protocol has been triggered by the White House. All we know is that I am not expected back any time soon."

Unlike almost all of his security and intelligence colleagues at NASA, Tom liked people and had a surprisingly high opinion of humanity in general. The very sunniness of his personality and his determinedly positive, upbeat attitude had been known to drive his colleagues crazy, even after only short exposure to it. That might perhaps explain why Tom so often found himself being stationed in the far-flung corners of the globe.

Despite his youthful appearance, however, Tom Olsen had risen swiftly, and for good reason, to the rank of Lieutenant Colonel in the US Marines. He was not someone to be trifled with.

"To be completely honest, I'm delighted to have been allocated as a field operative." Tom stared down at his shoes, a perplexed, somewhat downcast expression clouding for a moment his boyish face.

"NASA has arranged for some kind of device to be shipped." Tom paused. "It's on its way." Tom understood the need to know, but he felt uncomfortable, when it was he, who was out of the loop. He felt like a pinball being bounced around randomly, or if not randomly, then according to a logic of which he was unaware. Come to think of it, nothing about his career history made much sense to him. Joining the Marines was certainly not a boyhood ambition. After a very successful and well-decorated active military career, Tom had been casting about for something new, that much was true, but it was as though some unseen process was at work, guiding his footsteps, channelling his interests and steering his decisions. Perhaps he was being shepherded by his spirit guide, or maybe he had a fairy godmother.

"What kind of device?"

"I don't know yet. I'm waiting to be briefed. All I know is that it's been in storage in the desert for decades." Conversation faltered. Neither man seemed quite comfortable with the direction things were taking.

"Where are you thinking of sending me? Although I'm part Comanche, I was born and brought up in Alaska. I know the wilderness well." Tom paused. He had a feeling it would be somewhere far away in the middle of nowhere. Now that the White House had pressed the button, some globally planned response would roll on regardless.

An uncomfortable thought began to form in Harry's mind. He paused before speaking. "Until this moment, I had not thought to include NASA in my plans. However, your arrival may not be a coincidence." He paused once more, gathering his thoughts, such as they were. "I, too, was born and brought up in the wilderness by the River of No Return, and the events we are tracking are mainly occurring in wilderness areas all around the world."

The two men remained silent, each waiting for the other to speak. It was Harry who broke the silence.

"I have often thought that the routes our lives take are not entirely of our own making." Tom nodded.

"Take your arrival today. I wonder if this current situation, this crisis, is somehow intended to connect us. Might there be some purpose behind bringing us together here?" Tom was not at all sure who might have entertained such a purpose or where all this was leading.

"But I was allocated as a field agent only last night. Some old emergency protocol had been activated, they said. Probably a false alarm."

The two men sat at a small, circular table with a view across the CDC complex. Modernistic, curved structures of glass and steel set in neatly manicured gardens. A vision perhaps of some imagined future in which disease had been conquered, and the human race lived in easy bucolic bliss. Tom Olsen could not help but squirm at the irony of it all. This was the setting from which the world would marshal the massive capabilities of the CDC, and a host of other security-oriented agencies, in the face of a potential 'attack' from humankind's oldest enemy, disease. They were far indeed from the imagined nirvana the architects may have envisaged.

"No false alarm, I'm afraid. There has been what, in CDC parlance, we call 'an outbreak'." Harry Soames, who had risen to his feet, paused to allow the import of his words to sink in.

"Only this time, the outbreak isn't exactly a disease." Pause.

"Intelligence agencies, including my own intelligence branch, have been receiving reports from all corners of the globe of a spate of mysterious child disappearances." Pause.

"These reports are mainly coming from the inaccessible wilderness areas around the world."

Tom smiled. '*Here it comes,*' he thought, '*where is he going to send me?*'

"According to our statisticians, the number and spread of these incidents of child disappearances cannot be ascribed to chance alone. Their beloved null hypothesis has failed them. Simply put, the disappearances are not random."

Tom Olsen shifted in his seat as though to ask a question but held his peace.

"The military, which often uses wilderness areas for training and other exercises, has disavowed all involvement."

Tom remained silent. Soames continued.

"Of course, if we wanted them to bomb an actual military threat, they would no doubt be all in." Tom shifted uneasily. Harry plonked himself back in his seat, brooding. *What was this device that NASA was sending? Why was NASA even involved? All in good time*, he supposed. Some kind of strange attractor seemed endlessly to determine the asymmetrical orbit of his contemplations. He endeavoured to bring his mind back to the matter at hand. The two men stared at each other for a few moments, unspeaking. It had become obvious to each of them that something unusual was going on. To intelligence officers, there is no such thing as a coincidence. Harry Soames snapped out of his reverie at Tom's next question.

"As a matter of interest, where in the US is the biggest hotspot?"

"Most of the chatter is not coming from the US at all. Surprisingly, it's Australia." Harry Soames pulled out a much-thumbed report and began to flick through, obviously looking for something. Tom had an uncomfortable feeling. Something a little too coincidental had come to mind.

"It wouldn't by any chance be the Wollemi National Park, would it? Near Sydney?"

Harry found the page he was looking for and scanned down a table of hotspots. Near the bottom, his finger stopped, and he looked up.

"Yes. It's the Wollemi National Park. How did you know?"

Tom paused before answering. He had been counselled more than once in his career against jumping to conclusions. Intuitive leaps, he called them.

"Well, I guess we country boys should stick together. I am going to let you in on a little secret. It's bound to be classified, so please keep this information to yourself."

Harry leaned in, intrigued.

"I've been running a series of AI tools against a variety of data that's been coming from that area. There is something going on down there, but we can't figure out what."

"You're using artificial intelligence?" Tom nodded.

"What kind of data, and who's 'we'?"

"I guess 'we' are NASA Security and Intelligence."

"NASA Security? How and why is NASA Security involved?" Until that moment, Harry had assumed this was purely a CDC matter.

"The NASA technical guys detected weird electro-magnetic fluctuations emanating from the Wollemi Forest. They put the word out across the community. Also, some of our other…" Tom hesitated for a moment, searching for the right word, "err tools, are flagging parts of the wilderness areas surrounding Sydney as worthy of further investigation."

"What tools? What are they flagging exactly?" Harry Soames was not about to be bamboozled with technobabble by some techie from NASA. Besides which, he had an innate dislike of chance. He didn't believe in it. Synchronicity, on the other hand …

Tom stared at Harry, looking for all the world like a rabbit caught in the headlights. Finally, he spoke.

"Well, we have a piece of software, a kind of linear regression algorithm that trawls incoming data of all kinds and seeks anomalies."

"Anomalies?" Harry frowned. This was just the kind of airy-fairy crap he hated. "What kind of anomalies, Tom?"

"The guy who wrote the algorithm no longer works at NASA, and no one else has been able to figure out exactly how it works."

"You guys don't know how your own software works?" Harry was beginning to tap his foot in frustration.

"Well, it's not all of it as far as I know; it's just this one program. It's a predictive algorithm. Nobody really knows how they work."

"What happened to the guy who wrote the program?"

"Well, that's the damnedest thing now that I think about it."

"What?" Harry was becoming frustrated.

"He went missing on holiday", Tom looked at his companion, "He wandered off the trail and was never heard of again."

"Where'd he go missing?" Harry Soames was beginning to suspect that he could already guess the answer.

"He went missing while bushwalking in the Gardens of Stone National Park in the Blue Mountains near Sydney." Tom paused for a moment. "It's right next to the Wollemi National Park. It kind of merges into it." The two men sat in silence for a long while until Tom came to a decision.

"Well, at least I know *why* I was seconded to you, even if I don't know for sure who made the decision or even when it was made."

"When it was made?" Harry looked confused.

"Well," Tom paused, staring straight back at the Director of Security at the CDC, "Was it made recently within NASA, or was it made twenty-five years ago back in Denali?"

"Or forty years ago by the River of No Return?" Harry acknowledged their shared fear.

"Or both." A brooding look passed across the Lieutenant Colonel's youthful face.

"I should send someone to the Wollemi Forest."

"I could go."

"No, no offence, but we need to keep this within the CDC. We need to treat it as a public health matter, not a matter of national security. And I believe I have just the person." Harry Soames leaned back. "A young researcher I've been mentoring. She's also a shaman. She's from Ireland. I think you'll like her."

"Technically, I'm a researcher and a medicine man, not a shaman. Not that the distinction matters right now. I could brief her. I'd be happy to do that."

"No," Harry leaned forward, suddenly earnest, "the less she knows, the better. What she doesn't know, she can't give away".

"Need to know, really?" Tom looked doubtful.

"We have to assume that a very long-term game is being played here," Harry caught Tom's eye and held it. "We have to assume that someone or some group has been manipulating us, perhaps many of us, for decades or more."

Tom remained silent, processing the idea. A sudden chill took him, and he shivered involuntarily.

Was that a warning? Did an ancestor spirit just walk past?

"The less she knows, the less she can give away. She's not intelligence trained. I've been training her, developing her skills, specifically for this."

"You've been expecting this?"

Harry Soames stared out of the window.

"Well, what's her name?"

"Kaitlin. Kaitlin O'Neill."

YOU WANT ME TO DO WHAT?

Kaitlin knocked on the Director's office door at precisely 6:45 am. The intelligence briefing at the CDC was different this time. Director Harry Soames was less confident than usual, less pugnacious and his orders were less specific. Essentially, his instructions were to "go take a look and be careful". What had he said exactly?

"Our allies are getting nervous. They think we've deployed something new or that we're testing... Something... Out of the public eye, in areas of low population density. They're pissed."

"Are we involved, sir?" There followed a long, slow look from the Director, punctuated, to his evident displeasure, by a shuffling of feet. Soames was uncomfortably aware that they were his own feet.

"Not that we know of...."

"Sir, with respect. If 'we' means the combined intelligence agencies of the United States of America..."

"It does..."

"And we are still just about the most powerful country on earth...."

"Debateable, but yes ..."

"And we do not know what's going on."

"Mm."

"Then either nothing is going on, or something strange is happening, something very strange indeed."

"Just take a look, poke around, see what you can come up with."

"Why me, sir? Why did you pick me?" Kaitlin's soft Dublin accent lay gentle across the room. Soames shuffled the papers on his desk. Kaitlin waited, never in a rush to fill a silence. A moment passed before the Director met her cool, unflustered gaze.

"I want you to be the wounded healer, metaphorically speaking."

Kaitlin stared at him in disbelief. *Why was he using such arcane terminology? What was he getting at?*

"I want you to be the one who sees through the dark."

"You want me to think like a shaman?"

"I read every one of your reports, Kaitlin. That's your training, isn't it? That's your background, right? I paid a fortune for you to spend months in Alaska with some Medicine Man or other."

"You sent me there, sir. You signed it off." Realisation came.

"You knew this was coming, didn't you? This... whatever it is?"

"I want you to take a trip to Sydney. To go on a journey of discovery, Kaitlin, into the Dreamtime. That's what they call it in Australia, isn't it?"

"Is this ... research... related to Indigenous Australian concepts of the Dreaming, sir?"

"That's for you to determine. That's why I hired you." Soames paused.

"Just see what revelations you can come up with. I think that whatever is going on around the world's wilderness places is all interconnected. Use your training and trust your instincts."

"Interconnected? How are they interconnected?"

"There have been stories. Rumours are starting."

"What sort of stories? What sort of rumours?"

"I'd rather not say. I don't want to create preconceptions or influence you in any way." The merest hint of a twitch stretched the muscles in his left eye and cheek.

Oh shite! Kaitlin thought. *This is even more messed up than he wants to let on.* Much to her own annoyance, she found herself silently repeating the women's prayer her mother had drummed into her as soon as she could speak.

Holy Mary, Mother of God, pray for us sinners, now and at the hour of our death.

Kaitlin contemplated the Director, who was again shuffling mounds of papers, trying to stop anything from falling off his enormous desk. *I'm scared,* she realised, not yet conscious of the depth of it, unable to name the fear, but somewhere deep in the human shared subconscious, she could feel something stirring.

There was a small plastic wallet lying on the desk. Kaitlin's name was handwritten across the label. Scrawled along the bottom of the label was a brief message or motto. "The fingers are connected to the hand." Kaitlin had no idea what that was supposed to mean. The Director waved in the direction of the wallet, indicating she should pick it up.

"A few toys to ease your way." Kaitlin had a quick rifle through the wallet. There were several different IDs, all in her name but identifying her severally as a news reporter, a veterinary surgeon, a schoolteacher, and a junior trade attaché at the American Embassy in Canberra. There were also several driver's licenses, boat licenses and other less immediately obvious bits and bobs.

"Very James Bond". Kaitlin wasn't sure if the package was meant as a joke or not. *Should I be amused? Perhaps not.*

"There's someone I want you to connect with." the Director looked up from his desk. "He works for us. He was a mentor to me years ago. He's a great guy. You'll love him. He lives in the general vicinity of where you are going. He could be a great source of local intel." The director looked away for a moment, apparently at a loss as to what to say next.

"What's his name? Where does he live?" Kaitlin's tone was matter of fact. The Director straightened and looked up, finally coming to a decision.

"This may not make a lot of sense to you right now, but I ask you to bear with me. His name is Max. He is an intelligence analyst for the CDC. You will meet him, and you will recognise that it is him when you do. The manner of your meeting will be part of your process. You will find your way to him. I do not want to give you his full name or address at this point. I do not want to contaminate your intuition."

Stuff this for a game of soldiers. Kaitlin was angry. She stood for a moment, expecting more, hoping for more.

"We hired you for your unique insight, Kaitlin." The director's tone was suddenly gentle, confidential. "We scouted you out. But a mind like yours is very sensitive to outside disturbances, to ideas, scenarios, and so on. You'll figure it out. I have confidence in you." And with that, it was abundantly clear even to Kaitlin that the interview was over.

"Well, thanks a million for the briefing", Kaitlin attempted to lift the mood. "Will I be able to expense some new hiking boots?"

The director looked baffled for a moment, then smiled, relieved by the banality of her request.

"Expense what you like, Kaitlin... and take care."

Not wishing to prolong the awkwardness, Kaitlin took her leave of the Director. He's not such a bad bloke for a patronising suit, she conceded. She'd known worse.

It had been a busy day already, and it was still not quite 7:00 am. First, Lieutenant Colonel Tom Olsen, then Kaitlin O'Neill, and any moment now the White House.

The phone rang. It was the White House.

"Yes. This is Director Soames."

There followed one of those conversations between the aids to the most senior executive in an organisation and a senior person in some other relevant organisation. It had been a bit of a shadow dance.

"Find out what the hell is going on. Keep us briefed." Pause, "Also, and most importantly, you handle anything, err… newsworthy. Let us know immediately if anything potentially damaging to the White House is headed our way."

The protocol for the call and its immediate follow-up actions had long been agreed. There was a script to follow, at least for this part.

"I can confirm that intelligence of a potential outbreak has been received. Its scope is possibly worldwide." Soames rubbed his eyes. He'd been up early. What he had to say next was going to be tricky. "This particular outbreak may be a little out of the ordinary. It might be different from previous outbreaks. Different from previous outbreaks, such as Ebola."

"Yes."

"There have been reports of missing children here in the USA and around the world."

"Yes."

"Um, many return after a day or two, apparently unharmed."

"Apparently?"

"Some few seem to experience a period of memory loss upon their return. Some of the children, we refer to them as 'changelings' to distinguish them, suffer longer term memory loss."

"Changelings. Are they not the same children, then? Are they copies, or substitutes?"

"Perhaps 'changelings' is not an apt term. Traditionally it refers to children returning from a stint in fairyland...." Soames' response crawled to a halt. "Unfortunate choice of words."

"Indeed."

"Coincidentally, NASA has reported distortions in an electromagnetic field that may be associated with the disappearances. The field has reportedly become somewhat volatile."

"Coincidentally? Volatile? Well, you had better get to the bottom of it and fast."

The Director held off any mention of a hidden people, probably for the best. To his credit, though, Director Soames followed the very letter of the protocol. The medical threat level was formally estimated. The extent and likely level of 'contagion' and speed of transfer were all spelled out. So far, so good. But the White House was not happy. They seemed certain that somehow the outbreak must be the CDC's fault. They were keenly aware of the difference between a natural disaster and a crisis.

"A disaster is ok, but we must avoid a crisis."

"There's a difference?" Soames was a wee bit out of his depth.

"Of course. A crisis is always man-made. It is always political and always has political consequences. Whereas a natural disaster, well-handled, is a triumph."

"I see." He didn't, not really.

Towards the end of the call, once the nature of the threat to the President had been assessed and the risk of impacting him personally had been decided, a new voice came on the line.

"Director Soames, this is the President. I appreciate your speedy and effective actions. The nation places its trust in the CDC. You are to stabilise the electromagnetic field or make it safe. Find out why these children are going missing. Call on whatever resources you need." And that was it. He was gone.

Once the President had left the call, there were some desultory questions and answers followed by short pauses. Finally, the junior aide of the previous evening was left to conclude the formalities. It was with significant relief that Harry Soames replaced the old-fashioned handset on its cradle, leaned back in his chair and mused.

All in all, that didn't go too badly, he thought. The inevitable meeting with the military would be another matter. They were not going to be happy. Not happy at all.

Reluctantly, Kaitlin pushed back from the kitchen table and, staring out at the slate grey Atlanta sky, turned her attention to the pressing matter of her imminent Australian trip. She really ought to pack, or at least tidy up so she could pack or make a list of things she might pack if she could find them or something. The usual contents of her small standard travel kit were not going to cut it. Her phone rang.

"Listen, pet. I've been thinking. Really, how about one of the boys at the office? What's actually wrong with them?"

"Hi, mum. The boys at the office are dumb. They're envious of me going to Australia. They think it's all buxom blonde babes and wide sandy beaches, and they won't for a moment accept that an assignment in the heart of one of the world's last remaining and truly forbidding wildernesses does not constitute a holiday down under."

"I understand, pet, but they are available, aren't they? And none too fussy by the sound of it."

"Thanks, Mum."

"Oh, don't take on so. I'm only thinking of you."

Had she noticed the boys at the office, which of course, she was far too bound up in her work ever to do, Kaitlin might have realised that there were, at the very least, a couple of potential, even ardent, suitors knocking around the place. Naturally, she did not notice.

"Maybe I'll find the tall dreadlocked doctor you have in mind for me."

"I'm just worried you'll waste your life away with all that mumbo-jumbo you keep wittering on about."

"Ok, mum. Thanks for the call. I've got to pack."

"OK, bye, pet, but think about what I've said."

Somewhere, in a lonely cottage on the north-west coast of Ireland, Kaitlin's mum stared out over the Cliffs of Moher at the broad expanse of the Atlantic Ocean and worried.

Sure, Kaitlin's not a cruel girl. She has more than a pinch of aristocratic arrogance, to be sure, and a bloody-minded indifference to anyone else's professional point of view... Something was not right, though. She could feel it.

Kaitlin was indisputably independent but not necessarily uncaring or malevolent – just a bit involved in her own stuff. She would, metaphorically and, in fact, build an obstacle course around herself to keep those who fell-not within her inner circle out. The route to her office desk was littered with spiny cactuses in large pots strategically placed to dissuade.

In summary, her close friends would acknowledge that though she might not be the best team player, she was strong and imperturbable in herself and that perhaps was her gift. The phone rang again.

"You've a double first from Trinity College. I know it's only in shamanism and whatsit, but still, you could have found a good job in Dublin."

"I'm happy in what I'm doing, Ma. I have a career."

"Of course, you wouldn't go for something mainstream, like medicine. I've come to terms with that, but still, you are a specialist and a double first, Kaitlin."

"Mum, I was more than happy to turn my back on those patriarchal bastards in academia and take a job in the real world."

"I'm worried. I'm getting my thing again. You know what I mean."

"Have you had a vision, Mum? Will I call you a doctor?" Kaitlin's mother's visions were something to be taken seriously.

"No. But I feel one coming on, Mother Mary willing like."

"Call me if you have one, Mum. I have to go now. I have to pack."

Kaitlin's mind returned to her nondescript office building in some undistinguished, potentially indistinguishable suburb of Atlanta. For reasons she found literally unfathomable (having tried a couple of times to fathom them), she worked under the auspices of the CDC in a department funded by the National Security Agency. She didn't like the

NSA. Nobody did. Her department had been established to look into things that didn't make sense. Well, that's what she told her mother.

As Kaitlin contemplated her imminent journey to the Australian wilderness, she once again felt the equivocal lure of a greater power. This was her soft spot, the fear and attraction of losing control.

There had been many sessions with a CDC staff psychologist during her onboarding. They had picked up on it pretty quick.

"How long have you had these feelings, Kaitlin?"

"Have you ever been tempted to act out your fantasy, Kaitlin?"

"Tell me about your relationship with your parents, Kaitlin."

Nosy bastards. Kaitlin got through the grilling, but she was sure one or two folks looked at her differently after that. *They never knew the half of it.* Kaitlin smiled to herself.

She remembered once standing at the very top of a deep escalator at a tube station in London. Watching the stair treads sliding out, form into stairs and slip relentlessly down into the chasm below. She had imagined simply letting go, throwing herself down into the pit, losing all self-control in an ecstasy of self-destruction. For some reason that she also remained unable to fathom, she found the thought compelling and seductive. The notion of giving herself up, wholly, body and soul, to some powerful, implacable power, some influence beyond her understanding, captivated and enthralled her. There was to it, perhaps, a kind of rapture, the bliss of capitulation, utter and complete. This was a chink in what she otherwise fondly hoped was a bulletproof shell. Hidden beneath that was an emotional fissure Kaitlin was at pains to hide and protect.

"Are you alright, love?" The security guard has asked.

"Yes, sorry, I'm sure I've forgotten something, and it's driving me mad."

"My wife's the same. She'll walk halfway home from the bus stop before she remembers what she's forgot. Anyway, you can't stand there, miss. You're blocking the way."

Kaitlin thought back over the various assignments she'd been given since joining the CDC. There was the so-called Galway Changeling, who, according to the authoritative Connacht Tribune, had been stolen by the leprechauns and swapped for a doppelganger.

There was the winter spent living with a medicine man in the Alaskan permafrost, and there were the many shorter investigations into the arcane and the unlikely that she had performed in almost every corner of the world. In every case, there was a link to the central theme of her work, mass psychosis or hysteria. In addition to that, there were her own private studies and experiments. Kaitlin was an experienced and adept 'Tree Walker'. A Kabbalist practised at navigating the Kabbalistic Tree of Life, a model of the psychological and esoteric, and she was a witch. Sitting back, Kaitlin came to a conclusion, her mum was right. This Australia thing felt different somehow, life-changing, perhaps fatal. Kaitlin stood up. She couldn't put it off a moment longer. It was time to pack.

PLAN B

The windowless meeting room, deep in the bowels of the Pentagon was small and cramped, badly ventilated and poorly lit. Harry Soames and Tom Olsen were squeezed onto a narrow, uncomfortable wooden bench along one side of a thin white plastic trestle table, feeble and unstable seeming, within the context of that fortress. Across from them sat a wizened and distinctly hoary army General, a full Colonel from the Marines, crew cut and straight as a rod, and a nondescript, crumpled-looking gentleman from the NSA. The military were not happy. The NSA, true to form, was never happy. The atmosphere in the bunker-like room was frosty.

"So, precisely how long have you guys known about the threat from this hidden, semi-human race?" The old General leaned forward belligerently, his enormously bushy eyebrows seeming to reach halfway across the narrow table.

Harry Soames took a moment to gauge his response.

"General, we do not know definitively that they pose any threat at all or if they constitute a different species or not."

The General cut-in. "The interim report which the Centre for Disease Control finally deigned to provide us with says that children are being abducted by them all around the world, a kind of electromagnetic shield is decaying around their centres of population, and there is a strong possibility that we humans have been manipulated and, in effect directed by these creatures for decades if not longer." The General stopped speaking and stared across the narrow table between them.

The nondescript man from the NSA began to speak, "Err, General, the report is largely speculative in nature …."

"Don't give me that NSA bullshit!" The General banged the table for emphasis. Several half-drunk beakers of coffee jumped in the air. "You guys have known about these creatures for years, and only now do you bother to mention them to us."

"General, the threat level…." The man from the NSA was cut short again.

"Don't talk to me about the threat levels! The NSA is not equipped and is certainly not competent to assess a military threat level. And neither are we yet because you (pointing at Soames) are withholding information of national, if not global, importance. The President is going to hear about this." The room fell silent. No one was willing to respond. Finally, the crew cut Marines Colonel spoke.

"Do we have an assessment of their numbers and the sophistication of their technology?"

Tom Olsen, a Marine himself, still carrying the rank of Lieutenant Colonel, stepped in where angels fear to tread. He stood nervously.

"We estimate that their numbers have been falling over the last hundreds of years and that they now number around twelve million individuals scattered across the globe, located mainly in the wilderness areas."

"Thank you", the Marines Colonel nodded graciously, "and their level of technological sophistication?"

"We estimate that their technology is roughly equivalent to that of the European bronze age, although there are anachronisms, err… anomalies."

"Anachronisms, Lieutenant Colonel? Please explain."

"Well, Sir, although their general level of technology is approximately bronze age, they have deep expertise in the areas of botany, basic biology and medicine. They have a highly developed and effective knowledge of herbal medicine based upon a deep understanding of plants and a firm grasp of the basic biology of a wide range of species."

"I see. Thank you. But they have no advanced weaponry?"

"As far as we know, Sir, they have no weaponry at all. They do not appear ever to have fought a war, Sir."

"Interesting. A human-like species that does not fight wars. What are the anomalies you mentioned?"

"Well, Sir, they appear to be telepathic."

"Telepathic? You mean they can read minds?"

"Err, yes, Sir. They appear to communicate telepathically amongst themselves, and they appear to be able to communicate telepathically with regular humans."

"They can read our minds?"

"Yes, Sir. They can read our minds."

"Anything else you think we might like to know about them?"

"They appear to be able to group together psychically to create a more powerful, more intelligent single group entity, a kind of group mind that is capable of influencing regular humans. We call it the One-Mind, Sir."

"Influencing humans? How exactly?"

"The group mind, the One-Mind, appears to have the capability of suborning and controlling an individual human mind, Sir."

"Controlling a human being mentally? For how long? How complete is their dominance and control once established?"

"We don't know how long the control can last, Sir. We assume it is indefinite, and the control appears to be complete, Sir, if the One-Mind mind wishes it – err… for as long as the One-Mind mind gestalt lasts."

"How many humans can this One-Mind control at any one time?"

"We don't know, Sir. We have no information or evidence on that point."

"But the One-Mind could potentially control a platoon, or for all we know, a battalion or even an entire division. Is that correct, Lieutenant Colonel Olsen?"

"We don't know, Sir. We just don't have the data."

"But potentially? The One-Mind could control a large number of our soldiers on the field of battle?"

"Theoretically, Sir, potentially perhaps."

"Well, no wonder they have no weapons. They don't need them. They can use our own against us."

The General, who had until that moment been listening intently, re-joined the conversation.

"They live in the wilderness areas, you say. Can you offer any reason why we should not simply carpet bomb them out of existence?"

No one spoke. The question suggested an extreme level of threat. Neither Soames nor Tom Olsen had ever really been sure if the hidden people behind the veil were a threat at all. Now they were having to reconsider, and fast. Tom slumped back into his seat, thrown by the direction the meeting had taken.

The nondescript man from the NSA spoke again. "General, these men," indicating Harry and Tom with an idle and dismissive sweep of his hand, "were all born and raised in areas where the enemy is strong. The NSA does not believe their coming together in this way on this particular issue is a coincidence."

"If not a coincidence, then what?" The General stared at the man over the rim of his glasses, his distaste evident to them all.

"We believe they may have been brought together by the enemy, sir. We believe they may have been suborned by the enemy, whether consciously or unconsciously. Sir, they may be compromised already."

While Harry considered how to respond, Tom jumped to his feet.

"Bullshit!" Breathing heavily, he continued. "It is true, General, that the Director and I have wondered at the apparent coincidence of our upbringing in wilderness areas, but there is absolutely no evidence to suggest that we have been taken over or brainwashed. After all, Sir, it was we who produced the report exposing the existence of these people and warning of a potential issue."

"How convenient." The NSA man sneered from his corner.

Silence once more fell across the room until the General spoke.

"Lieutenant Colonel Olsen, as of this moment, your deactivated status is suspended, and you are placed once more on active service."

"Sir, Yes, Sir." The Lieutenant Colonel, who was in any case still on his feet, snapped to attention.

"I am allocating you as my personal liaison to Director Harry Soames of the Centre for Disease Control."

"Sir, thank you, Sir."

"You will retain your current title of NASA Liaison. No need to raise any more eyebrows in Washington."

"Sir, thank you, Sir."

"You will report to me weekly on any and all information available on these people."

"Sir, Yes, Sir."

"Do they have a name, by the way? What do you call them?"

Harry Soames cleared his throat, "Homo Occultatum would be the Latin name General, if we were following the established naming convention. We refer to them as the Wollemi since that's where they first came to our attention. The Wollemi Forest near Sydney, Australia."

"Wollemi. Strange name, does it have some meaning?"

"In the local Indigenous language, it means something like 'watch out, keep your wits about you, look around'."

"What do the Indigenous Australians call them?"

"Sir, there are around 250 Indigenous languages and perhaps 800 dialects. Languages are specific to a particular place and people, known as 'country'. Sometimes many different languages are spoken in a small geographical area. So, there are many names depending upon the district. We chose 'Wollemi' as a temporary name, and it seems to have stuck."

"Um, thank you, Director."

The General turned his attention to the Marines Colonel sitting next to him.

"Colonel, will you develop a plan for dealing with this menace and assemble as required Marine Corps expeditionary units to neutralise any threat?"

"Sir, Yes Sir." Ignoring Harry, the Marines Colonel turned to Tom. "Is there a centre to their organisation, Olsen? Do they have any discernible headquarters?".

Soames took the opportunity to regain his seat.

"Sir, as far as I know, and Director Soames will be able to correct me, the nearest thing they have to a centre, their largest population centre is in the Wollemi Forest and contiguous forest areas near Sydney, Australia."

"Perhaps if we cut off the head, the body will die." The Colonel was thinking out loud.

This was getting out of hand. Soames stood again to speak.

"We have no information on that aspect, Colonel, but I have two specialist researchers currently in the field. We will bring you more information as soon as we have it."

"Thank you, Director. We appreciate full and early disclosure of all information concerning these people, the Wollemi."

"Please be assured, Colonel, you will have our full cooperation."

Soames squeezed back into his seat.

"Noted, and thank you, Director." Tom raised his hand.

"Sir, it is our understanding that their population numbers worldwide have been declining slowly while ours have grown exponentially. We have also speculated that this drastic change in the ratio of our relative numbers is somehow connected to, or even responsible for, a detectable weakening in the veil they maintain between our worlds."

"The veil between the worlds? What inference or conclusion do you draw from that?" The Marines Colonel looked a little confused.

"Well, Sir, one might infer that a substantial and catastrophic reduction in their numbers in any one location might trigger a collapse of the shield in all locations, Sir."

"Are you saying if we bomb the hell out of the Wollemi Forest, we might so reduce their numbers that they can no longer maintain their shield, veil, or whatever you call it?"

"Yes, Sir, but…"

"But what, Olsen, spit it out."

"Well, Sir, have we yet, as a matter either of political policy or military strategy determined whether the shield veil should be brought down and destroyed so that our two worlds merge or should instead be slammed shut forever."

The room fell silent once more. It was suddenly obvious to everyone that before any battleground tactics could be developed, some kind of policy and strategy would have to be developed. Harry Soames, who had remained silent throughout, got to his feet once more. Genuine fear now gripped him. He was afraid that the Wollemi might indeed represent an existential threat to humanity, and he was afraid, too, that if they did not, then the military certainly represented an existential threat to the Wollemi. Soames cleared his throat again.

"General, if these people are intelligent as we believe them to be, and they turn out to be a distinct species from our own, then we are no longer alone. I believe NASA has developed protocols for contact with intelligent non-human species."

The nondescript man from the NSA shifted as though to speak but was silenced by a savage look from the General.

"On the other hand, if they turn out to be just a different, perhaps lost tribe, of human beings, then to destroy them in large numbers might feasibly be construed as an act of genocide." Harry Soames resumed his seat. The meeting was effectively over. The General spoke.

"I will liaise with the joint chiefs of staff. Thank you, gentlemen. That will be all for now."

JACK

The swirling call of the cicadas rose and fell across the outback afternoon. Jack was cagey about the location of his newest mine site. Near Gumbalie was all he would reveal, halfway between White Cliffs and Lightning Ridge. A flinty smell of sun-baked quartz tainted the air across Lightening Ridge. Clouds gathered on the horizon, portending rain. The lowering sun blazed golden bars across the gum trees, oozing like liquid toffee through their silvered fingers, amber against the ice-blue sky. A storm was coming.

Jack surveyed the detritus of the season's opal mining. Like his father, he was one of those rare individuals who had 'the knack'. He could 'smell opal'. People knew it and watched his comings and goings when they could. An almost supernatural, lifelong ability to slip from sight and merge into the backcountry had always served him well.

Summer was coming to an end. It would soon be time to head for Byron Bay to cut and sell the opal 'nobbies', and after that, a trip down to Sydney to see Emma, Jerry and Dad. It had been a pretty good season for Jack but not for many of the other guys camped in the bush nearby. There had been trouble already, sporadic claim jumping and even straight theft. Opal mining was not for the faint-hearted.

Jack was big like his father and strong. At nearly six feet tall and broad-shouldered, he was not built for the enclosed spaces of an opal mine. With black hair perpetually grey from clay dust, he appeared older than his years. His skin was weathered from a lifetime of physical work in the Australian sun. His oval eyes were a deep, dark brown, almost black, his features strong and sharp against olive brown skin.

Marked at the corners with white pegs, fifty-meter claim squares dotted the surrounding countryside. Grey piles of clay tailings indicated those that had yielded signs of hope to the nine-inch drill. To one side, the burnt-out engine of a big Calweld rig lay in pieces in the dirt near the top of Jack's most recent and possibly most profitable shaft. He left it where it lay, not worth his while repairing. There were opals still to be had in one of the shafts. Jack was sure of that. Pulling out the old phone Jerry insisted he use. Jack punched out a familiar number.

"Steveo, it's Jack. I need a new Calweld drill, mate. I'll bring you the old one. You might be able to do something with it."

"Hi Jack, good to hear from you. I've got a reconditioned rig I can let you have, but the new stock is ordered for next season now."

"Sounds great. Can you have it delivered to the roadhouse? I'll pick it up there."

"Sure thing. Err, how bad is your drill?"

"Bad."

"Mate, what do you do to them?"

"Don't ask. When can I pick it up."

"Ah, probs tomorrow." The conversation wandered this way and that for a minute or two longer until all the details were agreed.

"Thanks, Steveo."

"No worries."

While he had been on the phone, the outback seemed to have fallen silent. The occasional bird calls had stopped, as well as the cicadas. Something had startled the bush creatures into silence. Jack looked around, seeking the source of the intrusion. The scene was familiar from childhood summer holidays spent drifting from opal mine to gem field, from Coober Pedy to Lightning Ridge, Sapphire to Anakie and the annual New Year's Eve Rodeo at Emerald. Insects swirling like snowflakes in the harsh showground lights. There was nothing obvious to the eye or ear, but there was the sense of a presence. An uncomfortable memory, half-remembered, threatened to surface.

For the most part, Jack remembered his childhood as idyllic. Work shorts, Blundstone boots, an old and typically torn t-shirt, and freedom. Things had changed a little when they returned to his birthplace deep in the Wollemi Forest. Summers were then spent fossicking for gold washed down from the Blue Mountains. His was a lonely childhood. For a long time, his older brother Jerry had been his only friend.

Jack would probably be the first to admit that he was not particularly fond of other people. He would list his priorities as his immediate friends, family, and mining. At need, however, Jack could dig into a deep reserve of emotion and intuition implanted in him in childhood by his mother, whom he loved and feared in equal portions. She had been a strange, silent woman. Deeply intuitive and caring, but displaying at times an implacable, unreasoning will.

Jack did not fear his mother physically. He never felt he was in any bodily danger. Emotionally, however, he felt deeply and inexplicably equivocal. His mother's love somehow represented a loss of self and the dilution, perhaps even abandonment, of his own identity for that of another or others. It was as though, in his mother's presence, his sense of self was diluted in a pool of being. She had simply disappeared one day. Dad said she had gone back to her family.

In rare moments of introspection, Jack had wondered if these evasive feelings were at the heart also of his abiding guilt regarding the death of Emma's mother, his wife, Karen.

The phone rang again. It was Jerry.

"Emma wants to speak to you. She insists."

"Oh, does she now?" Jack laughed, "Ok, put her on."

"Hello baby, how are you going?"

"I'm going ok, Daddy, but when are you coming home?"

"I've got to polish and sell a few opals, and then I'll come for a visit. I promise."

"Will you stay this time?"

"You know I can't, honey. I'm a miner, and a mine is no place for a child."

"Uncle Jerry says you, and he used to go opal mining with Grandpa when you were kids."

Thanks, Jerry. Jack made a mental note to speak to Jerry about that.

"Times have changed, Emma. It's just not safe anymore."

Jack was sufficiently self-aware to know that the problem was with him, not with Emma's age. *Perhaps if I had been willing to give up more of myself for Karen, perhaps compromise my own wishes more, she would still be alive today.* He had a nagging sense of guilt, or perhaps it was only shame, that Karen's accidental death may somehow have been symptomatic of his own failure to have been a truer partner to her. Such thoughts, should they arise, would be unceremoniously pushed aside.

Something caught Jack's attention. Scrabbling sounds were coming from the bottom of the nearby shaft.

"I've got to go, honey. Talk soon."

"Bye, Daddy."

Jack turned his attention to the mine shaft.

"Probably just rats!" he shouted, making sure that anyone nearby would hear. A sensible precaution if there really was someone down there trying to steal his opals. Jack emptied a twenty-litre can of petrol down the dark mine shaft and waited a minute for the fumes to spread, filling the cross tunnel. Dropping the oily remains of a lit work shirt down the shaft, Jack jumped back and waited for the whoosh of hot air and smoke as the petrol ignited in the confined, methane-rich atmosphere. There was a deep rumble underground as part of the roof collapsed, and the anticipated whoosh of smoke and flame belched biliously from the hole. The sound of the explosion and the whoosh of black smoke and grey clay dust from the shaft, coupled with the smell of petrol, triggered some deep intuition in the stolid backwoodsman. A deep sense of foreboding gripped him for a moment and was gone.

That could've gone better. Still, with no one to witness the partial destruction of the mine shaft, Jack felt no loss of face.

He turned and walked to the truck, slung the broken drill rig in the back and checked the Main Roads report for any accidents or snarl-ups. The old Toyota motor growled into life first time, and Jack swung the wheezing Landcruiser ute towards the coast and the fleshpots of civilisation if the roadhouse could be considered civilisation. He eased his way along the narrow bush track. A little under half a day's drive away, nearer the coast, the roadhouse would be pleasant this time of year. If nothing else, he'd get a very hot shower and an ice-cold beer. He'd give Jerry a call once he got there.

JERRY

Wet mud, blood red, smelling of diesel, dripped from the otherwise pristine car door onto the man's immaculate black shoe. Reflections of ancient stone cliffs, bathed in the warm gold of late afternoon, swayed in the sleepy anthracite flow of the great Hawkesbury River. The drone of cicadas, instantly silenced when he slammed the car door, began slowly to return. A lone, desultory cockatoo flopped above the water, cawing gloomily towards the high old gum trees standing like sentinels across the darkening skyline. The aftertaste of a Havana Corona lay bitter on his tongue. Jerry looked around carefully, checking out the locale. He was not anticipating a showdown with anyone, in any case, not yet. He tapped one perfectly manicured index finger impatiently on the gleaming, highly polished roof of the Mercedes executive sedan. He was expecting someone, and they were late.

The agreed meeting place was discreet, a suitable spot for a rendezvous with the man from the New South Wales Department of Industry. There was no phone coverage out here, a distinct advantage these days, as there would be no electronic record of anyone's presence. Jerry was seeking to extend a couple of petroleum exploration licences at St Alban's Common and within the Yengo National Park. Just small, exploratory drill sites, nothing major, nothing environmentally impactful. Jerry was a careful businessman, not a corrupt one. He was not about to offer a bribe or test the narrow bounds of probity in these matters, but it never hurt to have a friend in the Department, and it never hurt to obtain a second and highly relevant opinion.

An old ute slowed as it approached and stopped. Headlights flashed. Jerry waved. The ute started up again and stopped metres from Jerry's gleaming Mercedes. A middle-aged man in a scruffy suit got out.

"Hi Jerry, good to see you again."

"You too. Thanks for coming."

"No worries. What can I help you with?"

Jerry handed over a sealed manilla envelope.

"Can you take a look at this proposal and let me know if it has legs?"

"Sure. You trying to extend your leases again?"

"Yep. I'm having an environmental assessment done. And I've offered to build new community centres at Wisemans Ferry and St Albans. I'm not expecting any objections from there."

"Yeah, we could do with a new community centre."

"It's the State I'm more concerned with."

"I'll take a look."

"Thanks. Any idea how soon you can get back to me?"

"Couple of days. How's Jack travelling? I haven't seen him around for a while."

"He's finishing off at some place called Gumbalie, near Lightening Ridge, as far as I can gather. He'll be back for a few days in a couple of weeks, I hope."

"And Emma?

"Same, still a Tomboy. Still climbing trees."

"Well, give my regards to Fiona."

"Will do. Thanks, mate."

"Talk soon."

Jerry watched as the ute made its way back along the gravel road, throwing up clouds of dust in its wake, then climbed into his Mercedes and drove away himself, smiling.

To the casual observer, there was something of the dandy or the fop about Jerry. However, in noticing that, one might well fail to notice the tempered steel hidden beneath. Jerry prided himself on his understanding of other people's emotions, their motivations, strengths, and weaknesses. He might concede that to him, these human traits were no more than handles, levers provided to him by a generous universe specifically, so he could manipulate or at least influence other people.

Once off the unsealed gravel road and back on proper tarmac, Jerry's phone rang.

"Hello." The in-car systems opened the line.

"Who's this?"

"It's me, Jerry. You know it's me. Your flashy car has already told you it's me." Jack could be grumpy at times.

"Hi Jack, good to hear from you."

"You sound happy. What have you been up to, you Machiavellian bastard?"

"I'm cut to the quick."

"No, you're ambitious. You're always driving yourself to close the next deal, open up the next mine."

"Machiavellian I may be. To be honest, I'm surprised you know the word, but evil, I am not. Just takin care of business, bro."

Jerry was definitely at the driven end of the spectrum but not un-caring. People, cars, trees, the laws of nature, emotions, desires, outcomes and so on were simply aspects of his business environment.

"That's true, I suppose, as far as it goes. I just wanted to say thanks for taking care of Emma."

"We love having her, Jack, and it's mainly Fiona, as you know."

"I called to say I'm going to offload my opals to a guy I know and head down for a visit."

"That would be great. Emma and Fiona would love to see you. And your mates keep asking after you. I should post a daily update of your doings on the Wisemans Ferry notice board."

"I'm sure you have people to do that."

"I'm trying to fit in, Jack, have been trying for years. People think I'm insular and aloof. I am, I suppose. But I do care, you know. I care about friends and family."

"Just not about the broader goings on of humanity, except insofar as they impacted your business interests."

"Cruel but fair. When can we expect you?"

"I'll call when I'm done here."

"Where's here?"

"I'll call from Byron."

"Ok, see you soon."

There was one thing Jerry did care about, though, one weak spot. That was his brother Jack. Since the 'accident', Jerry had felt deeply responsible for Jack even though Jack soon grew taller and physically stronger than he. Since the day Jack became lost in the forest. He could have drowned. He could have died there, his body never found. Jack was Jerry's Achilles heel. His point of vulnerability kept hidden. Jerry would willingly die to keep Jack safe. It was his unspoken truth.

There was one other defining characteristic of Jerry. Something that set him apart. That was his tendency under pressure to enter a trance-like state. A state in which unique, even peculiar, capabilities emerged. Jerry seemed to be able to tap into some broader network, to process large amounts of complex data, and display an extraordinary ability to summarise it all into a simple, clear pattern. Although this ability could make him appear very smart a lot of the time – the results were sometimes capricious.

On this day, Jerry was uneasy. The bush fell silent for a moment. Jerry shivered. *Something evil this way cometh*, he thought, not quite remembering where the phrase came from. When Jack was back, they would go together to their father's shack in the forest for a visit. It was well past due.

Jerry hoped Jack would indeed return soon. It was fine having Emma to stay. She was more than welcome, but she needed her dad. Jack's endless wandering was beginning to take its toll. And their dad wasn't getting any younger either. Jerry cast his mind back several years to that particular time he and Jack had ventured together to the shack in the forest. The time they finally learned the truth about what had happened to their mother.

The old man had been where he always was, down by the creek, under his tree, gazing out across the water. Although his health was still reasonably good, he was getting too old for full-time work. Jack knew it, the old man knew it, hell, even Jerry knew it.

There had been rumours going around again. Strange goings on out in the Wollemi Forest. A child had gone missing from Wollombi Village. That's why Jerry and Jack had come, really, to check up on the old fella and make sure he had everything he needed. Perhaps to encourage him to slow down a bit or at least start thinking about it. Old age alone didn't mean he would slow up, of course, even for a minute. His research was everything to him, his life's work. Jack and Jerry believed it was all that kept the old man going, really, since his wife had left.

The old house had seemed just the same, perhaps a little wonkier and ramshackle if that were possible. A lifetime of events was written into every brick and plank. A family history scribed in un-planed boards and homemade, yellow clay bricks. The rust-stained corrugated iron roof needed repair again.

Jerry's mind wandered back further. Twenty years or more to the summer's afternoon, they had all gone out scavenging and found a huge pile of corrugated tin sheets piled up on the grass verge next to a golf course near Gosford. Jack and Jerry were still in their teens. It was immediately 'evident' to all of them that the corrugated sheets had been discarded. Unfortunately, there was no one about to ask. Ten minutes later, with the ancient Dodge ute seriously overloaded and wheezing, they headed back to their private redoubt deep in the vast and anonymous Wollemi wilderness. The old man had caught Jerry's gaze and smiled. He didn't smile that often these days.

More recently, Jerry remembered an afternoon sitting on the porch, gazing towards the river and cliffs behind. Jack had wandered up. He reached down, placing a strong suntanned hand upon his father's shoulder, and squeezed gently. There was little family resemblance between the three. Though both Jack and Jerry were dark-skinned and dark-haired, Jerry was lithe and a little below average height, while Jack had inherited his father's heftier physique. The old man was tall and bulky, the fair hair of his youth long gone. The boys took their skin tone and the cast of their features from their mother. No pictures of her had survived a house fire some years before. No stories about her were ever told. Others said she was of Indonesian or Malaysian descent and had died when Jack was only a few years old.

"Got any grog?" Jack had asked. The old man nodded.

"Under the porch."

Jack and his father had strolled back up the gentle slope to the old house and settled themselves on the porch. While Jerry picked his way through the detritus of his father's wilderness life, his sleek Armani suit of woven lapis lazuli glistening and glittering in the afternoon sunshine, Jack stomped off to see what he could find. He had reappeared a few moments later with an odd assortment of bottles, including an unlabelled bottle of red wine.

Time passed. The sun began to set. Lubricated by several assorted bottles of home brew, Jack finally put the question he had come all that way to ask.

"Dad, what really happened to Mum? Where'd she go?"

"That's not something I talk about. You know that."

"It's important, Dad. Emma wants to know about her grandma."

The old man sighed heavily. He had always feared this day would come.

"She was different, your mother. You knew that?"

"Yeah. I guess we've always known."

"You won't believe me if I tell you."

Jerry had removed a pristine purple silk handkerchief from his breast pocket and begun assiduously to clean a drinking glass.

"Try us. You never know."

After years of delaying, deferring, and generally obfuscating, it finally came as something of a relief to be letting the secret out.

"People used to say she wasn't from round here. It was meant as a joke."

"Where was she from then?"

"Well, that's just the point. That's the whole damned point. People think I've stayed here all these years because of my work, and that is true enough as far as it goes. But it's not the whole reason." The old man was breathing heavily. Silence fell across the group. The two boys, now men, knew not to interrupt their father's thoughts.

"You see, she *was* from round here. She *is* from around here, exactly here. She never went anywhere, really."

Jack stared across at Jerry, neither quite comprehending the significance of what they had just been told.

"I've stayed here because your mother is here, right here, and I just cannot bring myself to leave."

Outside, night was beginning to fall. The sounds of the forest, as it settled down to sleep, drifted across the river from the cliffs and indistinct hills that rambled into the distance as darkness fell.

"We were very much in love, you know, each in our own way. She never spoke, but she could read my mind. I had only to think of something for her to understand. I learned to read her, too, in a way. I learned to interpret the nuances of her behaviour. Ours was a very easy, peaceful relationship, but in the end, she needed to return to her people. She needed to belong again. I wish I had gone with her. I wish I had had the courage, but I couldn't take you, boys, with me. It wouldn't have been fair, and I couldn't leave you behind."

"So, you stayed, for our sakes?" Jack had placed an arm gently over his father's shoulder.

"Yes. It was the right choice. I believe that, and I have never regretted it." Their father was staring into the growing gloom, staring at the cliffs across the river.

"I can't explain where she is exactly. Even after all these years, I don't have the words."

He nodded into the darkness across the water.

"But listen, and watch."

From under his collapsing, moth-eaten armchair, the old man retrieved an ancient and much-used item. A long, almost flat, almond-shaped piece of wood, with deep carvings worn smooth by use, traces of red ochre still visible in carved crevices, attached at one end to an old rope, silky with age. The old man rose to his feet, apparently gaining in strength and resolve as he did so. Slowly, deliberately, he unwound the short rope that held the old wooden blade, leaned over the balustrade a little, and began to twirl the blade round and round in the warm night air. Faster and faster, he spun the blade. A low thrumming sound rose and swirled in waves across the evening, redolent of some night creature staking out its territory. The thrumming continued, on and on, louder and louder. Jack and Jerry turned to their father, disturbed and uneasy. Something tugged at them, at and just below the level of consciousness. They were somehow being pulled into this summoning.

Their father's face, glowing now with energy and the deepest yearning, lost all focus in the here and now, staring back and past and through – something.

"Watch", they heard him whisper, then more strongly, "Watch, the cliffs, across the river! Look."

The boys turned and stared into the blackness of the Wollemi Forest at night. Tiny blue flickerings could be made out against the jet black of the cliffs. Sounds could be heard. Lights were coming on. People could be seen across the river, moving slowly. A deep feeling of unease grew, turning slowly to dread. A community emerged from the blackness. A village appeared where no sign of habitation had been before. As the three men watched, a woman turned, appearing to hear the wild thrum of the bullroarer. Separating herself from the group, she began to take a few hesitant steps in the direction of the sound. She was carrying a small lantern. Lifting it ahead of her to light the way, she peered into the darkness towards them. Her face, lit by the warm yellow light of the lantern, appeared at once alien and familiar to Jerry. Jack had turned to Jerry in that moment, older and perhaps wiser, better able to make sense of the alchemy of everyday life. Jerry's stare was intense. Recognition and yearning competed with loss and fear.

"There." Their father's voice was quiet, almost whispering. "There she is."

"Mother?" the brothers spoke together, each lost in their own thoughts, confusion, and amazement. A face much like Jerry's - feminine where his was male - but with the same impenetrably dark almond-shaped eyes and olive-brown skin, fine features, and slight build stared back at them across the gulf. A look of recognition flickered across her face, followed by sadness and loss. Tentatively, the woman held out a hand towards the three men, fingers grasping.

There was a sudden stirring in the encampment. All faces turned as one towards the decrepit house across the river. A sense of overwhelming dread tore through Jack and Jerry. The sound of the bullroarer stopped abruptly. The lights of the village snuffed out in an instant, leaving the men silent and alone, and darkness fell once more. Only the ragged sound of their breathing testified to humankind's ineffectual challenge against the implacable darkness of the wilderness.

It was after that incident that Max had taught them the summoning ritual. And it was around that time that Emma had taken to visiting her grandad as often as possible. She sensed a presence in the forest. A connection.

HENDRA

Jerry was not a happy man. Not happy at all. Sitting in front of him on his oversized, highly polished mahogany desk was a neatly typed letter on official-looking headed notepaper.

Jerry scowled at the letter once more, willing it to disappear. One thing he could not abide was letters, especially nasty, rude letters suggesting that he was not going to get his way. Such letters were, to Jerry's somewhat binary mind, a) an affront and probably a lie and b) almost certainly against nature. Furthermore, a letter could not be manipulated or influenced the way a person could. Give him a real-life person to work with, and he could achieve wonders of 'positioning'. Those business associates who knew him well resorted to printed communications delivered by Australia Post and rarely accepted in-person meetings.

On any other day, the pervasive scent of Gilly Stephenson's patented Liquid Beeswax Polish filling his office would have settled his mood, but not today. Jerry scowled again. To no effect. There in black and white was a short, crisp and pitiless note from the New South Wales National Parks Service explaining that due to an outbreak of Hendra virus in the vicinity of St Albans Common, his mineral exploration licence had been suspended until further notice.

'Hendra Virus, my arse.' Jerry muttered to himself. The 'Forgotten Valley', as it was known to the locals, had, quite unexpectedly, been identified by his geologists as a prime potential location for mineral sands and rare earths exploration. If there was any justice to be found in an otherwise cruel and indifferent universe, then these sites were rightfully his. The fact that the sites his geologists had identified were situated both in the middle of a National Park, and in a conservation area, was neither here nor there. It had taken some superlative positioning to obtain the exploration licenses in the first place. Demonstrable proof, in the face of an increasingly fickle universe, of the righteousness of Jerry's cause. The smaller rig was already at work a few kilometres south of St Albans Common area. However, all recent geophysical evidence suggested it was beneath the Common itself that the richest treasure lay.

Red Earth, the mining company he owned with his brother Jack, specialised in what Jerry called 'scientific' mining. He liked to suggest that other miners, particularly the huge 'globals' that made their money by strip-mining the continent, employed a process little better than random fossicking, drilling hither and thither until they hit pay dirt. Jerry's rigs rarely came up empty-handed. He, too, had the knack. To an objective observer, it might have seemed odd that Jerry never questioned it, but he didn't. His was a divine right bequeathed by Almighty Providence, chance, or his invisible fairy godmother – he couldn't have cared less which.

Of one thing Jerry was certain though, there was no outbreak of Hendra virus on St Albans Common. Something was going on. Someone was messing with him or trying to. This was not necessarily such an outrageously self-centred point of view as one might think. Jerry was not much liked within the mining fraternity. Nor amongst the mining regulators, for that matter. A feeling that he fulsomely reciprocated in both cases. Red Earth was a private mining company, unlisted on any stock exchange and without debt. It, therefore, Has-Mat-suite had its detractors. No one knew how much it was worth or what it was really up to. No one but Jerry.

Jerry came to a decision. He needed to get someone on the ground to take a look for him. Someone to poke around the Common and find out what was going on. Someone who could get around the biosecurity checkpoints. The whole area, from the edge of the village of St Albans all the way to the Yengo National Park, was closed off by teams of white Has-Mat-suited busybodies. Jerry's macchiato lay cooling horrifically, unnoticed in its exquisite, pale blue 'Trésors de la Mer' Versace coffee cup.

Jerry pulled his crumbling Thales phone from his jacket pocket. His desire for encryption and, above all, security overcame his usual obsession with elegant, expensive trinkets. His slim brown fingers tapped out the familiar number. The phone rang several times before a gravelly Australian voice answered.

"Yep."

"It's me, Jerry."

"Yep."

"Something's come up."

"Yep."

"Could you please try saying something else? Something other than 'yep'?" Jerry was easily irritated, and Jack knew all the buttons to press.

"Yep." There followed a long pause during which Jerry refused to speak.

"Ok. Bro, how can I help you this time? Is it standover-man or burglar?" Another pause. Jerry's extended, long-suffering sigh punctuated the silence.

"Neither. And I wish you'd be more circumspect over the phone."

"Thought these phones were supposed to be secure?"

"They are, but that doesn't mean someone isn't listening."

"Whatever. What do you need?"

"Where are you now?"

"Byron Bay. Chilling. Well, waiting for my mate to show up and buy my opals, you must know."

"I need a favour." Jerry paused, his brotherly protective instinct vying with his need for information and the certainty that if anyone could get it for him, Jack could.

"A favour? That doesn't sound good."

"I need you to poke around St Albans Common. Find out what gives."

"There's a bloody Hendra outbreak. Find some other mug."

"There's no outbreak. I'm telling you. It's a sham. Someone's messing with me. Messing with us."

"What do you think it is, then?"

"Dunno." Jerry sighed.

"No idea at all?"

"Not this time." There was another pause, then, "Except there's been some weird stuff going on in the Wollemi Forest. Rumours."

"Oh great. What kind of rumours?"

"Weird stuff."

"You already said that."

"People have gone missing. Some have seen lights in the forest at night. Just creepy stuff."

Jack did not respond. He was thinking back, remembering some creepy stuff of his own.

"Well?"

"Well, what?"

"Will you take a look for me? For us?"

"Yeah. Ok. I'll start driving back soon as I've offloaded the opals. Meet you at the pub in a few days."

"Ok. Thanks, Jack. Anything you need?"

"Coming up time for a new ute."

"No worries. You take care, Jack. There's something weird going on, that's for sure." The call ended. Jerry set the phone down on the gleaming surface of his desk and leaned back, satisfied. Jack loved his utes. It was the least Jerry could do. Something red, with ostentatious roll bars and a V8 decal. Maybe even one of those snorkel things at the front.

On the desk, the offending letter lay unperturbed. Jerry smiled. Jack would find out what was going on. Despite his lumbering size, if anyone could get in and out unnoticed, it was Jack. He was born to the wilderness, and he knew the country from Wiseman's Ferry to Mudgee like the back of his hand.

LAX

Kaitlin was sitting in Starbucks at LAX, waiting to catch the fourteen-hour Qantas flight to Sydney. The place was crowded and noisy and smelled very slightly of stale milk. She was hungry and tired and acutely aware of the griminess of long travel. Her dried-up chocolate croissant, lying stranded on a lightly smeared side plate, looked for all the world like some unfortunate crustacean marooned above the high-water mark. It had failed to entice. Furthermore, she needed a shower.

Recent events had rendered Kaitlin some uncomfortable insights that she was attempting to internalise. She was tired, but sleep was far away. A day spent with her shaman 'guru' in the Alaskan wilderness and the five hours grudgingly made available by NSA for Kaitlin to query their intelligence databases had given her plenty to think about.

As Kaitlin spread the dot matrix printout on the small Starbucks tabletop, that last "Take care" from her boss nibbled tentatively at the edge of thought. Foreboding settled in the deepest recesses of her mind.

The printout was large, on cheap paper, with irritating perforated strips down either side. *Who uses printers like that anymore?* Someone had told her once that it was something to do with document security. Sounded like the usual old bollocks, but one never knew.

What she had in front of her was, in effect, the hot-spot countries from which various Agencies had recorded 'quirky' stories. The 'quirky story' algorithm, legacy of a PhD analyst with a penchant for Jung, was used by everyone and understood by none, as a consequence of which the Agency had 'classified' it. Whatever, it just worked.

What lay before her now, soaking up spilled chai-latte, was a list of countries coincidentally also identified by the UN as containing significant areas of officially designated wilderness. Kaitlin stared at the report blankly.

Taking a sip from her long-since cooled, overly sweet chai-latte, Kaitlin scanned the list again, hoping she'd missed something. The intelligence databases of a dozen Agencies revealed a pattern in the media chatter. Something was happening in the wilderness areas across the globe, from tropical rainforests to savannas, wetlands to deserts, and even the Arctic and Antarctic. Strange stories were beginning to emerge from these wastelands and from the marginalised peoples who inhabited them. Folks were going missing, it seemed. Children were disappearing, often returning unable to explain where they had been or what had happened to them. Lost children, at least, she could deal with.

That's when she received the phone call. Private number. A man's voice, strained, very quiet, saying her name. It took Kaitlin a moment to realise it was her boss, the Director. Kaitlin shuddered. *Perhaps someone just walked over my grave* – that's what her mother would say.

"Good afternoon, sir," Kaitlin managed, "what's up?"

"Stay where you are. Someone's on their way to meet you. They'll be with you in a few minutes."

"Why? What's happened?"

"NASA contacted us. They've come up with something."

"NASA?"

"Yes, just stay exactly where you are. He'll be there in a minute."

"I'm in Starbucks at LAX."

"Yes, we know. Sit tight." The Director hung up.

Kaitlin sat back down. For some reason, she always stood up to take the Director's phone calls, some residual fight-flight response perhaps. "*We know, he'd said. How the hell did he know?*

The laptop was still open on the worn Formica tabletop. Kaitlin began to search the web for some kind of clue. Focusing her thoughts, she managed to block out the cacophony around her. From long experience, she had learned that, for her purposes, bizarre juxtapositions made the best search strings. She tried 'NASA LOST CHILDREN' and many similar combinations until, after a minute or two, she tried 'WEIRD NASA'. A story appeared entitled 'NASA observations defy inverse power law distribution'. Not very promising. Kaitlin was about to attempt another search when her eye settled upon a paragraph near the bottom of the screen. A specific phrase grabbed her attention, 'the effect is most intense in wilderness areas.'

What effect? What on earth was this tedious, arguably learned, scientific article actually about? Kaitlin pulled the laptop closer and began to read in earnest. The science of climate change was not her area, though she did like to think she was as carbon neutral as the next person, probably more so. Struggling through the obscure writing style and deliberately dry delivery, she managed to piece together the gist of the matter. NASA scientists, comparing historic Earth observation data with more accurate readings from their newest and most accurate satellite, had noticed two or three, frankly peculiar, facts.

Firstly, there were growing asymptotic fluctuations developing in various electromagnetic fields routinely monitored by NASA. Kaitlin had a rough idea of what that meant – the earth's magnetic field was getting wobbly in places. Secondly, the distribution of these fluctuations no longer followed a typical inverse power law distribution (she had to look that one up). It turned out bigger fluctuations were now more frequent than smaller ones, rather than the other way around.

And thirdly, these fluctuations appeared to be strongest in wilderness areas. The list of countries affected closely more or less matched the list Kaitlin had compiled from the NSA databases. What did it all mean? Kaitlin had no idea, but, as her downstairs neighbour's annoying teenage daughter would say, it sure sounded spooky.

Kaitlin sipped the dregs of her chai latte and waited dutifully, as instructed. Her new hiking boots were beginning to chafe. When would she learn to break them in before going on a field trip? Not that there had been time.

A quick check of her watch showed there was only about half an hour until her gate closed for boarding. Kaitlin was getting a bit jumpy by the time her contact arrived.

A youthful man approached her table, carrying a thin manila file held closed by an oversized paperclip. On closer inspection, his surface appearance - about twenty-five years old - gave way to the realisation that the man was much older. He was wearing a dark blue suit which, although tailored, still managed to appear oversized on his impossibly slim and wiry frame. The man, though unshaven, did not appear to have yet reached the point where he needed to shave regularly. He was wearing thick, square, black-rimmed glasses that Kaitlin associated with the British National Health Service. He was, at best, an unprepossessing soul.

"Kaitlin O'Neill?" The man-boy voice was surprisingly and incongruously deep and mellow. He had a Texas accent. Kaitlin was a sucker for a Texas accent.

"Yes"

"Hi, Kaitlin. My name's Tom Olsen, NASA Liaison. Pleased to meet you."

"Hi"

"May I sit down?"

"Be my guest." Kaitlin was not expecting so well-mannered an encounter. Had she taken the time to mull it over, she would perhaps have admitted to expecting a stereotypically tall crew-cut Marine with a no-nonsense manner and very little small talk – not the amiable boy-like man who now sat across from her.

"I was expecting someone more military," Kaitlin spoke before really thinking. "Oops, Outside voice, my bad."

"Not at all." Tom leaned over the small table, eager to deliver his message, "I have something top secret to tell you. Hot off the press, as it were."

"Is it about the asymptotic electro-gravitational changes in the wilderness areas?" Kaitlin almost laughed out loud. Tom's expression managed perfectly to combine both outrage and disappointment. It was beyond price.

"How do you know about that?" The man's somewhat hurt demeanour making him look uncannily like a chastened Labrador puppy. "That's supposed to be top secret."

Kaitlin turned the laptop around and showed him the article she had been reading.

"It's on the web. It's common knowledge." Kaitlin immediately regretted her unnecessary cruelty. "But you must have something more up to date than that, right?"

Tom brightened slightly, "I have." Then with a growing enthusiasm reminiscent of a galumphing Labrador scenting a treat, he went on.

"We detected a rhythm to the EM pulses. They are coming closer together like... birth contractions, and the sine wave is closing in on zero." Tom looked up expectantly. Kaitlin tried to look intelligent and engaged, but truth be told, she had only the faintest notion what the NASA Liaison officer was going on about.

"What do you infer from that?" Kaitlin hoped the question was at least ballpark relevant. Tom's response suggested that it might have been.

"We infer," Tom was rising to his topic now, sensing he had the edge at last, "that the pattern will complete in a little over a week when the sine wave finally decays to zero."

"And then?"

"And then," Tom paused for effect, "and then it will either fall apart completely or shift to a new, higher energy pattern, err... or not." Tom's voice petered out, "We don't know for sure."

"Do you know how long exactly until this sine wave reaches zero?"

"Best guess?"

"That'll do."

"Seven days.

"What do you think will happen then? Your personal best guess?"

"Well, one of two things, I suppose."

"Yes?"

"Either nothing at all, or else," Tom paused, uncertain, almost childlike, "or else, all hell will let loose."

"One week to save the world." Kaitlin smiled uncomfortably, not a happy girl.

"Here's something to read on the plane." Passing her the manila envelope, the NASA Liaison Officer stood up, turned abruptly, and walked away. Katlin watched him go. He was soon lost in the endless crowd of shiftless humanity that permanently populated Los Angeles Airport.

Fourteen hours to Sydney. What the hell was she travelling into? Fear of some nameless dread, archetypal and ancient, lurking in the wilderness began to grow inside her. Thankfully, she was travelling business class.

Jack left very early, well before it was light. Careful to leave no electronic trace, he loaded the old ute with half a dozen large diesel cans, turned off his phone and headed off via the back roads. From Byron, he cut across country NSW, wiggled his way down past Armidale on the lesser-used inland route and then took the Thunderbolt Way across country towards Gloucester. The backcountry had already dried to the yellow-brown and ochre of summer. Hardly a blade of green grass could be seen. Everything was tinder dry, biding its time, awaiting the inevitable spark that would trigger a raging bushfire. Jack picked up the pace.

Side roads took him around the Hunter Valley town of Cessnock and into the Yengo National Park near Wollombi village. After that, he left the tarmac and took to dirt tracks, sometimes used by drug smugglers and other ne'er-do-wells, winding his way right up to the old common-law boundary of St Albans Common. The last kilometre was slogged out on foot across the wilderness of sharp-peaked hills and deep forest until at last the country opened up, the trees thinned, and he could see, from an ancient sandstone escarpment spread out below him, the serene patchwork, and peaceful pastureland of St Albans Common. The green had returned. Various creeks and tributaries fed the floodplains. Neatly fenced paddocks slept under the late summer sun.

Nothing much seemed to be going on. Jack took out his camera and inserted an old-fashioned SD chip. Best not to store clandestine photos on the internet. He began to take photographs of lazily browsing cows and occasional peaceful farmsteads. The scene was bucolic, a reminder of a childhood spent freely wandering the hinterland of these forests with their higgledy-piggledy patchwork of small farms and pastureland, from the ferry to the Table of the Gods and all the way through Central Mangrove and Peats Ridge to the enigmatic Egyptian hieroglyphs carved into a rock face near Gosford. Jack made a mental note to look into those again sometime – too weird. Previous explanations from the Park Rangers had been vague and evasive, to say the least.

He began to make his way down to the plain below. The weather was warm but not yet hot. The whirring sound of insects suddenly picked up. He supposed that his intrusion into the vast silence had been accepted. He was now a part of the landscape rather than an imposition upon it.

As he neared the level pastures, Jack began to notice more and more the total absence of people and the signs of their presence. There was no distant sound of motors, no smoke drifting idly from chimneys, and on the roads, nothing moved.

Jack made his way along Wollombi Road, tracking the banks of Mogo Creek. No one was about. The place was eerily silent. In a few moments, he rounded a bend approaching Perry's Crossing and began to notice signs of recent human passage. Muddy tire tracks filled with brown water splashed over the ill-maintained, fragmenting tarmac, steaming gently in the warming air as it evaporated.

Suddenly, there were sounds up ahead. The unmistakable disgruntled purr of a diesel engine and human voices. Jack slunk silently into the overhanging trees and approached with caution.

As he neared the source of the sound, he removed his camera from his pocket and prepared to record whatever he saw. What met his eyes as he emerged from the shadows and lay flat and still on the banks of Mogo Creek was far beyond his immediate expectation or understanding. The camera shutter clicked and clicked as he recorded the scene. His eyes could not characterise or label things, to begin with. What appeared at first to be a logically inexplicable and possibly fantastic optical illusion gradually settled down somewhat into something merely utterly strange and peculiar.

Jack sat back, hidden by the long grass, and tried to make sense of the image before him. There was a shimmering curtain of light, reminiscent of the swirling rainbow pattern in a soap bubble, translucent and fragile looking, hanging low in the sky. At one point, it dipped beneath the brown, slow-moving waters of Mogo Creek. Beyond and through this curtain, the trees and hills were partially visible. A large electric generator sat on the back of a truck. Cables snaked away from it in all directions, leading to clumps and clusters of intricate-looking scientific instruments and paraphernalia.

Soldiers stood guard in plain black uniforms, unmarked, without insignia. Their stance gave them away, however. These were professionals, alert, suspicious and oddly nervy.

Beyond the truck, and somewhat hidden behind it, stood a large dish-like structure attended to by several white-coated technicians. This was the centre of activity. A number of people stood around, watching, chatting, and waiting. Jack inched closer on his belly, hoping to get a better look. He crawled his way under an ancient weeping willow, out of place in this landscape of towering gums. Planted perhaps by some early settler, displaced and homesick.

From this new vantage point, Jack had an excellent view of the technicians and their instrument as well as of the object of their investigations. Directly in front of the dish, perhaps seventy metres off, and behind the shimmering curtain, there appeared to be a large cave mouth leading into a hillside. Jack snapped off a few shots. This was weird.

Upon further examination, it seemed that an old, much-used stone staircase had been carved into the sides of the cave mouth, deeply cut into incorporeal limestone walls. Upon one of the lower steps, there sat a large basket fashioned from woven reeds overflowing with vegetables. To Jack's eyes, both basket and vegetables looked real as real could be.

In truth, there was nothing remarkable about either the carved steps or the vegetable basket except for the curious fact that they, along with the cave mouth itself, seemed to shimmer and pulsate as though phasing in and out of existence. In that, thought, their appearance was not of this earth.

Tantalisingly, at the very edge of memory, Jack could almost recall a similar tunnel. What he and Jerry thought of as 'the dragon's lair' encountered one childhood summer's day long, long ago. The same sense of foreboding filled him now as had filled him then. Fears and memories, carried around unnoticed for a lifetime, emerged from their secret hiding places to stalk once more the soft underbelly of Jack's mind. Slyly poking and probing, seeking his weak spots. He felt the hair prick up on the back of his neck.

There was a sudden commotion around the dish-like instrument. Jack took up his camera and began once again to record the scene. Several additional white-coated men and women rushed up. They were followed by three or four armed men, one of whom had a large panting German Shepherd dog straining against its lead.

Jack lifted himself on one knee supported by a low-hanging tree branch. From his new vantage point, he could see that the curtain of light was shifting and changing. The material of the curtain became thinner, attenuated and at last disappeared. A sound was heard from the cave's mouth. A child was laughing. He could hear the echo of footsteps down the passageway. Suddenly, someone appeared on the steps, a young girl, perhaps twelve years old. She stooped and picked up the basket. As she stood once more, placing it upon her head to carry it up the stairs. She caught sight of the people watching her from the other side of the creek through the now invisible curtain.

The German Shepherd began barking savagely, straining once more against its lead, desperate to break free. The girl screamed, an animal sound, unhuman. She dropped the basket and ran up the stairs. Jack shifted his position, trying to see where the girl had gone. She resembled the almost human face glimpsed once in the undergrowth all those years ago. A feeling of dread washed over him, a primal fear, threatening panic. At that moment, the willow branch he had been leaning on snapped with a loud crack. The dog turned and began barking once more, this time in his direction. There was a snapping tearing sound, and the curtain, which had disappeared completely from view only moments before, reappeared, thickening as it did so. Within a few moments, the cave and stairway had disappeared. The scene across the creek had returned to normal. The opposite bank was once again visible. The hills and trees once again receded into the distance.

The soldier with the German Shepherd on a lead began to walk towards the spot where Jack was hidden, trusting the animal's instincts and superior senses. He was no more than ten meters away when one of the technicians suddenly cried out.

"Look. Look in the water. The vegetable basket."

The soldier turned and made his way back to the group. There, afloat in the slow-moving water, was the archetypal image of a woven reed basket drifting slowly towards them across the creek.

One of the technicians waded into the shallow water to retrieve it. Jack chose that moment to slip quietly away, disappearing into the gloaming as evening approached.

BLOOD TIES

The brief ferry crossing failed to soothe him as it always had previously. The greasy Hawkesbury slid past like liver, water black as evening fell.

Jack trudged the five hundred metres up the lane to the Wisemans' Ferry Inn, where Jerry would be waiting. He wondered, as so often before, about the differences between the two of them. Jerry the success, the smart one, the one with university degrees, who drove a chic European car, drank fine wines and holidayed in Barbados. Jerry, the 'entrepreneur', and Jack, the backwoods boy, the sometime opal miner and gold fossicker. Jack, the one not to be crossed. Jack who liked a drink and never started trouble but had never backed away from a punch-up either. Often questioned by the police, always managing to avoid the courts. Good with his hands. Jack the Fixer and Jerry the financier.

The smooth black outline of Jerry's latest Mercedes stood out, incongruous amongst the parked utes and motorbikes. Headlights flashed while Jack was still two hundred metres away. He gave a brief wave and mimed the sign of someone drinking from a glass. The lights came on in the Mercedes. Jerry stepped out, slighter of build than Jack, svelte in his trademark black Armani – and with him came someone else. There, emerging from the back seat, previously unnoticed, was Emma.

Jack's heart skipped a beat. He couldn't run. He couldn't turn and walk away. She had already seen him. She was running towards him, smiling happily, waving her arms.

Emma crossed the intervening yards in seconds, flinging herself into the arms of her father.

"Surprise." Emma hugged Jack tightly and pressed her face into his neck. By the time Jerry had checked his appearance in the side mirror and locked the car, Jack was standing over him, Emma's arms clamped firmly around his neck.

The brothers walked in silence into the old pub. A few friendly nods of recognition in Jack's direction. A few sardonic looks cast at Jerry. The barman approached.

"Evening Jack. Cooper's Pale Ale?"

"Thanks."

"And for yer brother?"

"Do you have a Barossa Shiraz?" Jerry's tone suggested futility.

"Sure do. Glass or bottle?"

"Just a glass, thanks."

"And for the young lady? What are you having, Emma?"

"Pink lemonade, please."

Jerry paid. The brothers carried their drinks towards a table in a dark corner of the bar. Emma scampered off to play with a few friends she had spotted out the back. Unnoticed by either Jack or Jerry, Emma paused in the doorway that led through to the rear deck and looked back. She wanted her dad back. She wanted a family again. Jerry and Fiona were great, but they weren't a mum and a dad. Perhaps Grandad could help, or maybe even Grandma, if she could only find her.

Jack took a couple of swigs as he walked across the bar, gulping noisily. Jerry sipped, shuddered involuntarily, and sipped again. The wine was actually very good, but a sudden chill had crept into his bones. Out across the Hawkesbury River, darkness lay, punctuated only by the light of the odd farmhouse or fisherman's shack. Beyond that, in the deeper darkness, flickered the occasional glimmer of faint blue light. Infrequent utes, trucks and four-wheel-drives made their way past the pub, down to the ferry crossing. From time to time, a few cars and trucks came back the other way.

"Did you get in and out, ok?"

"Course I did." Voice low and level. Jack's baleful eyes were cast down at his beer.

"Anyone see you?"

"Course they didn't." Jack smiled now, relaxed.

"What did you find?" There was tension in Jerry's voice.

"You wouldn't believe me if I told you, and I can't really describe it." Jack placed an oil-stained manila file next to Jerry's glass.

"I took photos. Heaps of photos."

Jerry, nonplussed, opened the folder. He pulled out the first image, colour printed on plain A4 copy paper – an image of a young girl standing on stone steps next to a reed basket. Even though the quality was poor, the implication was immediately obvious to Jerry.

"Wollemi?" Jerry's voice was quiet, almost whispering. 'Wollemi', their name for the secret people, never spoken in public. The hidden folk who lived in the wilderness, behind the veil.

"Never seen the veil this erratic." Jack leaned back in his chair, sipping his beer. Silence stretched easy between the two brothers, both lost in private thoughts. A moment or two later, Jerry spoke, changing the subject.

"You really should come and see us in town." Jerry's voice sounded sincere, "Fiona would love to see you, and you've seen how much Emma misses you. She keeps asking when she's going to see her daddy."

Jack shrugged, ignoring the renewed ache in his heart.

"She's better off with you and Fiona for now. A mine is no place for a child."

Jerry met his brother's gaze. "You have to forgive yourself, Jack, if not for your own sake, then for your daughter's. Emma needs her dad. You know she's always welcome with us Jack but running around the outback isn't doing either of you any good. It won't bring Karen back."

"Leave her out of it!" Rage and hopelessness flared, momentarily blurring his vision. Jack, breathing heavily, regained control. Shame alone he might have mastered by now, but shame and guilt together had so far proven too powerful a combination for his limited emotional resources. It was his fault Karen was dead. It was his fault that his daughter was left without her mother. Jack couldn't seem to get beyond self-accusation. He changed the subject.

"I'll be opening up a new claim, up Anakie way, the old gem fields east of Rockhampton – sapphires. I can feel them. Feel their presence - you know?" Jerry knew - Jack's affinity for country, for the land, had always been a mystery to him, just as Jerry's ability to read people had always been a mystery to Jack.

"You don't need the money. You know that, right? You have a half share in Red Earth."

Jack sipped his beer in silence. Jerry waited.

"How is she going anyway?"

"She's fine, still a tom-boy. She practically lives in the Moreton Bay fig in the garden."

"I made something for her." Jack rummaged in his pockets, eventually producing a small carved wooden toy – a wombat.

Jerry examined the smooth, hardwood animal.

"Jack, as your brother, and with only Emma and your own best interests at heart, I have to tell you this. Emma believes that the reason you won't take her with you is because you blame her for Karen's death. She believes that she is at fault in some way and that if she can only find a way to fix her fault or repair the damage she has caused, then you will love her again, and you will accept her."

Jack stared across the table at Jerry, struggling to deal with what he was being told, horrified at the implications of what Jerry was saying.

"Jack, Emma spends hours on her own in the forest. She stays with her granddad whenever she can, but she needs to know that you love her. That you accept her just as she is. She needs her dad back."

Jack struggled to speak. He could hear the truth in Jerry's words. He knew that Emma's needs should come first. But he felt impotent, unable to act.

"I'll try, Jerry. The mining season at Lightning Ridge is over. I'm polishing opal in Byron right now, but I will come back and spend some time with Emma over winter." Jack shifted in his seat, preparing to leave.

"Another time, then. Can I give you a lift?"

Jack shook his head.

"There's a ute on order for you. Top of the range, V8, this one's even got a snorkel."

"Don't suppose you have any idea what the snorkel is actually for?" Jack's tone was gentle. There was strong affection still between the pair and a deep connection.

"Snorkelling?"

They both laughed. Jack chugged down the dregs of his beer.

The two brothers stared out at each other from the certainties of their separate worlds, tied by blood.

"Thanks for your help today."

Emma returned from playing and plonked herself down in Jack's lap.

"Here, I carved you another animal for your collection."

"Oh, I love it. Thanks, Dad. How long are you staying?"

"I have to head back straight away. I'll see you again soon."

Emma threw her arms around her father's neck, saying nothing. The sadness all too evident on her young face. Jack hugged his daughter then, holding her tight.

"I will find a way to make more time with you. I promise." Jack stood and, lifting Emma up for one last kiss, gently placed her on the bench across from Jerry.

"Be seeing you then." Jack nodded to Jerry, turned, and walked from the pub into the waiting night.

Kaitlin's hire car was waiting for her at Sydney Airport. A newish Toyota Landcruiser showing minor signs of abuse. Checking her itinerary, Kaitlin discovered, much to her surprise, that she was booked into 'Sophia's Grand Bedroom' at the Wisemans Ferry Inn. After fourteen hours in a plane and an hour getting through quarantine and customs, Kaitlin couldn't have cared less about how grand Sophia, or her bedroom were. She just wanted a comfortable mattress and sleep. Lots and lots of sleep.

Fortunately, the Landcruiser came with a comprehensible GPS. Kaitlin keyed in 'Wiseman Ferry Town Centre' and started the V8 diesel engine. Following the irritatingly triumphal instructions given in a warm, somehow condescending, Aussie accent, Kaitlin began to navigate her way through the early morning Sydney traffic. Even more fortunately, as it turned out, it was early Saturday, and traffic was light. Driving on the wrong side of the road, however, proved to be a bit of a challenge.

Sydney looked just as she had imagined it would - just like it did in the tourist brochures. The city was ravishing to the eye, laid out in mid-summer sunshine under a cloudless blue sky.

Eventually, motorway gave way to suburban roads, and they, in turn, gave way to the Old Northern Road, snaking this way and that across the increasingly hilly countryside northwest of Sydney. Once past Glenorie, civilisation seemed to melt away, peeled back, revealing miles and miles of native bush, dense and impenetrable on either side. Way off to the left, in the distance, Kaitlin could see the Blue Mountains rising like broken teeth against the skyline. Within less than an hour, she felt she had meandered back through centuries. Here was Gondwanaland, or what was left of it, the most ancient continent on Earth. Had Kaitlin noticed, it was probably at around that time that a vague feeling of unease began to insinuate itself into those cunning little corners of self-doubt and uncertainty that loiter, skulking, at the edges of the mind. There was something out there, and it was expecting her.

Her phone rang. Kaitlin pulled over to answer it - figuring out how to connect her phone to the ute had seemed too fiddly to be worth the effort. Who would be calling her anyway? It was her mum. *Of course.*

"Now, don't be getting all aspirated pet. You told me to call."

"I did?"

"Yes. If I had one of my visions. You said to call."

"Yes."

"Well, I've had one, haven't I."

"Ok."

"But there's more. I read something in the paper."

"The Irish Times?"

"No, of course not, you'd not find me reading that loaded, lefty rubbish."

"Ok."

"It was in the Connaught Tribune."

"What was."

"Well, the thing I read, obviously."

"Mum, please. I'm in outback Australia, I'm tired and hungry, and I couldn't sleep on the plane."

"Sorry pet. Listen now while I tell you."

"Please, Mum."

"You'll never believe it. There's been another changeling."

"Where? When? Please tell me exactly what the paper said."

Kaitlin quickly called up the Connaught Tribune on her phone, searching for the story. A triumphant tone crept into her mum's voice.

"It was on Toraigh."

"The island you mean."

"Yes, obviously. What other Toraigh's do you know of?"

"Sorry, Mum, please go on."

"Well, the boy went missing, and at first, the Guards thought it was the father. They always do. Not very imaginative. Then they thought it was the uncle. The uncle was fond of a drink, it says, and they had him fully convinced he must have done it while he was drunk."

"Done what, ma?"

"Well, the deed, of course. Killed the boy."

"But why ma, what would be the motive?"

"Think about it pet. There's only about a dozen people even live on the island, and it's ten miles off the shore at least. Not a huge pool of suspects. The motive could come later."

"I see."

"Yes, well, they had the man confessing to the terrible deed and promising to remember where he done it, and why, and where he hid the body. Then the young fella wanders back into the village large as life with no memory of where he's been or what has happened to him."

"Thanks, ma. I've found the article myself now."

"You have a copy of the paper with you in Australia?"

"No ma, online, on the internet like."

"I thought it was all porn and conspiracies?"

"It is mostly, but there are one or two useful bits."

"Now, would you like to hear about my vision?"

"Yes, ma."

"Our Lady blessed me with a horrible vision of a water monster carrying you away. There was fire all around and ash falling everywhere."

"Was that it? Was that the whole vision, Mum?"

"Well, there was one other bit, but I don't like to tell you about it."

"Mum, please. It could be important."

"A young man carried you up some narrow stairs and placed you on a large, old-fashioned four-poster bed."

"Was I dead?"

"You didn't feel dead, in the vision like. It was more like you were in a deep sleep or unconscious or something. I didn't like it, Kaitlin."

"Was there anything more?"

"He carefully undid your boots and took them off you. Then he gave you a very chaste kiss on the forehead. Gentle like."

There followed several more admonishments to take care and watch out for water monsters before Kaitlin finally managed to end the call and get back on her way.

The road rose and twisted along the backbone of a spiky ridge through rocky gorges overhung by elegant, warped, and misshapen gum trees. Then, on both sides of the road, glimpses of a deep valley and a broad, slow-flowing river began to appear.

Eventually, the tiny hamlet of Wisemans Ferry swung into view. There was something genuinely primeval about the scene. Here, Kaitlin felt, was mankind's primordial home. This is where it all began, or so it seemed. The road down from the ridge was narrow with many zigzag turns, each revealing more of the stately river and murky forest below.

Kaitlin brought the four-wheel drive to a halt in front of the quaint old police station at the crossroads immediately above the town proper. The engine grumbled into silence, and Kaitlin got out. It was hot, she realised. The Toyota's climate control had shielded her from the harsh reality of Australian summer. The sound of the cicadas rose and fell around her as she gained her bearings.

From where she was standing at the top of the village, Kaitlin had an almost one-hundred-and-eighty-degree view of the river, the flood-plain, and the endless native forest. It was breathtaking, awe-inspiring, and more than a little daunting. Fascinated, she gazed out and across the seemingly endless forest. Her eyes seemed to gain a new sharpness of vision. It was as though she was being drawn into the forest. Some-thing, some force, seemed to tug her focus deeper and deeper into the trees. Perhaps something silent in the depths of the forest had sensed her gaze. She fancied she could hear it calling to her, pulling at her, almost physically, drawing her towards it. Caught off-guard, Kaitlin felt a sudden panic rising. She had experienced the arcane before. She had faced dark forces in the past, but this was different. Here was a singular kind of power. She was unprepared. She found herself mumbling, 'Holy Mary Mother of God, blessed are thou amongst women....'

Fortuitously, the loud banging of the gate behind her wrenched her attention back into the here and now. Something snapped. A connection was broken. For a moment, Kaitlin almost staggered.

"Can't park there, miss." A New South Wales police officer had emerged from the cute, old-world police station and was facing her, hand on hip, a little frustrated if not yet entirely pissed off. Kaitlin was speechless, caught between the extraordinary and the mundane for a moment.

"Oh, sorry," she managed, snapping back into the moment, "I'll move it right away, of course."

"Not enough room for trucks, see." As if on cue, a massive military six-wheeler wheezed its way warily around the corner and came to a complete stop, air brakes hissing angrily.

Kaitlin jumped back into the Landcruiser and drove the last few yards to the Wisemans Ferry Inn, its old limestone façade warm and inviting in the summer sun.

"You have reached your destination!" The GPS chimed in, stating the bleeding obvious. The river curved around the hamlet of Wisemans Ferry and slid smoothly past, basking in the summer heat. Above, on the other side of the river, cliffs rose like sentries, bastions of the wilderness. Involuntarily, Kaitlin shuddered. Foreboding welled up from some hidden crevice, riffling the edges of her conscious mind. The ubiquitous sound of cicadas rose and fell, swirling this way and that, like a hymn to the outback.

HAPPY FAMILIES

Snoozing in her tent, dimly aware of the buzzing of the cicadas, and the chatter of the protesters all around, the Elder felt the 'Connection' steal upon her once more. It was a dream, yet not a dream. It was like listening in on the slow, plodding thoughts of some great mind. The Elder imagined a blue whale or something similarly slow and massive. Sometimes it made sense, and at other times not. The dream-thought became clearer. The Elder became more attentive. One never knew when something truly important might be shared. This was her gift, one of the reasons that she had been elected an Elder of her people. She could sometimes hear the voice of the One-Mind in the forest.

[The woman is close now. The father will come. Drawn by duty and [untranslatable idea]. The girl safe within the people. That is good. The girl is the key. She draws the men who bring the [thing]. The girl is the pivot, the reciprocal. She is the [untranslatable idea]. She brings assimilation and harmony.]

From deep within the vast Wollemi Forest, the One-Mind reached out. The Elder sensed the merest tendril of thought, directed not at her but at someone else, someone nearby. The lightest possible touch as it made contact – with …. *Who is that?* An unknown woman, somewhere not too far off.

[Great care is needed. She has sensed our presence. After all these years waiting and preparing. The time is coming. Now the end game. [untranslatable idea] is foreboding. Our moment of doubt and pain. We must prevail.]

The Elder felt herself baffled by the multilayered, evolutionary, and cultural gulf that lay between her and the One-Mind. She was made an observer as, deftly and with practised skill, the One-Mind insinuated itself into the deepest, darkest corners of the strange woman's mind. Secreting itself in those places where consciousness seldom pried. Wrapping and integrating itself into the subconscious processes that drove her, that drove all humans - were they but aware of it? Priming her, readying her for a triggered response. The Elder listened, focussed. This was a message that could not be ignored.

"[There is no room for error. The woman must fulfil her part of the plan. Whether she wants to or not.]

There was a terrible implacability to the thought. The Elder felt the subtle impulses as they were implanted, delicate and elusive, and she was afraid. This was an irresistible power driven by indefatigable intent. Matters were coming to a head. She could feel it. Time to prepare was short.

Insubstantial, seductive, and infinitely refined, the seeds were set. *[It is done. There is everything to play for. We shall not fail.]*

The Elder sat bolt upright in her bed. The Dreaming was in flux. The great mind in the forest was on the move once again. The time was approaching when she must raise the peoples. Their final duty awaited.

GESTALT

It was a short drive to his Wisemans Ferry house. Jerry paused for a moment after he parked the car, allowing his eyes to grow accustomed to the gloom. Emma jumped out and ran inside to show Fiona her new toy animal. Jerry made his way down the hill to the small sandy beach by the river. He needed some air. He needed time to think.

Synesthetic patterns once again began to form in his mind. Jerry allowed the configuration forming at the back of his mind, beneath the level of full consciousness to complete. He had learned to trust his 'gestalt' as he called it, a name picked up from some university psychology primer. It was his secret weapon, the foundation of his success, trusted, relied upon, unquestioned, but never fully understood. Other people didn't have it. He had come to realise that much. Some had something similar, less developed, not quite listened to. It was more than cleverness, though. It was a kind of insight, more sophisticated than instinct, more reliable than intuition. Oh, Jerry was smart alright, used to being the smartest guy in the room, but that wasn't it. The gestalt was not so much a different way of thinking as a different way of knowing. The slow pattern, when it formed, layer upon layer, voice upon voice, inference upon inference when it made itself known, was always complete and final, beyond question.

Jerry listened to the sounds of the river, the faint rustling of animals fidgeting in the undergrowth, the buzz of the cicadas. He realised that he was worried about Jack and about Emma. He was worried, too, by the image of the Wollemi by the creek. Something was very wrong. He could feel it. He could no longer stand aside and wait. He would need to be more proactive and perhaps a little bit more forceful. He needed time to figure things out. He doubted he would be afforded any.

It was now dark. Only the line of the cliff top was visible across the river, and then only as a difference in grain against the night sky. For an indeterminate moment, Jerry thought he saw lights moving against the blackness of the cliffs. He sensed or, thought he sensed, a presence prowling the night-time hinterland beyond the river.

Jerry wandered back towards the house, fiddling around for a moment inside his jacket pockets, seeking the slim metal box containing his most tolerable vice. He lit up an illicit Havana Cigar and inhaled deeply. Having given up smoking many times, he allowed himself to pretend the occasional cigar was merely an innocent indulgence, not an addiction.

Suddenly, sooner than usual, he felt the familiar prickle at the back of his mind, slithering beneath and between the levels of consciousness. The thing was forming more quickly than expected. His 'gestalt'. It would not be long now.

Quickly, Jerry strode back through the garden to his car, keeping his cool, trying not to hurry. He felt uncomfortably exposed now that Jack was gone, out of place in this rural idyll. Jack had always been a reassuring presence amongst these people, living as they did along the periphery. Eyes always seemed to watch him as he went, some curious, some hostile. He was glad to shut and lock the car door. A Mozart Piano concerto he had been listening to swelled and enfolded him as he settled back in the driver's seat. He felt the numbness on his tongue now and the grittiness in his teeth and gums. The gestalt was almost upon him. He slipped the manila folder under his seat.

Jerry fumbled for the central locking, making certain the car was secure before the seizure hit him.

What am I in for this time, he wondered. *What new revelation will come?* Colours, brilliant and impossible, tasting of almonds and blood, swept him up as the synesthetic pattern engulfed him.

PICNIC

"I know I promised you a picnic Emma, but I just have to make a phone call first. Ok?"

"Ok. But don't take too long, grandad." Emma wandered out onto the veranda to stare across the river at the limestone cliffs opposite. She wondered if she might catch another glimpse of the elves. She fancied she had caught sight of them once, beneath the fern trees as darkness fell.

Max Hexenkreige picked up the satellite phone. It and his laptop computer were probably the only modern items in the whole shack. Provided by Harry Soames himself, with a note saying, "Remember to keep the damn thing charged".

The phone had one stored number, too long to commit to memory. Max pressed the button.

A few moments later, after some crackling and buzzing, a familiar voice came on the line.

"Hello, old friend."

"Hallo Harry."

"Your long wait is almost over, my friend. I'm so sorry it's been this long."

"Who knew? No one could predict."

"How are you feeling?"

"I'm good. I'm taking Emma for a picnic in a minute. I just wanted to get the latest. When's the woman arriving?"

"She'll be there by now. She's staying at the Wisemans Ferry Inn. She needs to find her way to you. That's part of the process, I think."

"I will try to contact the One-Mind this evening, at sundown."

"Sundown?"

"Ja, for some reason, the veil seems weaker at sunrise and sunset."

There was silence on the line for several moments. There was so much to be said, yet neither man could find the words.

"Just try to find out what it wants. Ask it what's going on."

"Understood."

"Don't trigger it, though. Just find out what you can."

"I'm too old to run, Harry. I'll be careful."

"I'd come over myself, Max if I could get away from the office."

"No need, but it would be good to see you. I still have that bottle of single malt, twenty-five years old now."

"I do want to come Max. I feel I need to be there, on the ground. It's as though my whole life has been leading up to this. All our lives."

"Ja. I have that same strange feeling. We must see it through to the end."

"How are Jack and Jerry?"

"Jerry just keeps on making more and more money, and Jack's still hiding down some opal mine over near Lightning Ridge, far as I know."

There was another pause, then "How's Emma?"

"She's growing up fast. Puberty is just around the corner."

"I never had kids. I would have liked some. Just never found the right person, I guess."

"She spends most of her time in the forest when she visits. She feels it, I'm pretty sure, but she's never said anything."

"Well, keep her safe. Keep her close."

Emma appeared in the doorway, hand on hip.

"Picnic?"

"Ok, Harry. I must go now. I have a picnic to attend to."

"Take care."

The line went dead. Max and Emma set off on foot to the picnic spot. Always the same place, high on a ridge under shade trees with a magnificent view across the Wollemi Forest. Hund, her grandfather's ageing gundog, foraged ahead.

At the appointed place, Max set out a large picnic blanket upon which he spread the picnic. It was warm and peaceful on the brow of the hill. A gentle breeze blew. The sound of the cicadas rose and fell in mellow waves. Emma busied herself, making a necklace of flowers.

Hund slept by his master's feet. They ate together, grandfather and granddaughter, bathing in the soporific warmth of the forest afternoon.

When the old man awoke, it was already late. The sun was headed towards evening. Emma was nowhere to be seen. Maximilian sat bolt upright, foreboding filling him. He stood and shouted Emma's name. He called for Hund. There was no response from either. Her flower necklace, now wilted and wan, lay abandoned a little way down the hill, towards the MacDonald River. Hund was gone too.

He made his way as swiftly as age, and the trackless waste would allow, down to the bank of the river, its flow reduced to little more than a stream at this altitude. A couple of impressions made by Emma's sneakers in the soft mud on the far side bore witness to her passage. Emma was gone.

As soon as he got back to the shack, Max called Jerry. Jerry would send word to Jack. As evening fell, the old man wandered down from the veranda to the banks of the river. Focusing his mind on summoning the presence in the forest, he began the call. Evening fell. Lights appeared in the limestone cliffs opposite, and in ones and twos, a few people began to emerge from the gloaming. A familiar face appeared same shape, same eyes as Jerry and Jack.

[Maximillian] He heard his name called though there was no sound.

"Do you have Emma? Is she with you?"

[Yes. She is safe now.]

"What is happening to the veil? Why is it weakening?"

The answer, when it came, was not given in words. It was a thought-image. Humanity growing in numbers squeezing the wilderness and the wild areas, corroding the barrier, somehow, psychically, degrading the veil.

[It is you] the silent voice sounded in his mind, *[your shattered minds think poison.]*

The presence began to fade. Max found himself wading into the water. Their eyes met. She smiled and waved and was gone. Behind him, Max heard a familiar snuffling noise. Hund had found his way home.

INTO THE WOODS

Sophia's Grand Bedroom was a revelation. What caught Kaitlin's eye first was the immense, heavily carved, four-poster bed. A relic of a bygone era. The room was set out as it would have been a hundred years before. An ancient sensibility permeated the chamber, recalling a time before telephones, aeroplanes, quantum mechanics and electronics, a time of sail and steam when life was lived on a human scale. An elegant, old-world mahogany washstand complete with an enormous wash bowl and jug, emphasised bygone days. Heavy dark-wood furnishings and thick red velvet drapes completed the effect. The massive stone walls of the old Inn soaked up the sounds of merriment from the bar below. Kaitlin threw herself down on the colossal bed, intending to grab a couple of hours sleep before exploring the, no doubt, many and varied exotic pleasures of Wiseman's Ferry.

When she woke, it was five a.m. The raucous calls of Sulphur Crested Cockatoos cavorting in the gum trees outside her window broke into her dreams and woke her. She still felt exhausted and jet-lagged from the flight, but sleep was now far away. There was nothing for it but to shower and begin her exploration of Wisemans Ferry, the Forgotten Valley and the Wollemi wilderness. The room had no *en suite* facilities. This omission served, perhaps more than anything, to emphasise the archaic charm of rural Australia. Kaitlin was certainly not in Kansas anymore. She found the shower down the hall and was soon refreshed and ready for anything, or so she thought.

Downstairs, the building was silent, apart from some tuneless humming coming from the public bar. Kaitlin stuck her head around the corner and smiled. A middle-aged woman with an open weathered face was busily cleaning up – she smiled back.

"You're up early. You with Red Earth or the protestors?"

"Err. Neither" Kaitlin was intrigued, "I'm a tourist. Who or what is Red Earth, and what's the protest about?"

"Red Earth's a mining company drilling near St Albans. The Greenies don't like it. Things will really hot up now one of the Red Earth kids has gone missing. Mind you, another one from here went missing over a week ago."

Kaitlin ascertained that the Red Earth drilling site was just beyond St Albans, obtained directions to it, and headed off. The missing children and the Red Earth protest were as good a place to start as any.

She decided to go the long way around via the old Settlers Road rather than the faster route along the recently re-tarmacked St Albans Road. Kaitlin wanted to get a feel both for the domesticated countryside and the forest wilderness beyond.

After half an hour roaming through narrow lanes and past occasional farmsteads, without warning, the road deposited her across from the St Albans pub at the centre of a cute little hamlet.

A few brave cyclists and perhaps half a dozen motorcyclists were eating breakfast at the scattering of wooden benches and tables set out around the ancient stone Inn.

Kaitlin ordered the 'big breakfast' and set to chatting up her intrepid fellow travellers and any locals who happened by. It was now around seven in the morning, and the day was already noticeably warm. There were a few raised eyebrows when she asked for directions to the drilling site, but Kaitlin flashed her News Media ID, and suspicions eased. It was only as she popped the ID back in her wallet that she noticed exactly which news outlet she was apparently accredited to – the Christian Science Monitor, Boston. Someone back at the office had been having a laugh.

Kaitlin was directed to take the Wollombi Road. "A few kilometres after Mogo Lake", was all she was told. "You can't miss it."

"Anything else going on around here?" Kaitlin asked, "Anything weird and wonderful I should know about?"

There were a few noncommittal grunts from the Lycra encased cyclists, but the motorbike crew fell silent. Meaningful glances flickered this way and that. The oldest of the group, a grizzled old fella in worn leathers sporting a red bandana, wandered closer.

"Stay away from Mount Yengo. The Dharug National Park is ok, but there's something not quite right going on around the mountain." There was a general muttering and some dark looks within the motor-cycle crew.

"That's enough," an unidentified voice said.

"Why?" Kaitlin asked. "What happened?"

"It's the Janjarri," someone at the back of the group piped up.

"The who?" Kaitlin had a sense that she was being told something important if she could only interpret it correctly.

"The little people," the old biker attempted an Irish accent. "The Aboriginal folk call them the Janjarri, or in some places the Mimih."

The same unidentified voice from the back of the group piped up, "In the far north, they're called the Rai."

The old biker continued, "They are supposed to be delicate, slightly built, elusive, magical beings, mischievous and hidden. Just like your leprechauns."

"The folks in the west of Ireland where I was brought up still leave out milk and cookies for them on Beltane and the Eve of All Souls," Kaitlin smiled encouragingly.

The old biker continued.

"The Aboriginal legends say they are always nearby, listening, hovering."

"Like the Japanese Kami?" Kaitlin was thinking aloud. "Ancestral spirit people, poised just beyond the edge of sight."

"Maybe." The man continued. "They're supposed to live in the wildest of the wilderness places, the red centre and the northern rain forests." The biker paused for a moment.

"And the Wollemi Forest?" Kaitlin ventured.

"Yes, they're here too - some say."

"Why are they here?" Kaitlin was transfixed. Here, at last, might be some answers.

"According to Aboriginal legend, they are kind of companion-beings to us or to the Aboriginals. They look after us in a way, but they are tricky, and they don't exactly share our interests."

"They're Faeries, then?" Kaitlin could work with that. "They inhabit the empty-seeming outback and bush. They are like Loki in the Thor movies - tricksters."

"Worse than bloody tricksters."

Kaitlin couldn't see who had spoken.

"They can control the weather," the biker paused, checking the sky, "they can also control the animals. They can piggyback on any living thing, so the stories go. They can see through the eyes and hear through the ears of any creature they choose. Watch out for large flocks of birds. They could be spies." The man gave a little wink and a smile, but fear lurked beneath.

The motorbike crew began to leave their table, preparing to get on their way. The older biker paused for a moment before heading over to join the others.

"There's rumours they steal kids."

And with that, he turned on his heel and mounted his motorbike. With exaggerated noise and revving of engines, the ageing kings of the road headed off across St Albans Bridge in the direction of Wisemans Ferry and civilisation.

As Kaitlin turned once more to her breakfast, she noticed a few dark glances being cast her way. The hidden people were not a popular topic of conversation locally. It would seem.

Kaitlin finished her breakfast and headed off to explore.

ST ALBANS COMMON

The Wollombi Road ran past St Albans Common, another spot Kaitlin wanted to check out. There had supposedly been an outbreak of the lethal Hendra Virus in the area a little while earlier, but no detailed reports of infection rates or human transmission had been forthcoming to the Centre for Disease Control. Kaitlin remembered the veterinary surgeon's ID in her wallet. Someone back at the CDC had been doing a bit of research too.

Kaitlin stopped for a few moments to read the historic St Albans Common sign. This was the only 'common land' on the entire continent of Australia, a relic of another world. Winds played in wild patterns across the dark waters of Mogo Creek. Flashes of sunlight sparkled upon the enigmatic surface of the lake. Other than the calls of various birds wheeling and dancing above the black water, and the sound of winds in the branches of nearby trees, the place was silent, deserted. There was nothing to see here.

A moment or two later, however, a few hundred yards away, a couple on horseback emerged from a paddock.

"Good to see the Hendra outbreak has been contained," Kaitlin called to the riders as they approached. The couple glanced at one another, clearly discomforted by the comment.

"Yes, turned out to be a storm in a teacup."

"Were many horses affected in the end?"

"None. Like we said, a storm in a teacup."

"So, there was no Hendra outbreak then – after all?"

The couple increased their pace and moved on out of sight around a bend in the road.

Kaitlin was a country girl herself - originally. It seemed out of character to her for country folks to miss out on the opportunity to chew the cud over their latest misfortune. If nothing else, it was always an opportunity to blame the government. Curious.

Kaitlin continued down the winding, often unsealed road, deeper and deeper into the Yengo wilderness. After about twenty minutes, the oil drilling site came into view. All that could be seen was a sea of brightly coloured tents, benders, and lean-tos. There, on one side of the road, was the typical rag-tag-and-bob-tail encampment so recognisable from eco-warrior protests over recent decades, and there, on the other side of the road, was a neatly set out portable village constructed of porta-cabins, various trucks, and shipping containers. A high, chain-link fence surrounded the drilling encampment. A large gate chained closed and locked with an enormous steel padlock blocked the way. A few children played between the porta-cabins, while at the gate, several large burly, looking men stood guard, eyeing with evident suspicion the brightly coloured protesters pottering about on the other side of the road.

Kaitlin parked the Landcruiser and walked slowly up to the gate, trying all the time to decide which ID to present. By the time she had walked the few remaining yards, she had opted to be the reporter from the Christian Science Monitor, realising as she did so that the paper was not regarded in any way as partisan or political. A smart choice, after all, she conceded.

"Hi." Kaitlin showed the men her ID. "I'm from the Christian Science Monitor doing a piece on rural Australia. I understand a child has gone missing."

One of the men stepped forward.

"Can I see your ID, please, miss?"

Kaitlin passed the plastic card back through the bars of the gate. The man photographed it and her with his phone. Kaitlin watched as he forwarded the images with a brief text message. He passed the ID back silently.

"What's the child's name?" Kaitlin had a notebook out and was beginning to scribble a few lines.

"We're not authorised to speak to the press." The man explained.

"Is there someone I can talk to then?"

"I've told the boss you're here." The man turned away from Kaitlin and lit a cigarette. Kaitlin headed off to talk to the protestors. Those encamped across the road had noticed Kaitlin's arrival and had begun to gather. Banners appeared. A desultory chanting of slogans began and then swiftly petered out.

"Red Earth means Dead Earth." The demonstrators had not yet decided who or what she was. Kaitlin showed her News Media ID. An olive-skinned, neatly dressed woman in her mid-thirties stepped forward from the crowd to examine her credentials.

"Good morning, Kaitlin." Her engaging smile and easy tone embraced Kaitlin like a warm towel after a cold dip.

"You're a long way from home." The woman stepped to one side, suggesting with a slight wave of the hand that Kaitlin should walk with her.

"I'm Alice Whalebone. I'm the elected spokesperson for the camp."

"Whalebone? That's an unusual name." Kaitlin was intrigued.

"I'm an Elder of the indigenous Darkinjung people. I am an Indigenous Aboriginal woman.' The reporter woman seemed somehow familiar.

This was the first Indigenous Aboriginal person Kaitlin had met. She didn't want to make a bad first impression.

"Is Whalebone a traditional Darkinjung surname?"

"Nah." Alice Whalebone replied gently, "It was my husband's surname. He was from the coast around Newcastle. He was a Wonnarua man."

"What's going on here?" Kaitlin indicated the protest camp and the drilling site with a broad sweep of her hand, "I heard a child went missing."

"You think it was us took the child?"

"No, not at all. I'm just wondering, what's your take on it?"

Alice didn't respond immediately, taking instead a few moments to size up her questioner. Was this the woman the One-Mind had been talking about?

"We're well supported today." Alice surveyed the brightly coloured assembly, "The head of Red Earth is coming for his weekly visit, and we like to greet him with a good display."

"Will there be violence?" Kaitlin doubted that these people were capable of anything serious, and her expression suggested as much.

"Nah, we're just here to register our disapproval of mining mineral sands in a wilderness and a National Park to boot."

Kaitlin wiped the sheen from her brow and fanned herself with her hat.

"Come and sit down, out of the sun." The Elder's voice was calm and assured. Alice led Kaitlin to a small, hastily assembled shack under the trees at the edge of the encroaching forest. Could this woman be the one? Alice decided to dig a little deeper.

"Children have powers we adults have lost." Alice continued once they were settled. "Children see things in ways we have forgotten. Don't you agree?"

Kaitlin nodded, "Yes, their innocence gives them a different perspective."

"Children can sometimes see things that we adults cannot see at all." Alice let the concept rest on the warm still air that lay between them. Kaitlin, who had learned patience overwintering in Alaska, was attuned to traditional ways of speaking. Although this was her first trip to Australia and her first conversation with an Indigenous Australian Elder, Kaitlin was aware that she was being taught, or maybe being offered the possibility of being taught, by an Elder, if her responses were harmonious. She fell silent, listening intently, eyes downcast.

Alice continued, "Some of our peoples believe that young children can perceive the Dreaming. Some even think that children can occasionally enter the Dreaming itself and walk and talk with the Dreamtime ancestors."

Alice fell silent, awaiting Katlin's reaction.

Kaitlin waited to speak, wanting to be sure that speech was appropriate. Allowing a moment to pass, she cleared her throat a little to indicate that she had something to say. Alice was watching her intently. Kaitlin sensed that much now hung on the next few moments and the words she would choose.

"I'm from Ireland." she ventured at last. "I was brought up deep in the countryside on the remote west coast, the Atlantic coast."

Alice sat still, waiting silently.

"Where I'm from, some people still leave milk and biscuits out for the 'little people', as we call them, the hidden folk."

Alice's eyes sparkled. Kaitlin could sense she was walking on sacred ground. She remembered the hours of coded conversation with a Medicine Man during the long dark Alaskan winter's nights. Kaitlin chose her next words carefully.

"Some believe that children have the power to see through the veil when, for whatever reason, it is fragile."

Alice watched and waited. *This may be the woman.*

"Some believe that children can walk through the veil and enter the faery world, where time runs differently and, as Shakespeare said, 'nothing is but dreaming makes it so'."

"And what do you believe?"

Kaitlin stared at her new hiking boots, afraid to answer and afraid not to. Drawing upon her deepest belief, she found the words.

"I have become aware of another world, one that parallels our own but where different rules apply. There, an older race resides, one whose minds tick to the rhythm of a different clock, who see and experience the universe very differently from us."

"The Elder brothers." Alice all but whispered. Then she offered her teaching, private knowledge that would not be shared except with someone who was able to accept it.

"The Dreamtime was in the past, a long, long time ago, but the Dreaming is also now, just a footstep, just an eye blink away, and it is in the future too, forever." Alice sat back in her chair, watching Kaitlin, waiting to see how she would react.

Kaitlin struggled to take in the concept and to encompass the once and future Dreamtime within her concept of the Faery world, seething and changing, just on the other side of that most fragile veil of understanding and perception.

"Is that where the missing child has gone?" Kaitlin stared hard at her feet, not wishing to suggest any confrontation or assume any unwarranted intimacy by lifting her eyes to the Elder.

"Is she in the Dreaming now? Walking with the ancestors in the Dreamtime?"

"That remains to be seen." Alice's look was far away, unfocused. "But we did not take her."

Kaitlin somehow knew that Alice included within 'we' and 'us', more than simply those encamped across the road from the drilling rig. She had in mind a larger community spread across the country far and wide, north and south, beyond the arbitrary confines of a National Park.

Jack was camped five kilometres along Russian Creek when the news came. Jamie Boyle, his neighbour, camped a few kilometres to the north, brought the letter from the post office in Emerald.

"Urgent, the bloke said." Jamie fetched the crumpled envelope from the pocket of his overalls and handed Jack the letter.

Jack turned it over a couple of times, noting the 'Red Earth Mining' logo on the back. *What did Jerry want this time?* Of course, he would send a letter to the nearest post office. The opal mining area was way off the mobile phone network, and the mine site had no address to which he could have sent a telegram.

Jamie sat down in the shade of a nearby gum tree and began to roll himself a cigarette. Jack stuffed the envelope into his pocket and turned to his friend.

"How's it going?"

"Can't complain." The man spat a damp wodge of unused rolling tobacco onto the parched earth. Ants gathered around it immediately, investigating the unexpected moisture. "And you?"

"A few cores drilled, nothing spectacular."

Silence spread easily between the two men, birdsong swelling evenly to fill the void. There was something unambiguously honest about the outback, and in particular about the deserts. It wasn't just the clean, empty expanses so much as the pitiless, if not overtly cruel, environment. Nothing and no one could survive that merciless ecosystem without showing it suitable respect. The categorical imperatives of city life seemed somehow pale and lacking in authenticity to Jack and his associates.

Jack sighed, pulled out the crumpled envelope and opened it. The letter was from Jerry. That much was obvious from the logo. Another brotherly attempt to bring him into line, no doubt, another appeal to paternal duty.

The hand-written letter was, however, short and to the point. Emma had gone missing. She and their dad had been picnicking near the upper reaches of the Macdonald River, near the shack on the edge of the Wollemi National Park, when she had disappeared. Late in the afternoon, she had gone off, perhaps to climb a likely-looking tree, not too far away, not far away at all really, and she had not returned. Max believed Emma was with her grandmother. He was to come at once. Jack looked at the date on the envelope three days ago. *Three whole days!*

Jack faced the terrible realisation. He had abandoned his daughter. This might never have happened if he had had the courage to stay. All other considerations were now unceremoniously stripped away. He had only one aim, there was only one thing he must do. He must get Emma back safe, and, remembering Max's warning, he must act swiftly before the Wollemi mind overwhelmed her completely.

Assuming the laid-back manner so often affected by Australian miners, prospectors and the like, Jack spoke. His casual tone belying the fear growing inside.

"Got to go." he turned to his friend. "Watch out for my gear, mate?"

"No worries."

With that, Jack was in the old Landcruiser Ute, gunning the grumbling engine into life. Going as fast as the back roads would allow, Jack estimated two days back to Sydney, a whole five days since Emma had gone missing. Once back on the highway, he would be able to pick up the phone signal and call Jerry. She'd probably have turned up. She'd have walked out of the bush on her own. She was a tough kid.

Jack felt bile on his tongue. An old terror scratched sharp claws into the soft tissue at the back of his mind. He supposed she was a tough kid, he hoped she was a tough kid, but if he was honest, apart from a few awkward meetings each year, he had almost no idea about her at all.

The journey back to the highway seemed like an eternity. About an hour out of Emerald, his beaten-up and much-maligned Thales phone picked up the network signal.

Jack pulled the truck over onto the grass verge, unable to manage the tiny keyboard while driving. Muscle memory kicked in. His fingers remembered the number, keying it in, in spite of himself. Dread filled his mind. Every sort of terror assailed him. After a seeming age, the connection was made. Jerry answered immediately, "Where are you?"

"Near Emerald just got the letter. How is she? Is she found?"

"Still missing, mate," Jerry sounded tired and flat, "everyone's out looking. I've pulled all the crews off the rigs, and the locals are pitching in. What with police, SES, and the volunteers, there's close to two hundred people searching for her right now, and I'm drafting in more."

"What's the weather been like? Did she have any water?" Jack calculated the odds of a little girl surviving three days in the forest alone.

"Weather's been on our side Jack, relatively cool and dry, and she did have a small flask with her."

"I'll get there as soon as I can. If I drive through the night, I can be there tomorrow."

"Fly from Emerald. There's a ticket waiting for you at the Qantas desk."

There were times when Jerry's obsession with organisation came in handy.

"Thanks."

"No worries. See you tonight. I'll pick you up from the airport."

RED EARTH

There was a sudden commotion in the camp. People rushed across the road to the fence surrounding the miners' compound. A car was coming down the road, ostentatious, sleek as a panther. The protestors recognised the vehicle and prepared to shout very loudly and wave their banners.

Alice hurried from the little shack, closely pursued by Kaitlin. The protestors had massed in front of the locked gates. Blocking the way. The heavy-set security guys were speaking urgently on their walkie-talkies. The stage was set for a ritual confrontation. Tensions were running unusually high. Anything could happen.

"Who is it?" Kaitlin asked, "Who's in the car?"

Alice Whalebone, Elder of an Elder people, took her place directly in front of the gates, her back to the security men, calm, unconcerned.

"Jerry Hexenkriege, head of Red Earth. You should meet him."

The car slowed as it approached the protestors. The sole occupant stared out at the assembled throng from behind the wheel.

Jerry Hexenkriege was in a good mood, not yet a great mood, but he had high hopes. When he was in a very good mood, he would whistle Beethoven's Ode to Joy tunelessly through his teeth, but when he was in a great mood, he would hum it. It was not that he was not concerned about Emma, but he was certain she was with her mother. She would be physically safe, thank goodness. The issue would be getting her back. But right now, fate had, he believed, presented him with a way of getting rid of the protestors and turning them into allies, all in one go. Killing two birds with one stone, as it were. As for the reporter, whatever her ID claimed and whoever she really was, no doubt there'd be a role for her too. And Jack would arrive later.

The crowd of protesters surged forward, passing Alice. Creating a human barrier between her and the car. Slowly, almost delicately, the car began to advance the last few metres up to the very edge of the protesting mob. There was a tautness in the air, as of nerves stretched tight, almost to breaking point. The black-clad security guys were apprehensive, enduring the stress, awaiting their orders, uncertain whether or not to unchain the gates and open the way through the fence or leave their boss locked outside with the protesters.

The cacophonous chanting spontaneously assumed an ordered rhythm.

"Red Earth – Dead Earth!
No drilling in the wilderness!"

And on and on, louder and more and more threatening.

Jerry, never one to lose his nerve, manoeuvred the massive, gleaming, black Mercedes as close to the gate as he could get without colliding with the protestors. He could have had police protection, but that would have cost money, and in any case, he knew Alice Whalebone of old. She was a commander like him. She would control her people. He hoped. As he inched forward, the crowd gave way, little by little, until there was no more than two or three metres between the lustrous, chromium-plated front bumper of Jerry's absurdly ostentatious ride and the dull grey zinc-coated metal of the fence.

Thus far and no further. The pack would give no more ground. The stage was set for a direct, physical confrontation. The security men had been joined by several colleagues, all now pressed against the towering fence, screaming at the protestors to piss off and get the hell out of the way. Scared to open the gate, terrified not to.

The door of the car popped open, and out hopped a small, wiry, elegantly dressed little man. His skin was olive brown like Alice's, but his features were, if anything, a little finer, a little more delicate. The man stopped for a moment to flick an imagined speck of dust from the cuff of his expensively tailored dark blue suit jacket.

The man straightened, caught Alice's eye and with a smile so broad and so white it seemed to light up the faces of the protestors, he cried out.

"Alice, how lovely to see you. We must talk."' And then, as if catching sight of Kaitlin for the very first time, he continued, "You must be Kaitlin O'Neill, reporter emeritus with the very excellent Christian Science Monitor of Boston? Yes?"

The crowd fell silent. At some all but imperceptible sign from Alice, the multitude pulled back, opening a wide path around Jerry and Alice.

"Good to see you too." Alice's voice was warm and modulated, poised as ever. "This is indeed Kaitlin. She's been telling me about growing up in Ireland. You should give her an interview."

"Of course, of course." Jerry made a flicking motion with one hand towards the gate, and the guards quickly removed the enormous padlock and chain. Miraculously, in the space of only a few moments, the mood of the crowd had changed. Gone was the growing anger and resentment, replaced now with a kind of wary disdain. The gate swung open with the painful and extended screech of unoiled hinges.

"Come on in." Jerry seemed to sweep the two women up with either arm, "Let's have a good old chin wag."

It was only then that Kaitlin appreciated just how diminutive a figure Jerry Hexenkriege was. Both women were taller, Alice Whalebone by a head at least and Kaitlin by a whisker more. Yet Jerry had a magnetism and energy, an undeniable power and authority, that swept them both along willy-nilly into what Kaitlin now realised she had already, subconsciously, begun to think of as 'the heart of darkness'.

I must regain my impartiality as a professional reporter, she began to think, until she remembered that she was not really a reporter at all but a scientist on a mission. *Well then, my scientific impartiality,* she chided herself.

Alice flicked Kaitlin a smile as though she somehow knew and understood her misgivings.

"You're such a charmer." Alice smiled at Jerry. "Still, I won't deny an air-conditioned trailer and a coffee wouldn't go amiss."

"Air con and coffee, it is." Behind them, the protestors slunk back to 'their' side of the road. One of the black-clad security guys sidled up to the big black Mercedes, slipped into the driver's seat and drove it slowly into the compound. The gates creaked shut, and the massive chain and padlock once more sealed the way.

Jerry led the two women to an opulently appointed porta-cabin on the far side of the compound under the shade of an enormous gum tree. "Away from all the noise and fuss," as he put it.

The room itself was set out as an office-cum-sitting-room. On the far side from the door was a desk and three-drawer filing cabinet, and on the side near the entrance were two comfortable brown leather sofas, a coffee table, and a fridge. The air-con was already pumping out gales of cool, dehumidified air.

Jerry plonked himself down on one of the sofas with an enormous sigh, at the same time patting the seat next to him with one slim, manicured hand, indicating to Kaitlin that she was to sit next to him. The two women exchanged the briefest of glances before Kaitlin dutifully sat down at the furthest end of the sofa, away from Jerry. Kaitlin fumbled in her handbag and produced a ring-bound notepad and a small digital voice recorder.

Jerry took in the look that passed between the two women, the gesture implicit in Kaitlin's seating position and the notebook and voice recorder in a single, expressionless glance. This was it. The moment Jerry had been waiting for. With infinite care, he began the exquisitely delicate process of reeling the two women in. Jerry reached inside his jacket, for a moment exposing a flash of turquoise silk lining and retrieved a large gentleman's leather wallet. He flipped it open, exposing two photographs. One was of himself standing next to an extraordinarily beautiful woman with pale skin and shoulder-length dark hair, and a larger, burly man, his face somewhat obscured by shadow, sporting a battered Akubra hat and a long, dark brown, Driza-bone oilskin duster coat. The other photograph was of a prettyish young girl, approximately eleven years old, barefooted, wearing apricot-coloured shorts and a grubby blue t-shirt, smiling down from her perch high in a spreading fig tree.

Jerry proffered the photographs to the two women.

"Alice, you know Fiona and Jack, of course." Turning to Kaitlin, Jerry continued, "This is my lovely wife Fiona, a countrywoman of yours, I believe. She's from a tiny little place called Foxrock, a little outside Dublin, near the Carrick Hills – do you know it?"

Kaitlin shook her head, "I don't know it, but I've heard of it."

"And that big brute is my brother, Jack," Jerry continued. "He's the co-owner of Red Earth Mining and Exploration Ltd". Neither woman responded. Jerry pressed on, "If you don't mind, I'd like to keep this conversation off the record for now." Kaitlin nodded acceptance. She leaned forward the better to see the two photographs.

"The family resemblance isn't that strong," Kaitlin mused, without realising that her comment might be thought rude, "it's difficult to see your brother's face clearly, but there is something in the eyes." Kaitlin paused for a while, leaning further forward to examine the photograph more carefully. "The suggestion of things seen a long way off or hidden. And you both have similar epicanthic folds." Kaitlin looked up, suddenly, abashed.

Both Jerry and Alice were staring at her.

"Epicanthic folds?" Jerry arched his eyebrows theatrically, for an instant resembling a disapproving maiden aunt.

"Err, yes, some people have them, and some don't. No one knows why, really." Kaitlin's voice petered out under the little man's unblinking stare.

"A topic of interest for the Christian Science Monitor, is it?" Jerry appeared mildly curious.

"Not particularly." Kaitlin hesitated, temporarily at a loss for words. "Who's the little girl?"

Jerry turned the wallet slightly so that he could see the picture too. This was the fulcrum moment, the finely balanced 'judo' instant when opposition can be pivoted and turned into support.

"Actually, that's what I wanted to talk to you both about." Jerry's voice began to falter. He even managed what he hoped was an authentic break in it when he went on to say, "That is Emma." For a moment, he appeared to be unable to speak. Into the awkward silence that grew between them, Kaitlin spoke.

"Your daughter?" The little girl's face looked familiar. Kaitlin was certain she had seen it somewhere recently.

"Jack's daughter." it was Alice who spoke. Kaitlin turned to her.

"You know Jack?"

"And Jerry, we grew up together - in the forest."

Kaitlin stared back and forth between her two companions.

Jerry began to speak. "It's about Emma." Jerry permitted one perfect tear to seep from a dark brown almond-shaped eye and trickle down his smooth, apparently ageless cheek. Mustn't overdo it.

"Why? What happened?"

"Emma has gone missing. She's the missing girl. You might have seen the 'missing' posters in town."

Kaitlin remained silent, taking in the information, adjusting to this unexpected turn of events. She realised she had glanced at the posters on her arrival at the Inn the previous evening but hadn't made the connection. Until now. Jerry looked up, dabbing his eyes and cheeks with a crisp white cotton handkerchief retrieved, magician-like, from an inside jacket pocket. He cleared his throat and sat up straight, regaining command of himself.

"I need your help." Jerry both looked and sounded like a little boy. He had their attention. This next stage was what Jerry privately referred to as 'positioning'. He began to speak slowly, rhythmically, hypnotically, with a cadence similar to that of someone reciting a catechism.

"Emma went missing a few days ago. I've had everyone I can spare out looking for her. The police and the state emergency service have been notified, but no one has seen sight nor sound of her since she disappeared. I need to put together another search party. We need to search deeper into the Wollemi Forest. We need guides, people who know the backcountry." Jerry turned to Alice. He reached across one slim olive-brown hand and touched her arm briefly.

"Can you help?"

Alice snapped upright in her seat. Kaitlin, too, felt the imperative woven into Jerry's speech. There was something archetypal in his delivery, something that hearkened back to the fireside at night, at the dawn of times. Something mythical and metaphysical that spoke to the shared experience that makes us all human.

"I will put the word out." Alice Whalebone was once again the Elder of an Elder people, "My people will come". And with that, she stood and walked from the little air-conditioned porta-cabin out into the humid heat of the afternoon.

Jerry and Kaitlin sat silent for a few moments. Taking the time to gather themselves.

Kaitlin suspected that her cover had been blown or, more likely, had never been believed in the first place. Nevertheless, she was not going to jettison it unless challenged.

"What can the Christian Science Monitor do? How can we help?"

Jerry's inscrutable smooth face looked back at Kaitlin. Observing her reactions.

"Perhaps you have other resources?" he suggested, "Maybe you know people who know people? You tell me."

Kaitlin looked back into those unfathomable eyes, wondering what schemes might lie beneath that enigmatic surface. The jetlag wasn't helping.

I have been manipulated, she thought. Alice and I both. We have been… influenced somehow. She may have been a professional researcher for the CDC when she took this mission on, but her personal interest had now been engaged. She had somehow gained a personal connection to the lost child. Something had changed deep inside her. Jerry had woven some magic spell. Kaitlin knew now that she would do whatever it took to get the little girl back.

"I'll see what I can do."

Jerry stood as she made to leave.

"My card," Jerry pressed a small black and red business card into her palm, "anything you need, you know, materially, just give me a call." The sound of the air-conditioning was loud and obtrusive in the confined space.

Outside, under the pitiless arc of the Australian sky, the sunlight struck Kaitlin like a bar of unbearable brilliance as she left the cool shade of the porta-cabin. Behind her, she could hear Jerry humming Beethoven's Ode to Joy tunelessly to himself.

Jerry watched the woman leave. Things were coming together. His priority was the safe return of Emma, nothing came before that, but for Jerry, it was essential always to be a player, not a spectator, and if he could turn some advantage for Red Earth at the same time, well then, all well and good.

CHANGE IS COMING

The gate was opened for Kaitlin as she approached. Across the road, the protestors' camp was a hive of activity. People were packing up. Alice stood still and unruffled in the centre of a cyclone of activity. She was gazing north and west into the endless wilderness of trees. In the distance, a tall, flattened peak rose above the rest, rising above the mantle of trees. Around the crown, a huge flock of birds wheeled and dived in perfect unison, searching this way and that, seeking who knew what? Their intent hidden. Their purpose masked.

"What's happening?" Kaitlin asked, "Are you leaving? Why are you leaving?"

Alice continued to gaze at the massive, synchronised display.

"Have you just given up your protest?"

Alice turned and placed a motherly arm around Kaitlin's shoulder.

"Change is coming beyond anything even Jerry could imagine. Beyond anything, even he could control." The Elder paused for a moment before continuing.

"We have been overtaken by events." Turning back towards the mountain, Alice Whalebone waved an arm, "Mount Yengo, something wakens."

Kaitlin stared at the flock of birds, for the first time realising its size and scale.

"There must be thousands of them, hundreds of thousands." Kaitlin almost whispered as her inherent awe at the powers of nature took hold. There was something undeniably ominous, if not directly threatening, in this perfect, effortless synchronisation of untamed nature. Was there a conscious purpose behind that glorious display? Could there be?

"Murmuration, that's what we call it back home. The starlings do it every year. Millions and millions of them, perfectly in sync. Amazing."

"I must summon my people." Alice took Kaitlin's hand.

"Jerry is not a bad man," Alice leaned close, almost whispering, "but he has a certain way about him. He can *persuade* people."

"Persuade people? How? What do you mean?"

"Jerry is not innocent. He is not a child. He cannot enter the Dreaming, yet the Dreaming is in him, somehow...." Alice faltered.

"I can't explain. He is an old friend. A childhood friend but watch your thoughts when you speak with him."

Kaitlin looked around. The camp had almost emptied itself. The security guards at the gate were staring in disbelief.

One caught Kaitlin's eye, "I don't know what you said, love, but there's a job here for you any time."

Kaitlin gave the man a smile. Why not. Then she climbed into the driving seat of the long-suffering four-wheel drive and gunned the engine into life. To the north and west, the birds were still swirling and swooping around the distant peak. What had Alice said? "Something wakens", that was it. Kaitlin pulled out the GPS and typed in "Mount Yengo" under "Places of Interest".

A track appeared on the little screen, not even a road, no more than a forest path. The name was written in a font too small to read. Kaitlin tapped the screen a couple of times to enlarge the writing.

"Old Convict Trail," the legend read.

Kaitlin was reminded of the endless low-grade horror movies she'd watched as a lonely teenager on the West coast of Ireland. This seemed like one of those "Don't go into the attic!" moments: weird goings on in the impenetrable heart of one of the world's most ancient wildernesses, a sinister and gigantic synchronised flock of birds, and the gloriously doom-laden phrase, "something wakens". *Not this time,* Kaitlin told herself as she eased the vehicle back onto the tarmac and headed firmly away from the mountain, still shrouded in its cloak of living birds.

Alice watched Kaitlin out of sight. Events were moving on apace. She had work to do. The time was coming when she must fulfil the long-held covenant of her people. Her priority now must be to protect the people and her friends and to attempt the safe return of Emma.

The terrifying truth was beginning to sink in. This was it. This was the time, foretold in legend when her people and the hidden ones would fight their final battle. And she must lead, she realised. She must fulfil the role that fate had placed upon her. For a moment, almost, she baulked at the enormity of what was being asked of her. A phrase came to mind, heard once, a long time ago, in happier times, "If not me, then who, if not now, then when?""

Well, she thought, *it's me, and it's now. Shit happens.*

Jack headed for the airport on autopilot, events he had believed long forgotten forcing their way into consciousness. Emma's disappearance had prised open memories he had hoped were shut to conscious thought forever. In his mind's eye, he was a child again, lost and frightened in the endless Wollemi Forest. He was dazed, he recalled, and suffering from concussion.

Once again, in memory, the female form stooped over him, momentarily blocking the savage mid-day sun. The sound of forest insects almost deafening in the small sunlit glade was equalled only by the powerful scent of eucalyptus. A slight blue haze rested in the still air. Her strong, smoothly muscled arms slipped softly around him, half lifting, half dragging him into the welcoming shade.

Jack twisted his torso, wincing at the pain, craning to get a look at her face. The woman stepped back, settling on her haunches, sunlight cutting a diagonal swathe across her body, arms wrapped around her knees, staring back at him. Her skin was a deep nut-brown, her body lithe and wiry, long dark hair touched with grey at the temples. Jack examined the smooth, high cheek-boned face. She was beautiful, he realised, in a way. He found himself gazing into her eyes, seeking the person inside. Looking for understanding.

Almond-shaped eyes stared back. Pitch black. And behind? Swirling seas of emotion, still, deep oceans of intuition and the quicksilver fleeting instants of body knowledge as she shifted an arm into the shade. Her movements were sensuous, catlike, and immediate.

She looked familiar! Did he know her? Shock took him. His sense of unease growing deep. He seemed to sink into her eyes and through them into a pool of communal understanding or shared memory, alive and pulsing. Hundreds, perhaps thousands of minds merged easily and without resistance into what? The group, the collective, warm and embracing.

Two things hit him simultaneously: A thought, "She looks like Jerry and Mum!" and a primeval fear. There was no soul in those eyes, little true individuality. In a sense, there was no one there, nothing, and at the same time, there was a vast, peaceful, implacable mind. Jack had felt then a wave of nausea strike him, knocking the breath from him. Rustling sounds at the edge of the glade gave way to a sea of faces, men, women, and children, all alike, all different, all silently staring with the same single, imperturbable intent. It was all too much, stress and shock, fear, and pain conspired against him. He lost consciousness. When he awoke, he was alone in the forest. The moon was full. It was not far to the road. He was perhaps nine years old, alone in the moon-light.

A truck horn sounded, bringing Jack back to the here and now. Traffic increased as he approached Emerald, wrenching his focus from long ago back to the present. The little car park was all but empty at this hour. On the tarmac, a small commercial plane was waiting. Jack showed his driver's license and was ushered swiftly on board. There were, perhaps, a dozen or so seats packed into the little jet. Jack was shown to a business class seat at the front, behind the pilot's tiny cabin. Here he had a little more legroom, and the seats were marginally wider. He was the only passenger. The cabin steward approached Jack as he settled in.

"Your brother left a message for you, sir. He says Emma is with her grandmother's people, and she'll be safe there for now."

"Oh. Ok, Thanks." Jack's mind was racing. If Emma had somehow wandered into the Dreamtime, then she would be physically safe, but her mental health was another thing. At her age, she could be lost to the Wollemi. She was part Wollemi too, and Jack had always suspected that she could feel their presence. They didn't all come back, the changelings. Some never returned, and those who did were often deeply changed. But Jerry wouldn't suggest it unless he was pretty certain. Jack felt a wave of relief wash over him that Emma was probably alive.

But it was mixed with the deepest apprehension. Within minutes the plane was headed for Brisbane and then on to Sydney.

END GAME

Alice had passed on the call to search for Emma. She was home now, trying to sleep. The air conditioner was playing up, offering her either a small breath of cooled air at the cost of a loudly rattling fan or silence and still, humid air enveloping like a warm bath. Alice chose silence. As she lay on the bed, trying to sleep, she felt once more the One-Mind, away in the deeps of the forest, mulling things over. Talking to itself as though justifying its actions or actions it was about to take. Or perhaps it was talking to her. Alice listened.

[*Conflict drove human understanding and [untranslatable idea]. Empires collapsed. [Untranslatable idea] leading inevitably to [untranslatable idea] and war.*]

There was a pause in the monologue.

[*Our lost children rebuilt their [untranslatable idea]. Each time learning from the past. We saw our opportunity to [untranslatable idea], we guided their greatest minds to a renaissance in understanding. We bent them to our will.*]

Was the One-Mind talking to her? Did it know she could hear its thoughts? The rambling 'explanation' continued.

[*Our children's greatest weakness and greatest gift was reason. Understanding itself. A double-edged sword. Time was short — a terrible reckoning. Reason unchecked by [untranslatable idea] or empathy was [untranslatable idea] to self-destruction. We feared for our own existence. We could not maintain the veil against the corrosion of billions of individual minds indifferent to the web of life they shared. We were afraid the humans would regain the power of the dream, that they would re-enter the Dreaming. They would have to be stopped. We would stop them.*]

Alice tried to decipher the message. *The One-Mind was afraid we humans would somehow break into the Dreaming. That we would bring down the veil and march in.* This was a very different perspective. She would have to share this with her people. They would have to take stock. The voice in her head continued.

[*If the veil failed, our two species would be thrown into confrontation and possibly war. The tipping point approached.*]

Alice's people had come to the same realisation themselves. Something had to give.

[*We needed a [untranslatable idea] to produce raw psychic energy to reconnect our lost children to the web of life and slam shut the veil forever. Though they have lost the power of telepathy, still the potential to awaken their dormant empathy remains.*]

A dawning realisation came to Alice then of the long, long game being played and of her people's part in it. Alice could feel the One-Mind's attention on her. It was talking directly to her now. She was being briefed for some reason. The One-Mind wanted her to know.

[*Your intense paranoia and fear drove you humans to develop a psychic engine designed to attack and destroy an unknown and non-existent enemy, malevolent aliens from outer space. An engine was built to deliver the blast of energy required. It was an [untranslatable idea], capable of [untranslatable idea]. It will provide the psychic energy so urgently needed to control you. Our final defence. A last resort if the veil was in imminent danger of collapse.*]

It had come to that then. The veil was finally failing. The worlds were about to collide. Unless something could be done to stop it.

[*Our plan will only work if we assimilate all the people everywhere. Only then can we marshal the resilience and capacity to absorb and direct it. It will be all or nothing.*]

The One-Mind is going to go all out, Alice realised. It's going to give it one last shot. She still had only a vague idea what it was going to attempt. But whatever it was, both peoples were possibly approaching an extinction-level event.

"*No rest for the wicked.*" Alice dressed and left the house. The shit was about to hit the fan. She must raise the people. A hundred thousand years of history was about to come to fruition.

RUBY

The first of Wisemans Ferry's missing children to return was the girl, Ruby. She appeared suddenly, walking out of the bush near the old Great Northern Road. Spotted by the Ferryman as she wandered through the early morning mist rising from the Hawkesbury River. The police and the girl's mother were called.

"Where have you been, Ruby? We've all been so worried. You've been gone two weeks!" Ruby's mother looked as though she had not slept in days. Her wild hair was a little beyond tousled. Her make-up, such of it as there was, had been hastily applied. She appeared to be wearing the clothes she had been sleeping in. This was a woman overwhelmed by dread, pushed way beyond her capacity for hope, given sudden reprieve. She was close to breaking point.

The little girl stared back at her mother, impassive, calm. Explanation concealed behind the otherness, willing her mother to understand. Her silent, wordless account left unperceived, unheard, lost.

At that moment, Ruby noticed a woman step forward. She had turned up with the police. She was not a local. Ruby did not know her.

"Hello, Ruby." The woman's soft voice betraying a lilt of something far away, "My name's Kaitlin. We can't hear you, sweetheart. You can hear us, can't you?" The girl gave a little nod. "We need you to use spoken word like we are." There was a pause to make sure the little girl understood. "Now, can you tell me your name please, using words?"

"Ruby."

"Yes?"

"Ruby McFarlane."

"Welcome back, Ruby." The woman gave her a warm smile, "You've had a bit of an adventure, haven't you? You must be hungry. You can tell us all about it over breakfast." The girl smiled. The woman offered Ruby her hand, and the girl took it.

In the background, a policeman whispered. "She's the one I told you about." The girl's mother nodded, confused and upset.

"She's the one who helped the other ones in Europe?"

"The changelings?"

"They're not changelings!" Kaitlin snapped, "Keep your thoughts to yourself." This was by no means her first encounter with the returned. The first few minutes and hours were crucial to resettling the child on the mundane side of the veil. Above all, the child should be encouraged to regard their experience as an exciting adventure rather than a trauma.

The girl's mother and the policeman held back, uncertain what was expected, not sure what to do. Kaitlin was thinking back to an earlier returnee, a little boy, son of a horse whisperer who lived no-one-knew-where exactly, to the north of the village of Béal an Daingin in Galway, on the west coast of Ireland. It had taken nearly a year for him to speak, and he had been gone only four weeks. Time seemed to pass differently on the other side of the veil.

Kaitlin looked at the girl as they crossed the road from the tiny police station and headed the few yards to the Wiseman's Ferry Inn and breakfast.

"I like scrambled eggs with buttered toast, do you?"

Ruby nodded.

"I have to have the toast buttered all the way to the crust, otherwise, I just can't eat it at all. Am I a bit fussy?" The girl smiled but made no answer.

"What's your favourite, Ruby?"

The girl hesitated a moment, "Vegemite fingers." She looked up at the woman holding her hand. "And scrambled eggs." Ruby turned, searching for her mother. She reached out with her free hand, beckoning her mum to come closer. She took her mother's hand and continued walking between the two women.

"That's ok, isn't it, mum?"

"Yes, my darling. You can have anything you want."

The small party made its way the short distance down the hill to the Inn.

"Will she be ok?" Ruby's mother appeared close to collapse. Kaitlin reached across Ruby giving the woman a reassuring squeeze.

"Ruby's fine, aren't you, pet? Nothing a nice breakfast, a shower, and a change of clothes won't fix. Am I right?"

Ruby turned to her mum, suddenly grave. "I'm sorry Mum. You must have been worried." Ruby's mum burst into tears, overcome with the stress and dread of the last two weeks. Ruby took her hand, stroking it gently, "I'm ok, Mum. I'm back. It's all ok."

The harsh, intrusive sound of a truck braking hard cut across the early morning stillness. The sound of airbrakes hissed angrily as a small convoy of military Unimog trucks appeared on the 'S' bend curve of the escarpment above and began their sluggish, wheezing descent to the village, their freshly painted digital camouflage looking oddly jaunty in the morning light.

DIRECTIONS

There was a voicemail message waiting for Jack when he landed at Sydney airport. It was from the manager of the Wisemans Ferry Inn. The message was short and sweet. One of the missing girls, a girl by the name of Ruby McFarlane, had just turned up safe and sound. The police were involved as she could not account for her whereabouts during her absence. Also, there was some foreigner, a Yank maybe, or Irish, who was somehow involved in the investigation. His usual room had been reserved for him if he wanted it.

Jack picked up a ute that had been left for him and called Jerry as he drove. He left a message as to his destination and intent.

The narrow winding Old Northern Road that had always seemed so welcoming and familiar in the past now seemed interminable and slow, and maddeningly twisty as Jack snaked his way across the hilly wooded countryside. At last, Jack swung the ute into the small car park of the Wisemans Ferry Inn. The sun was already thinking about setting as he grabbed his bag and jumped out. He was tired after the rushed journey from the Queensland gem fields, but he was also anxious to hear any news and desperate to join in the search for Emma.

Jack grabbed his stained and much-worn old rucksack from the passenger seat and made his way into the cool, shady interior of the pub. The manager greeted him as he entered the front bar and handed him the key to his room. As Jack thanked him for his message and the key, the manager leaned forward, nodding his head in the direction of a youngish red-headed woman wearing muddy walking boots and an old hiking jacket, sitting on a bench in the corner of the bar.

"That's her," he whispered. "That's the Yank." Both men turned, attempting to gain a surreptitious glance at the foreign woman.

"What's her name?" Jack spoke quietly, not quite deigning to whisper. She was not bad-looking, Jack had to admit. There was something a little prim about her, but there was depth too, and he recognised in her a deep inner strength to which he was also strongly drawn. Despite himself, and to his great surprise, he found he was immediately attracted to her. She was, he realised, the first woman he had thought of in that way since Karen died. Jack found himself wondering if Emma would approve, and that thought brought him back to the moment at hand and the role and interest of this foreign woman in whatever was going on.

"Kaitlin, something. It's written in the register. I'll check for you later."

As if sensing that she was the subject of someone's attention, Kaitlin looked up. She noticed the two men staring back at her and smiled.

"Trying to decide which one of you will buy me the first drink, are you?"

The two men were momentarily nonplussed, caught unawares by Kaitlin's sudden attention and forthright approach. Jack broke the silent impasse.

"That's simple," he smiled his broadest, most engaging smile, "He will." indicating the pub's manager.

"He most certainly will not." The manager was having none of it, "You can buy your girls your own drinks."

"Well, what are you having?" Jack appeared serenely indifferent to the manager's comment.

Kaitlin wasn't quite sure how she felt about being described as one of this man's girls. It wasn't that he was unattractive. She had to admit he had a certain rustic, Aussie charm, but she would never consent to being one among several of anyone's girls. She could see the man was waiting for an answer and, she admitted to herself, she could do worse than have a drink with him. He did look familiar somehow, or maybe he just had one of those faces.

Kaitlin was not much of a drinker, but she cast her mind back to an earlier era and a night out with friends in Dublin's Temple Bar district.

"I'll have a rum and black, please." It was the only drink whose name she could recall. The black currant cordial hid the bite of the rum.

Jack glanced over at the barman, "Coopers Pale Ale and a rum and black for the lady, please".

Jack squeezed his bulky frame onto the hard, wooden bench next to Kaitlin, stuffing his rucksack under the bench. He placed the drinks on the scarred old wooden table and turned to get a good look at the woman.

"Don't mind me, will you? Just look me up and down, why don't you, like I'm a prize heifer."

Jack remained impervious. "I'm Jack, and you are?"

"Feeling distinctly disrespected at the moment."

Kaitlin gave up after a moment and responded more gracefully. "Kaitlin O'Neill, pleased to meet you."

"Pleased to meet you too," Jack was never one for small talk, "I understand you're over here investigating the disappearances."

Kaitlin did not respond immediately. Instead, she took a moment to size the man up.

"Yes," she ventured after a second or two, "I'm doing a story for the Christian Science Monitor".

"Why would the Christian Science Monitor be interested in a few kids going walkabout in Australia?"

"They're not. Well, they weren't very keen. I sold them on it."

"Why?"

"Well, because I was interested, am interested, in these and other disappearances. There have been others recently, too, around the world, usually in wild or wilderness areas."

"You think they are connected?"

"Well, no, err, yes, possibly, or not. I don't know." she finished off lamely.

"Why would they be connected? How?"

"We don't think they are, necessarily, but then, they may be."

"We? Who's 'we'?"

Things were getting a bit out of hand. Kaitlin had not expected such a direct forensic onslaught from someone she had taken to be little more challenging than a local farm hand.

"Who exactly are you, Jack? You seem to have more than a casual interest in all this?"

Jack took a moment to compose himself before he answered.

"I'm Jack. My daughter Emma is the missing girl."

And as chance would have it, if it was chance, that was when Jerry, who had driven hard from his office in the city the moment he heard Jack's message, burst into the crowded bar.

"Kaitlin O'Neill," Jerry was standing in the doorway, incongruous and out of place in his silky svelte Armani suit, "I see you've met my brother Jack."

Kaitlin stared from one man to the other, mouth agape.

"You're the man in the photograph? You're Jack Hexenkriege?"

"You know this woman?"

Kaitlin and Jack spoke over each other, both amazed at the sudden turn of events.

"Yes." Jerry was smug, as only Jerry knew how, "Indeed. We had coffee together out at the drill site."

Jack looked dumbfounded.

"With Alice." Jerry continued, "Alice Whalebone. Her people are joining the search." Jerry was, if anything, even more smug, almost, one might say, to bursting.

"She seemed to feel the protest had run its course." Kaitlin chimed in, "We've been overtaken by events. That's what she said."

"You turned Alice Whalebone into an ally of Red Earth?" Jack was bewildered and, despite himself, more than a little impressed.

"Yes. Well, not exactly an ally, but she's called off the protest." Jerry was fairly fit to explode with pride.

"I felt it was something more personal than that," Kaitlin spoke up again, "I think she wants to help you guys and Emma. For personal reasons."

Jerry scowled for a moment, unwilling to have his moment of triumph taken away so easily. Then he brightened.

"Yes, Jack and I go way back with Alice."

"You all grew up together in the forest. In the Wollemi Forest."

Both men were silent, each recalling what was meaningful to them of those happy, halcyon days.

"Kaitlin, would you join us for dinner?" Jerry was once again the attentive host, "They do a good steak here, and the chips are hand cut and crunchy," Jerry paused, "but I warn you, Kaitlin, by all means, keep well away from the chicken schnitzel! It would take two grown men to finish one."

The three made their way through to the restaurant. Enormous plate-glass windows revealed an expansive deck crowded with customers, and beyond them, a paddock leading down to the river and, in the middle distance, massive sandstone cliffs, bathed in the golden light of evening, reflected in the slow-flowing water.

Orders eventually placed, they settled down in a corner of the deck to watch the sunset and let the evening draw its dark veil across the forest and the day.

"Katlin's doing a piece. Did she tell you?" Jerry sipped from a large glass of red wine, "on the missing children."

Jack nodded.

"She's with the Christian Science Monitor," Jerry was attempting small talk, always guaranteed to irritate Jack.

"Yes, I know," Jack snapped back, "she told me already."

"Kaitlin's a journalist." Jerry was on a roll. Jack rolled his eyes.

"Brothers always know exactly how to wind each other up, don't they?" Kaitlin was enjoying the exchange.

"Kaitlin was going to explain to me who she's working with on the story, I mean." Jack's tone was light, offhand, but his eyes were bright and focused under his dark, brooding brows.

"Oh, let a girl have her secrets, won't you?" Kaitlin adopted a bantering tone in reply, "I have my contacts."

"Yes," Jerry piped in, "Kaitlin has access to extensive, untold resources." This was aimed at Jack, a caution to him, suggesting perhaps that Jerry would reveal more later when they were in private.

The three fell silent for a few moments, watching as the sun began slowly to sink and the filtered Australian sunlight fell full upon the cliffs towering over the broad reach of the river, oblique and golden-orange in the early evening. Every rock, every nook and cranny and every tree and leaf appeared in sharp relief, each gilded, ancient and yet somehow fresh, as if newly wrought when the world was made, perhaps only a moment ago.

In the end, it was Jerry who broke the silence.

"Kaitlin, you and Jack should take a look at the picnic spot where Emma went missing. Jack knows the place, in the forest above Upper MacDonald, near Dad's place." Jerry looked to Jack for confirmation.

"There's a few chores I need to attend to in the morning." Jack, habituated since boyhood to evading Jerry's manipulations, appeared less than enthusiastic at the thought of guiding this Irish/American woman into the Wollemi Forest. "Tell you what. I'll write detailed directions. You've already found your way out to St Albans?"

Kaitlin nodded.

"Well then, you take the Webbs Creek Ferry and the St Albans Road and turn left just after the St Albans Bridge. Follow the MacDonald River up into the hills. You can't miss it."

Kaitlin, who was not overjoyed herself at the prospect of a long drive into the wilderness with the younger Hexenkriege brother, was even less impressed at the idea of being sent out into the uncharted forest with nothing but a hastily scribbled set of directions.

"Don't you want to see where your daughter disappeared?" Kaitlin was deliberately provocative now, irritated by the suspicion that she was being manipulated by this unlikely pair.

"Of course, I do." Jack half lifted out of his chair. "What the hell do you mean by that? Find your own bloody way then." Jack grabbed his beer and sipped on it sullenly. Jerry attempted to smooth things over.

"Go later in the day when Jack's had time to sort out the things he needs to do. Two sets of eyes are better than one."

"Sorry, I meant no offence." Kaitlin was contrite. "It must be a terrible strain, not knowing where your daughter is, or if she's lying hurt somewhere, or …."

Jack cut in, not wishing to hear what further awful scenario Kaitlin was about to posit.

"Ok, meet me out the front of the Inn at noon."

"Ok. Thanks." Kaitlin smiled sheepishly, not sure if she had been manoeuvred into something or had manoeuvred herself out.

The food arrived, and the three of them ate in silence. Kaitlin was surprised at just how hungry she was. As Jerry had suggested, the food was excellent. Jack ate with the dogged determination of a lumberjack on his lunch break, and Jerry toyed with his meal, turning it over with his fork and turning his nose up.

"Would you, gentlemen, please excuse me for a moment?" Kaitlin wanted to check for messages from the Director, and a trip to the little girl's room seemed like an inobtrusive excuse.

Once she was out of sight, Jerry turned to Jack.

"Information coming back to me from Alice and other sources suggests that Emma is visiting the Wollemi."

"Suggests?"

"Well, I'm pretty much certain that's where she is, Jack."

"Then she's safe. I mean, she's in no immediate physical danger."

"That's my feeling too. We need to get her back, of course, and quickly, but that still needs careful planning and execution."

Jack took a swig of beer and leaned back in his chair. His calm exterior hiding a maelstrom of emotion beneath. He was terrified that she would be assimilated by the Wollemi, and at the same time, he was reassured that she was most likely alive. The idea of Emma spending more than a few hours with the Wollemi filled him with dread. Though time passed differently behind the veil, she could come back much changed, and she might not come back at all.

Jerry sat back humming to himself, the thick purple-red Shiraz staining his lips like blood. From his point of view, things were coming along nicely. He was concerned about Emma, of course, but she was with her grandmother's people, of that much he was certain.

"What do you think of Kaitlin?" he asked, feigning nonchalance.

Jack thought about it for a moment, "Apart from being annoying, she seems smart enough, and she's not bad looking."

"I haven't been able to find out exactly who she's working for yet, but it's only a matter of time." Jerry took another sip of Shiraz.

"Do you reckon she's married?" Jack was as surprised as Jerry to hear himself asking such a question.

Jerry raised one eyebrow knowingly. A gesture perfectly designed to piss Jack off.

"It was just a question." Jack fumed into his beer.

"She's not married, I'm sure of that. She's not wearing a ring, and she just doesn't seem the domesticated type."

Kaitlin returned to find the two men deep in contemplation. There had been no messages from her boss.

Jerry's phone began to ring, and he wandered off to take the call.

"Can I get you another drink?" Jack moved a little closer to the Irish woman.

"Sure. I mean, thanks. Another rum and black would be grand."

When Jack returned from the bar, Jerry had reappeared.

"I've got to go home. Fiona and I are staying at the Wisemans Ferry house tonight, so we can be close to the search teams in case they turn up anything. You're both welcome to stay. We have heaps of room, as Jack can tell you."

"Thanks for the offer, but I'm staying in Sophia's Grand Bedroom here at the Inn." Kaitlin was firm but polite.

"I'm booked in here too, thanks. Give Fiona my love." Jack examined his fast-emptying glass. Jerry gave the two one of his most annoying, knowing looks and walked from the bar.

"He's my older brother, and you're right. He knows exactly how to wind me up."

"It's my understanding that older brothers always do." Kaitlin found herself warming to this brusque backwoodsman.

"My shout". Kaitlin manoeuvred her way past Jack. He watched her go, noting as she walked away that she didn't have a bad figure either.

Kaitlin returned with a Cooper's Pale Ale for Jack and a rum and black for herself. The atmosphere in the bar had reached the noisy but convivial point. It was a long time since she'd had a proper drink with a fella in a pub. Kaitlin had to admit she was enjoying herself.

At some point, Kaitlin mentioned the events in other wilderness areas and the other missing children. They had both enjoyed quite a few drinks by this time, and her account was a little fuzzy. In any case, Jack got the point that something way bigger than he had realised was probably going on and that Kaitlin believed the 'hidden' people were somehow involved. The sheer scale of it was all a bit much to take in after such a long day.

It was past midnight before they staggered upstairs to their rooms. Kaitlin, who was unused to drinking, gratefully accepted Jack's help on the stairs. There was a moment of disentanglement when they reached the landing outside her room. For a moment, they stood close, almost touching. Then Jack turned suddenly on his heel and stalked off in the direction of his own room.

"Good night," he called back, "see you in the morning."

The next morning, before he set about his allotted tasks, Jack stuffed a note under the windscreen wiper on the passenger side of Kaitlin's four-wheel drive. Just in case, perhaps, he could offload the strangely compelling woman. You never knew.

"In case you want to head off early and take a look on your own. Take the St Albans Road from Wiseman's Ferry. There are two crossings at Wiseman's, you take the Webbs Creek ferry to the St Albans Road. Follow the MacDonald River past St Albans and up into the wilderness. Keep going through Upper Macdonald, past the house with the shocking-pink roof, carry on through Higher Macdonald past the old weatherboard Kirk of St Phillip, through the farmyard with the geese and the next one with the two psycho border collies. Follow the track up to the 'four-wheel drive' sign (remembering to close the gate behind you) and continue on, fording the river three times. Watch out for livestock. The track is unfenced from the gate onwards. Watch the road as the track switches back this way and that as you go higher and deeper into the forest. Continue up the track as far as you can beyond the last ford. You will come to an area of beaten earth under a copse of tall trees. Park right under the trees and cover your vehicle with old branches and leaves. You will see the mountain in the distance. Walk towards the mountain. Follow the river. You'll see police tape if it's still there. That's where they were picnicking when Emma disappeared. P.S. Thanks for an enjoyable evening, Jack."

In the morning, Kaitlin found the note under the windscreen wiper. The day was bright and sunny, not too hot, and having checked out her route online. She thought she might just take a look at the picnic site herself, just to spite him.

However, when she jumped into the four-wheel drive, it wouldn't start. She had left the cabin light on, and the battery was completely dead. It wouldn't take a charge, and the punctiliously polite Indian proprietor at the petrol station said he didn't have a spare. The earliest he could get one was the next morning. The hire company couldn't get a technician out to Wisemans Ferry that day either. In the absence of any better option, Kaitlin began the painstaking task of talking to everyone in town, introducing herself, showing them her Media ID and asking them about the missing girls.

After a while, a pattern began to emerge. Firstly, no conversation about the disappearances would progress for more than a few sentences without the Hexenkriege brothers being brought into it. It wasn't that they were in any way 'implicated'. It was more that their engagement in the issue, and even the fact that the Hexenkriege girl was one of the missing, seemed, if not inevitable, then certainly unsurprising. The brothers were almost assumed by most of the people to be in some way integral to resolving the matter, especially 'now that Jack's back'. The phrase was repeated time and again in many different contexts. A conversation would often end with Now that Jack's back.' Sometimes, in dribs and drabs, occasional references were made to Jack going missing too once, long ago, when he was a boy.

After a long morning chatting with everyone and anyone Kaitlin could engage in conversation, she ended up at the Wisemans Ferry Grocer, which, along with the Inn, was one of the social centres of the isolated hamlet.

"I'd like a Caesar salad, no chicken but extra fetta, please."

"Sure thing," the cashier rang up the bill and passed Kaitlin a small stand with a number on it while she paid.

"You're the lady who got Ruby speaking, aren't you."

"Err, yes. That was me."

"You a psychologist then?"

"Not exactly. I'm a journalist. I'm from Ireland originally, and I came across a similar thing once before."

Kaitlin grabbed her number and stalked off to find a table.

A few minutes later, her salad arrived, delivered by the cashier.

"We've had some other odd goings on around here. I'm glad Jack's back. He'll get to the bottom of it."

"What about his brother, Jerry? He lives in the village, doesn't he?"

"People around here prefer Jack to Jerry." The woman grimaced. "We're suspicious of Jerry, to be honest. Folk don't trust him."

"Why is that?"

"We don't trust his money and power."

"Yes."

"But there's something else too, something deeper, underneath."

Kaitlin waited a moment for the woman to continue.

"Jack's one of us. He belongs here. Everyone likes him."

"He's not here often, from what I've heard."

"That's true since Karen died, but even though he's away a lot, always travelling, he's one of ours."

"And Jerry?"

The woman smiled awkwardly. "Jerry has always seemed a bit 'alien' kind of. Even though he was born and brought up in the area and keeps a home in the village."

"Alien?"

"Well, different. He's always been different. He's not a bad person. I don't think anyone thinks that. He contributes generously to community projects."

"What is it then? Underneath?"

"He's a smooth talker, manipulative maybe. Some folks are a little bit afraid of him, too, I reckon. Just a little bit."

A posse of cyclists pulled up outside, and the cashier jumped up and ran off to her station. Kaitlin wandered around and chatted with a few more people.

She turned up one other curious fact, confirmed by several locals, the original settlers of Wollombi village believed that 'the little people', as they called them, lived in the forest. Every Halloween, on the Eve of All Souls, they would put out effigies intended to ward them off and keep bad luck at bay. It was just a tradition, they claimed. But no one wanted to talk about it.

By the end of lunchtime, Kaitlin had a pretty good sense of who was who and what was what within the little township of Wisemans Ferry and the surrounding countryside.

The facts were clear. Only two girls had gone missing from Wisemans Ferry. Emma and Ruby, who had recently returned, unharmed physically but still unable or unwilling to talk about her experiences.

Kaitlin met Jack outside the Wisemans Ferry Inn at noon. *Precisely as ordered*, she thought to herself.

"Can you help me collect my equipment from the hotel, please? It's more awkward than heavy, and the stairs are narrow. I don't want to damage anything."

Up in Kaitlin's hotel room, Jack saw her bed was covered with weird and wonderful bits and bobs. As Kaitlin threw items into a hold-all, she explained what each item was, if not its precise purpose. There was a silver knife and a gold cup, a small Persian rug, and a collection of dried plant and animal parts. There was an aluminium bottle containing red wine and an assortment of powders and potions. Last of all was a large plastic bottle of plain kitchen salt.

Jack laughed when he saw Kaitlin place the salt in the holdall.

"It's like something out of Harry Potter. Are you planning on casting a spell to find Emma?"

"It's a sideline." Kaitlin smiled uncomfortably. "I find it helps to engage the intuition."

Jack laughed uneasily, things were becoming stranger and stranger by the minute.

"Never underestimate a woman's intuition Jack Hexenkriege."

"This is all a bit unexpected. You'd have to see that."

"You may laugh Jack, but salt is a key ingredient in any protective spell."

Jack realised that there was nothing for it but to consent to Kaitlin's wishes. He carried the holdall back down the narrow stair stairway to the ute. Realisation was beginning to sink in. He was heading out into the forest to search for his daughter with an Irish witch, posing as a reporter from the Christian Science Monitor, who was proposing to cast a spell to find Emma, who was living with the little people, using kitchen salt. This was a situation he could not possibly have imagined only a few hours before, back in Russian Gully. In the desert, everything was clean and clear. There was little in the way of ambiguity.

As they approached the Ute, some unaccustomed spirit of gallantry encouraged Jack to open the passenger door for Kaitlin. Jack slung Kaitlin's holdall on the back seat next to a beaten-up old esky. As they were travelling well off the beaten track, and the ute was a hire, Jack drove the few yards to the petrol station to check the oil and tyres. While Jack was fiddling about with the ute, Kaitlin quickly slipped across into the driver's seat. By the time Jack returned, it was a *fait accompli*.

"You don't mind if I drive, do you?" Kaitlin smiled sweetly, batting her eyelashes in an obvious and comical display of 'girlie charm'. It was too ridiculous. Jack laughed, defeated for the moment, and plonked himself down in the passenger seat.

"Sure, I don't often get to sightsee."

The ferry crossing was uneventful. They drove in silence at first. The dense forest seeming to hunker down on either side of the road. Kaitlin turned the windscreen wipers on and the headlights on full beam as the sky darkened and heavy late summer rain began to beat down. Lightning flashed, and thunder roared its primal warning. No cars came the other way. Neither spoke, to begin with, an unexpected shyness overcoming them both.

After a while, Jack began once more to question Kaitlin, determined to ferret out what exactly her interest was in the disappearances. Was she going to be a help or a hindrance in finding Emma, or just a hanger-on? Last night's conversation was a hazy blur, half-remembered.

"Sorry, but I just didn't get it." Jack's frustration was an almost palpable phenomenon hanging in the stuffy air between them. "Would you explain it again, one more time? Please."

Kaitlin opened the driver's side window an inch, letting in some fresh air. Raindrops pattered against the glass. The ute creaked and moaned its way along the narrow track. She took a moment to order her thoughts, gauging how much Jack could take in in one go.

"It's like this," she began, searching her mind for another way to explain, "There is evidence, and the evidence is growing, now that we are taking the time to look for it, that there was a thriving global civilisation prior to about 10,500 years ago, and it was destroyed."

"Ok, now hold it there." Jack butted in, determined this time to take it slow and examine each piece in the puzzle thoroughly as Kaitlin placed it in front of him.

"What evidence? Can you give some examples?"

"Well, the earliest pieces that we began to put together..."

"Who's 'we', who's putting the pieces together?"

"Well, that's another story in itself, but suffice to say, I am, in a small way, and many colleagues. Scientists and linguists and all sorts, really. Academics and enthusiasts like me." She paused. Jack remained silent.

"There was Stonehenge, of course. There's always Stonehenge. And there was New Grange in Ireland. Everyone knew they were ever so old, but nobody ever bothered to find out exactly how old or exactly who had built them. Not the druids, of course. Everyone knew that." Kaitlin paused again, casting her mind back.

"The first break came when people put together the Indus Valley Civilisation and the Vedas."

"The what?"

"There's a river in the Pakistan-India border region called the Indus, and along its banks, there had once been a great civilisation, but nobody knew who they were. They left no written record. None, that was, until some bright spark suggested that the Indian Vedas, which are a written history looking for a civilisation, belonged to the Indus Valley people, who were a civilisation in search of a history."

'What was so special about that?'

"Gosh, aren't you the impatient one? I was coming to that... Anyway, the Vedas describe a number of cities along the course of a river.

Now not all these cities could be found along the Indus." Jack began to stir. Kaitlin thought better of describing the fascinating detective work that had led to the next discovery and cut to the chase.

"They discovered that the missing cities were under the sea."

"Under the sea?"

"Yes, off the coast a little way. Fishing boats used to get their nets caught in the spires and rooftops of the sunken cities."

Jack made as if to speak but then fell silent.

"Anyway, if we assume that these cities were not built underwater but somehow ended up there, then either the land sunk or the sea level rose."

Realising that her audience was beginning once again to shift in his seat, Kaitlin decided to cut to the chase once more.

"Well, to cut a long story short, once people knew to look for them, artefacts started to come to light from all around the globe. Like the megalithic society that spanned Europe from Africa to the northern tip of Scandinavia. And not just artefacts, stories too and fragments of histories, ancient oral traditions all started to point to some hugely widespread civilisation destroyed by some global disaster. A flood. Possibly 'The Flood'." When after a moment or two, Jack remained silent, Kaitlin continued.

"The flood caused a leap in human evolution, we think, or a split in it or something. Anyway, after the flood, everything was different."

"Bugger me."

"Quite."

"So, what has all that got to do with me and my missing girl?"

"That is exactly what I'm here to find out."

Jack sighed heavily. The forest slipped past on either side, illuminated in glimpses as they passed by.

"Maybe some of them survived."

"Some of who?" Jack was becoming used to her random changes in direction.

"Some of the ancients, the people who built that civilisation."

"Survived how? That was thousands of years ago."

"The pines survived." Kaitlin settled back in her seat.

"That's true." Jack was one of very few people who knew the exact location of the remaining two hundred-million-year-old Wollemi Pines.

"If the wilderness can hide them for hundreds of millions of years, then who knows what else is out there?"

Jack tried a different tack, "But what about the weird animals? What's that all about?" Kaitlin had taken great pleasure in filling Jack in on the very many internet reports of strange animals turning up on beaches and elsewhere over recent years. None of it was making sense to him. The look of frustration on Jack's face was a site to behold.

Kaitlin smiled. The urge to laugh was all but overpowering. To her credit, she managed to keep her composure until Jack, a few moments later, his face the very image of wounded dignity, attempted to offer some smart alec comment. At which point she, and eventually Jack, broke into fits of uncontrollable laughter.

Kaitlin pulled the ute to a halt, struggling to catch her breath. Jack, who by this time had pulled himself together, was leaning back in his chair, tears still wet on his cheek. On impulse, Kaitlin leaned over to briefly dab his cheek with a scrunched-up tissue paper. Their faces, close together, intimate, glowed in the illumination offered by the dashboard lights.

I'm growing closer to this vagabond by the minute. Kaitlin found herself thinking. I must admit, I do like him.

Jack sat passively while Kaitlin dabbed his cheeks with the tissue, drying his tears. It was a sweetly intimate gesture, maternal in a way and distinctly feminine. Jack surprised himself by permitting it, but permit it he did.

The road surface had become seriously uneven. Kaitlin restarted the engine, engaged the lower range gearbox, and moved off again slowly, the vehicle jogging along at around ten kilometres an hour.

"They're from beyond the veil."

"Beyond the what?"

"The veil" Kaitlin arched an eyebrow knowingly.

"What veil? What are you talking about?" Jack was once again pissed off. The woman knew more than she had shared thus far. Jack was once more on his guard.

"Jack." Kaitlin slowed the ute almost to a halt and turned towards him, making eye contact, ensuring she had his full attention, 'the world is changing. Something important is changing.' Jack, unsure of what Kaitlin already knew and still unwilling to open up to her, dissembled.

"You're not on about the climate again, are you? I know all about that. I didn't just crawl out from under a rock, you know!"

"Not the sodding climate Jack. Don't pretend. It's the veil between the worlds. I believe you already know. It's weakening. That's why the weird animals are appearing. They're breaking through the weak points, where the veil is thinnest."

"The veil between the worlds?" Jack stared incredulously at the Irish scientist-witch whatever she was. How the hell did she know about that?

Frustrated at his lack of response, Kaitlin slammed on the brakes. Once again, stopping the ute dead in its tracks. This time the motor stalled.

"It's true, Jack, you know it is. You've seen it yourself."

Kaitlin took his brawny right arm in hers. Flicking on the tiny overhead light, she turned his wrist and hand this way and that, examining him carefully, searching for some kind of a sign or mark.

"You've met them, haven't you?" Kaitlin's stare was probing, intent.

Jack was about to proffer some glib, sneering reply, but something in her manner stopped him short. He did know what she meant. He recalled the almond, black eyes beneath the fern tree, the slim dark brown woman who looked like Jerry and his mum. He recalled the weird ghostly cave at St Albans Common. He was not ready to talk about them yet, not to her, and certainly not now.

Kaitlin leaned forward, turned the key in the ignition and gunned the engine, exasperated. Jack attempted a further diversion. "Why are you driving my truck anyway?"

"Oh, stop your whingeing. Women are better drivers than men. It's a fact. You can look it up."

They carried on, once again in silence, as the bitumen gave out and the gravel took over. They had been climbing steadily since leaving the village of St Albans, nestled in a broad loop of the Macdonald River. No signs of human habitation could be seen now, no lonely farmsteads, just the track ahead and forest to either side. To Kaitlin, it seemed as though they were driving back in time. There was no mobile communications network here, no TV signal and no mains electricity, indeed none of the accoutrements of modern civilisation. None but the hardiest people lived here, and none but the most ancient rules of life applied.

After a while, Jack tried again, "Even if some survived, what have they got to do with Emma and the other missing children?"

"Have you heard of changelings?"

"Changelings? No, I don't think so."

"In my own country, we have a long history of changelings, children taken away by the elves and returned very changed, or perhaps swapped for a doppelganger."

"You're losing me again – you're not saying we have child-stealing elves in the Wollemi Forest?" It was clear that Kaitlin knew much more than he and Jerry had thought possible. Their secret was perhaps not so secret after all. Jack's resolve began to weaken.

"Well," Kaitlin paused longer this time, uncertain how to proceed, uncertain for her part how much of this, no doubt classified, information she should give away, "I am, and I'm not."

"What? You are, and you're not what?"

"I am saying that, and I'm not, and now I've said too much."

"The elves are stealing children in the Wollemi Forest. My Emma has been stolen by elves." Even as he spoke, forcing as much doubt and incredulity into his voice as he could muster, Jack knew full well the underlying truth of what Kaitlin was suggesting. But he was still not ready to talk about it openly. Some old and deep inhibition still held him back.

"They are, and they aren't, well they may be, but they don't see it that way."

"Who don't see it that way? The elves? You are off your head! What have you been smoking?" Jack, never one for deep introspection, was angry now. Fear and doubt taking the form of rage, suspecting she had been playing him for a fool, at the same time afraid that she hadn't. If Kaitlin knew all about this and had encountered the Wollemi herself in Ireland, then all this was much bigger than he had thought. Whatever was going on was way beyond his current frame of understanding.

"I've lived in the Wollemi Forest all my life, and I've never seen any sign of any bloody elves!" He knew this wasn't true. His words rang false. He knew what she meant by elves.

"Haven't you?" Kaitlin was serious, studying Jack's face intently. Jack paused, breathless, halted by the intensity of her stare.

"What do you mean?"

"Think back. Think hard. Have you never encountered something, some phenomenon, that seemed out of place, just plain wrong somehow?"

"What are you getting at? What do you know or think you know?"

"As you say, Jack, you've lived here all your life. Nobody knows the Wollemi Forest half as well as you do." The silence stretched out between them, each alone with their thoughts. The track became more uneven and bumpy. Kaitlin once more slowed the vehicle to a crawl.

"I've heard stories." Kaitlin continued, "The villagers talk. About a boy who got lost once a long time ago. About a boy who lived deep in the forest alone with his father and brother until the age of nine or ten." As the conversation had become more intense, the ute had slowed almost to a complete halt.

"Me. You're talking about me." Jack fell silent, trying not to assimilate the idea, trying not to make sense of Kaitlin's questions. He looked up, deep into the eyes of this strange, intense Irish woman.

"You think I'm a changeling."

Kaitlin stopped the ute and met his stare, unflinching.

"Are you?"

Jack did not speak at once. This woman was the first person other than his father and brother with whom he might be prepared to discuss the secret hidden in the forest. Jack studied Kaitlin's face, making up his mind. Despite the irritating twists and turns of her conversation and the unnerving directness of her questioning, Jack realised he felt closer to this woman now than he had to anyone since Karen's death.

"Ok, I did have a kind of an experience many years ago. I suppose I could tell you about it".

It was not long before they reached the point where they needed to ford the shallow river. The geese and psycho Border Collies that Jack had warned her about were, thankfully, left some kilometres behind. The track had thinned out to a couple of rutted lines on either side of a grassy centre. Kaitlin stopped the ute at the edge of the shallow slope leading down to the water.

"Ok, this is as far as I'm driving. I don't do rapids and I need to set up the satellite mapping thingy." Someone back at HQ would be able to track her sat-nav signal. At least someone would know where she was.

Jack and Kaitlin observed the shallow, swiftly flowing water for a moment or two. The river, at this point, was maybe a few inches deep.

"Rapids?" Jack smiled as he jumped out of the car and began to walk round to the driver's side. Kaitlin slid across from the driver's seat and was already rummaging in her pack by the time he jumped in and gunned the engine. She attached a small electronic device to the windscreen with a suction cap.

"Ok." Sitting back and watching the birds-eye images moving across the tiny screen, "Let's hear it. From the beginning, Jack."

The four-wheel drive rumbled down the shallow slope and into the clear running water. Jack concentrated on navigating the few yards to the further bank before responding.

"There's not that much to tell." The vehicle lurched up the opposite bank and wobbled its way along the rough track.

"I was born in a little house, not much more than a shack really, in what they call an 'enclosure' in the Wollemi Forest."

"What's an enclosure?"

"An enclosure is a privately-owned piece of land within a larger government-owned area or within common land." Jack appeared to be quoting from memory, "It's an English legal concept, I think, from the colonial days. Imported with the convicts." Jack turned and smiled at Kaitlin, sizing up her reaction.

"The reason it matters is that the state government wants to get rid of them, all enclosures in wilderness areas, and the owners naturally want to hang on to them."

"Why doesn't the government just ban them or compulsorily purchase them or something?"

"You'd have to ask Jerry that. There's some kind of federal government deed to them or something, outside the state's authority maybe."

"Anyway," Kaitlin was impatient to get on with the story. "You lived in this shack in the wilderness. With your mum and dad and Jerry? Yes?"

"I don't really remember my mum." Jack sounded almost wistful as he reached back in time to early childhood. "I barely remember her."

"Yes?" Kaitlin was keen to encourage him to keep talking.

"She was small and warm." Jack paused for a moment, summoning up a memory or attempting to. "I can't remember her voice, just her warm arms holding me and the peace and silence of the place."

"What happened to her?"

"She left."

"Was there a row? Did your parents have problems?"

Jack was momentarily annoyed at these intrusive, probing questions, but eventually, he continued.

"No, I don't remember any strife. I don't remember any arguments at all. After she left, my dad was very quiet, now that I think about it. I guess he was lonely."

"Where did she go?"

Jack paused for quite a while before answering.

"She returned to her own people, I guess."

"You guess?"

"No, I'm sure. She went back to her people."

"Where was she from?"

Jack didn't reply. The track was thinning out to a narrow grassy way between overhanging trees. Branches occasionally scraped the roof or sides of the vehicle.

"Was she Indigenous, an Aboriginal woman?" Kaitlin had been wondering at the brothers' dark colouring.

"No, she wasn't." Jack slowed the vehicle almost to a stop. He turned to the woman sitting next to him, wanting to take her measure.

"You better ask my dad about that. He lives a little way past the picnic spot."

"After your mum left, you lived just with your dad and Jerry? Your dad never remarried?"

"Yep. Just me, Jerry and Dad. He never remarried."

The car hit a bump in the road as it began to edge its way under the trees. The satellite mapping device fell from the windscreen into Kaitlin's lap.

"We'll walk from here." Jack turned off the engine. The four-wheel drive was hidden deep under the overhanging branches of an old tree.

The couple grabbed their packs and jumped out of the air-conditioned vehicle into the humid, insect-rich shade of the forest. Within seconds mosquitos started to bite. Jack sprayed himself with jungle strength mosquito repellent and then offered the can to Kaitlin. She nodded without taking the can. Jack took a moment to spray her exposed skin, arms and hands, ankles and neck. He sprayed a little of the aerosol onto her hands, and Kaitlin applied it to her face and ears.

Kaitlin attached the satellite mapping device to her belt.

"I got lost once," Jack continued unprompted, "Jerry and I were playing deep in the forest, and I got spooked."

They walked together in silence for a few minutes before Jack picked up the tale.

"We were hunting the dragon that lived in a cave in the heart of the forest." Jack smiled at the memory, "We were fierce and intrepid."

"I bet you were." Kaitlin laughed lightly, "How long were you missing?"

"I wasn't missing, not like Emma and the other girl. I was just lost. For the afternoon only. Someone found me and took me home."

"Were you frightened?"

"I guess I must have been. I had a powerful imagination back then."

"What did you imagine? What did you think you saw?"

"Yes," Jack's voice was quiet, "Eyes staring out from deep within a cave, and a face."

"Did you see who it was? Did you recognise the face?"

"Sort of," He paused. "No, not really recognise, but there was something familiar about it."

"Did it scare you?"

Jack paused again, unwilling or unused to talking about events from so long ago, "Yes. I must have been scared. I ran hell for leather into the forest."

Up ahead, a few strips of yellow plastic ribbon were visible, strung around a couple of small gum trees, indicating the site of the picnic.

"Were you really lost? How did you find your way out?"

"I fell." Jack almost whispered as if talking to himself. "I fell from a height into cold clear water." He was lost in memory, "I was sinking, drowning. Someone grabbed me. Pulled me out."

Kaitlin remained silent. After a moment more, Jack appeared to snap back to the present.

"That's all I remember. It was someone from Alice's husband's people, another Whalebone, the guy who found me." Then, looking around, "This is our picnic spot." Jack turned around, taking in the well-remembered scene. To the south and east, the forest could be seen sweeping away in endless waves across the low hills, a seemingly infinite expanse. A sea of trees. To the north and west, the tall, flattened peak of a mountain could be seen, rising above the trees, like a blunted tooth. A narrow little-used track wound away from the picnic site into the deeper forest.

"Is that where she went? Where Emma went?" Kaitlin indicated the narrow track.

"Yes, Dad told Jerry and Fiona that she wandered off to pick wildflowers or climb a tree or something. She knew the area pretty well. We've been here many times."

"You weren't here?"

"No," Jack scuffed the dirt with the toe of his boot, "I was up north, mining."

Kaitlin did not speak.

Jack looked up, catching Kaitlin's eye.

"Opals this last time, sapphires next, and emeralds if I can find them. Even rubies sometimes."

"Emma doesn't live with you?"

Jack, stung by the question, took a moment to answer.

"I live a nomadic life, out in the bush most of the time. I'm not married, and a mine site is not a safe place to bring up a child. She's better off with Jerry and Fiona." The explanation sounded both defensive and well-rehearsed in Kaitlin's ears. She knew better than to probe the point at that moment.

"You're a part owner of Red Earth Mining, yet you prefer to mine gems on your own account?"

"I reckon there are probably two kinds of miners. Those who go after precious metals and gems and those who go after minerals. Jerry is into resources, commodities, and minerals, he's a businessman. I like the pretty stuff."

The pair looked around the site, poking about with the toe of a boot, not sure what they were looking for. The police had been all over it at the time.

"Shall we walk down the track a little way?" Kaitlin was keen to lift the mood a little, "It's a lovely spot right enough."

"Sure." Jack took one more quick look around the picnic site before following Kaitlin into the shade of the trees.

They walked on under the deep green canopy for perhaps twenty minutes in total silence. Neither speaking, both focussed deep within their own thoughts. The whirring of the cicadas rose and fell in waves of sound as they walked, sometimes rising to almost deafening crescendos, sometimes falling away to silence.

Finally, the trees gave out, and the pair walked into a little clearing. The sun could be seen beginning its slow descent into the distant west.

"We should head back soon. We don't want to navigate the track in the dark."

"You said your dad lived near here."

"We can go see him tomorrow. I'll ask Jerry if he wants to come along."

Kaitlin, lost in her own inner world, spoke her thoughts aloud, more to herself than to Jack, "What happened to Emma's mother? Where is she?"

Jack froze. This was the question he dreaded most. He knew it was coming at some point. People always asked, but still, he dreaded the answer and the silent accusation he always felt in giving it.

"Emma's mother is dead." Jack stared into the middle distance, hoping Kaitlin would leave it there. Knowing she wouldn't. No one ever did.

"Oh, how awful," she responded immediately, "how did she die?"

This was it. This was where the silent accusation rose up and smacked him straight in the face. This was the part he hated and feared most.

"We were camping. Up near the Table of the Gods."

Kaitlin had heard mention of the place, but she had little idea where it was – somewhere in the Wollemi Forest, that's all she knew.

"Um…" Kaitlin was anxious to keep him talking.

"We'd been there before, a few times. She knew the layout. We all did."

"Yes."

"It was getting dark. I was looking for the stuff to light a fire. Karen went off to get something from the ute."

"That was Emma's mother's name, Karen?"

"Yes."

"Go on."

"I had the only torch." Jack was breathing heavily, forcing himself to go on.

"As I said, it was getting dark. She tripped and fell. She died."

"I'm so sorry." Kaitlin could see the pain and grief on Jack's face, plain and fresh and new as if it had happened only yesterday.

"It was my fault." Jack's voice was emotionless, flat. "Karen asked me to pack three torches, but I forgot."

"How old was Emma?"

"She had just turned seven."

"You can't blame yourself."

"Don't you ever try to tell me what I can and cannot blame myself for?" Jack was incandescent with rage. "You know nothing about it."

The anger faded as suddenly as it had come. "I'm sorry, I don't know where that came from. That was uncalled for."

"It's understandable," Kaitlin placed a hand lightly on his arm, "I apologise."

"She was afraid of the dark."

"Karen?"

"Yes. She said she saw eyes staring back at her. She didn't like camping much. I think she only agreed to it to please me."

Thinking back on that terrible night from the vantage point of all that had transpired recently, Jack wondered if Karen had been right all along, that there had indeed been eyes staring back at her from the forest.

The sun was lowering in the western sky. There was still plenty of time to get back before dark, but there was no point stretching it. Not with the two psycho Border Collies and the farmyard full of geese to navigate.

"Let's get back to the pub and get pissed," Kaitlin suggested.

"Bloody good idea." Jack smiled, pulling himself together. There was nothing immediate he could do to find Emma. If she was with the Wollemi, then they would need to plan her retrieval carefully. It would take a small team to get her back.

The pair made their way back to the picnic spot. They took one last look around and then headed back to the ute.

The drive back to Wisemans Ferry was uneventful. The lights were on at the lonely farmhouse where the dogs lived. The animals must have been taken inside. There was no welcoming committee on the way home. As if to make up for it, however, the farmyard appeared to be full of geese, augmented by a thousand undisciplined and skittish ducks. Nevertheless, they made it through, arriving at the ferry as dusk was falling.

As they slowed to join the short queue of cars waiting for the ferry, Kaitlin noticed a large red octagonal stop sign at the side of the road. Someone had painstakingly painted a brief message below the word 'STOP'. As she was on the passenger side Kaitlin was able to read, in a clear and neat typeface, the following message:

"NSW ROADS AND MARITIME SERVICE
PLEASE DRIVE CAREFULLY GOANNA LEGS"

There were times, Kaitlin thought, when rural Australia took a bizarre turn. Kaitlin glanced over at Jack, who seemed distracted, staring across the river at the approaching car ferry. Australian culture was different from American culture, or Irish culture, for that matter. Their sense of humour was oddly different. There was something not just dry but desiccated about the delivery. It was not just that someone in this remote, perhaps forgotten, community had taken the trouble to amend the STOP sign in the first place. It was the fact that they had gone to such lengths to do a professional-looking job of it. It took a moment for the casual passer-by to notice that there was anything odd about the sign at all.

A few moments later, the ferry slipped into its berth. The heavy steel drawbridge clattered and clanged as it fell into place and slid noisily up the concrete ramp. A few cars rolled off before the signal was given for Jack to drive onto the ferry. A few minutes after that, Kaitlin and Jack were sitting in the front bar of the Wisemans Ferry Inn, contemplating a schooner of Cooper's most excellent pale ale and a double rum and black. It had been an eventful day for both of them.

They had a few more drinks in the bar before heading into the restaurant to grab something to eat. The atmosphere between them was easy, almost domestic. The events of the day demanded their attention. Both had plenty to think about. They decided to turn in early. It was going to be another long day tomorrow.

Back in his hotel room, after a quick shower, Jack found himself once again reviewing recent events. He liked Kaitlin, he realised. Oh, she could be as annoying as hell, but he enjoyed her company. He liked the way she looked too, and the way she carried herself. She was strong and intelligent, and she could make a good partner in life. Perhaps she would make a good stepmother to Emma. Somewhere, Jack mused, out in the deep forest, Emma would be settling down to sleep with her grandmother's people. Silently, he sent her his love and wished her a good night's sleep. Perhaps it was time to end his wandering ways. Perhaps it was time to stop running and come home. And perhaps, just perhaps, Kaitlin O'Neill might have a part to play in that.

THE SHACK IN THE FOREST

The next day Jack and Kaitlin headed for the shack in the forest. The geese were not as bad this time around, but the psycho dogs were worse. It seemed they were making up for missing the ute on its way past the evening before. One dog ran ahead of the vehicle, trying to slow it down by leaping up at the front grill, snarling and biting, while the other jumped up at the driver's window, growling and snapping, trying to open the door with its teeth. This palaver carried on for nearly a kilometre until the couple forded the river. The river, it seemed, was the boundary of the dogs' territory. Although it was shallow enough for them to cross, the ravening beasts would go no further. Instead, they ran up and down the far bank of the stream, barking and howling like banshees until the ute disappeared into the trees.

Jack, Kaitlin and wheezing ute passed the yellow tape surrounding the forlorn-looking picnic site and continued under the canopy of the forest. It was not long until they reached an open glade and then dove once more under the trees. The track thinned still further, becoming ever more winding and uneven. The forest on either side of the narrow way became increasingly dense and would have been near impassable for anyone on foot. The canopy hunkered down over the rough pathway giving every impression of a narrow, dimly lit tunnel cut by hand through the living trees. The sense of the wild crept in. It felt to Kaitlin as though they were travelling beyond the end of civilisation into some primordial territory governed by primeval laws derived directly from the elemental heartbeat of creation. As the track gradually thinned, threatening to peter out completely, Kaitlin began to feel that her last connection with the modern world was being taken away. Were it not for the satellite tracker attached to her belt, she would have felt lost and very alone, despite Jack's presence. She took a moment to check the tracker was working, watching the regular flickering of the tiny green dot marking their passage.

"Not far now," Jack answered Kaitlin's unasked question, "from here on, we must use low gear and engage the four-wheel drive." The path dipped precipitously as the hillside fell away from the ridge.

Finally, as the muggy and all but lightless tunnel grew unbearably oppressive, the ute broke through the trees into a wide cleared area dipping less steeply towards another river and a small, apparently collapsing house, visible in the distance. Something about its dilapidation and isolation reminded Kaitlin of childhood stories of isolated witches living in the woods.

On the far side of the river rose a tall sandstone cliff, ancient and worn, covered with eucalyptus trees of all sorts and sizes. Jack stopped the ute. He needed a moment to reset his focus and take in the view. Kaitlin stared across at the bucolic scene, so different in spiritual feel and emotional tone from the journey through the tunnel in the trees.

"This is where your father lives?" Kaitlin was unable to keep the tone of incredulity from her voice.

Jack realised it was only now, perhaps seeing his old home through Kaitlin's eyes, taking a look at it as if for the first time, that he noticed the obvious signs of decay and neglect. Despite Jerry's many offers to fix up the old house, their father valued his solitude. "I don't want a bunch of tradies ferreting around the place," he would say. And that would be that.

The weatherboard was grey from the battering of sun and wind, any paintwork long since weathered away. The chimney, from which wisps of thin grey smoke were wafting, was cocked at a crooked angle inviting the viewer to believe it could collapse at any moment. One side of the wrap-around veranda had collapsed, and there appeared to be a large, healthy gum tree growing through the roof of the shed. There was, however, a new-looking water tank to one side and a sparkling array of solar panels perched precariously on the rusting corrugated iron roof. Jack started the engine and began the slow descent to the house.

"Home sweet home." Jack looked a little embarrassed as the ute bounced its way painfully down the uneven slope towards his ancestral pile. He pulled the vehicle up a few yards from the house.

"Safe enough to avoid damage if the place should collapse unexpectedly."

"Well," Kaitlin was at her least discreet after the bone-shaking ride down the slope, "you couldn't say unexpectedly."

Jack turned off the engine, allowing it a few final coughs and splutters before he threw open the driver's side door and stepped down from the ute. A tall thin man in a wide-brimmed and well-worn Akubra bush hat appeared around the corner of the house. He was carrying an old shotgun and was accompanied by an ageing gundog. Jack and Kaitlin walked over to greet him.

"Miss O'Neill, I believe." The old man's voice was strong and firm. There was the faintest hint of an accent, but Kaitlin couldn't place it.

"Err, yes, but please call me Kaitlin." the Irish woman was somewhat taken aback. Everyone around here seemed to know who she was.

"Kaitlin, it is then. And this is Hund." The dog paid no attention.

Jack and his father shook hands silently, a curiously formal gesture it seemed to Kaitlin. Stepping into the Wollemi Forrest was like stepping back in time. The little group made its way round to the front of the house, which faced the river and the distant cliff, and climbed the steps to what was left of the broad shady veranda. More formal introductions were forthcoming. Jack and Jerry's father was Max Hexenkriege, and he was originally from Berlin, although that had been over fifty years before. Kaitlin O'Neill was indeed Irish, although she was now also an American citizen working for the Christian Science Monitor.

"Does Hexenkriege mean anything? In German I mean?" Kaitlin was curious.

"There's no direct translation," Max replied, "you could interpret it as 'Witch War' or perhaps 'Witchcraft War'. My granddaughter tells me there's a character in a computer game of the same name. What can you do?" Kaitlin couldn't help wondering how a family would come by such a name but thought better than to press the matter.

"Let's get out of the heat, where we can talk comfortably." Maximilian led the pair into the house.

The first thing Kaitlin noticed was how cool the interior was, and then, once her eyes had adapted to the lower light levels, that the place was spotlessly clean and tidy. Somehow this was not what she had been expecting. Not that she had assumed that Max Hexenkriege lived like a tramp, but the place was substantially cleaner and tidier than anywhere she herself had ever lived. The next things she noticed were the books. The house was virtually a library. Every available inch of wall space appeared to house a bookcase, and every bookcase was filled to the gunnels with neatly arranged and colour-coded and catalogued books.

"You have a lot of books." Too late, Kaitlin regretted the banality of the comment.

"Yes, I read a lot."

"What does the colour coding signify?"

"Black is physics and the earth sciences. Green is the life sciences, blue is mathematics, and yellow is the science of the mind and consciousness."

"Are you a scientist, Mr Hexenkriege?"

"Max, please."

"Well, Max, are you a scientist?"

"In a way, yes I am."

"What do you study? What is your speciality?"

"When I was young, many years ago, I was a geologist and a bit of a physicist."

"And now?"

"Now, I focus on the interrelationship and impact of consciousness on the other sciences."

None of this was what Kaitlin had been expecting. She was not sure how to proceed.

"How about a beer?" Jack cut in.

"In the fridge. Kaitlin, what can I offer you?"

"Err... nothing for the moment, thanks."

Jack wandered off in the direction of the kitchen to see what he could find.

"You're not what I expected." Kaitlin found herself wishing she could hit a pause button before speaking.

"What did you expect?"

"I don't know. You're not very like Jack or Jerry, although I can see the family resemblance."

"No." Max Hexenkriege smiled. "Jack is a commissar, a man of action, and Jerry is a bon viveur and an entrepreneur." Max paused and shrugged his shoulders, indicating the interior of the house and perhaps its remote location.

"I live very simply, as you can see." Kaitlin began to suspect that the outward appearance of the little house was by design. Perhaps Max didn't want anyone wondering what went on inside. What was this old man up to, alone, deep in the forest?

"Is there a specific topic you are studying or researching at the moment?"

Max Hexenkriege did not respond immediately. Instead, he pointed to his small study, indicating that Kaitlin should follow. The study was compact, full of papers and books. The desk itself was clear. On it sat a smallish computer, a large, expensive-looking screen, a keyboard and mouse, and an array of old hard disks piled up in unsteady-looking towers leaning against the wall for support.

"Most people see the sciences as a stack, the foundation being physics and the earth sciences, which support the life sciences, which in turn support the sciences of the mind."

Kaitlin nodded.

"I see the whole thing as a continuum, with physics and the earth sciences bleeding into chemistry, biology and the life sciences and the life sciences bleeding into the sciences of the mind."

Kaitlin nodded again, not sure where all this was leading.

"Somewhat uniquely perhaps, I see the science of the mind as providing feedback into the sciences that underlie it, both the life sciences and the earth sciences."

"I'm sorry." Kaitlin decided that honesty was going to be the best policy, "You're losing me. I think you may have lost me already."

"No one would argue that economics, the ebb and flow of the market, is influenced by human expectations?" Max paused, seeking confirmation.

"No."

"And no one would argue that a person's health and longevity can be influenced by their outlook on life, their attitude and happiness?"

"No."

"Well then, what I am saying is that the human mind, all our minds together, can, through such phenomena as culture, shared meaning and so on, influence the physical world… Influence reality might be a better way of putting it."

"Are you talking about quantum mechanics and consciousness?"

"Well, that may be part of it, but no, not really. My focus is not about that. What I am studying is real, macro level, physical effects created by human minds in combination."

Jack chose that moment to reappear with a bottle of homebrew in his hand.

"Oh dear," Max pretended embarrassment, "looks like you'll be staying over."

"Why is that?" Kaitlin was found she was nervous about spending the night in such a remote location with two men she hardly knew.

"I'm just teasing." Max was contrite. "The homebrew is quite strong."

"I'm ok to drive," Jack cut in, "I'll just have the one."

The tension in the room eased.

"Your father was just telling me about his studies into the physical effects of human minds *en masse*."

"Beyond me I'm afraid." Jack took a sip of the homebrew, "But I can testify to the effect of dad's homebrew the human mind." Jack smiled and left the room. A few moments later, the sounds of wood chopping could be heard coming from the back of the house.

"I have been reading quite an interesting paper," Max continued, "written by your namesake from Trinity College, Dublin. It's about shamanism and states of altered reality."

"Oh."

"Yes, it's an older paper, a Ph. D thesis I found on the Trinity College website."

Kaitlin froze, realising it was her own Ph. D thesis, feeling trapped, wondering once again if her cover was blown or if it had ever been believed in the first place.

Fortunately for her, the peace and tranquillity of the place was shattered by the deafening thwop-thwop-thwop of a helicopter engine. Max and Kaitlin ran outside to see Jack bent double, leaning into the wind as a small chopper landed lightly a few metres away on an area of flattened grass.

The door of the little aircraft opened and out jumped Jerry, impeccable as ever in a sleek navy-blue business suit carrying a large and shiny black leather attaché case.

Jerry took a few steps away from the helicopter and gave the pilot a wave. The small aircraft immediately leapt into the air and swung away over the trees.

As the sound of its engine attenuated with distance, Jerry smiled.

"So sorry I'm late. I got here as soon as I could. What have I missed?" Jerry looked keenly from face to face, the very picture of earnest enthusiasm. For a moment, Kaitlin fancied she could see in him the schoolboy he must once have been.

Jack and his father laughed.

"Always have to make an entrance." Jack smiled indulgently at his older brother.

"Well, Red Earth had chartered the chopper anyway for some aerial photography and technical imaging. Seemed like a shame to waste the opportunity."

The party headed back into the crumbling old cottage.

With Jerry's arrival, Kaitlin was hoping that Max would be diverted from the unfortunate direction the conversation appeared to have been taking previously. Kaitlin was not about to revive it.

"Let's eat. I've brought Baum Kuchen, Kassler Braten, Schinken, Kartoffelsalat and Roggenbrot." Jerry tapped the attaché case. Jack responded to Kaitlin's obvious bemusement by translating.

"Cake, literally 'tree cake', roast meat, ham, potato salad and German rye bread."

Kaitlin and the two brothers headed out onto the rickety front veranda while Max went indoors for plates and cutlery.

Kaitlin's stomach rumbled loudly. She realised she was starving. It was well into the afternoon, and she had eaten nothing since an early breakfast.

Jerry placed the attaché case down on the table and flung it open with evident glee. It soon became clear that Jerry had prepared a feast. There were olives and nuts and many more items and condiments than he had mentioned. Max appeared and set the table. The two brothers dug in furiously, piling food onto their plates. Soon everyone was chomping away. The sun was sliding down the sky on the other side of the house, casting the shadow of the crooked chimney across the grass.

Jerry opened a bottle of Shiraz, and Jack slipped off to find another bottle of home brew. Max turned once more to Kaitlin and continued the conversation exactly where they had left off.

"I thought perhaps you might have written that paper?"

Kaitlin was not sure how to answer. It didn't feel right to lie to the old gentleman, yet she was supposed to keep her true purpose and allegiance firmly under wraps.

"You were at Trinity at the time, weren't you?"

Kaitlin remained silent.

"There's a photo of you in the yearbook."

"Yes."

"Yes, there's a photo of you in the yearbook, or yes, you were at Trinity at the same time, or yes, you wrote the paper?"

"Well, yes to all three, I suppose."

"So, you are a scientist too?" Jerry, who had been listening to the exchange while quietly sipping his wine, continued, "I knew there was more to you than just a reporter."

Jack came back with a large pewter tankard filled to the brim with beer. He seemed very pleased with himself. Catching the gist of Jerry's comment, Jack stepped in. Although he already knew the answer, he wanted Kaitlin to come clean. "So, are you a reporter or not?"

Kaitlin looked from face to face. The three men were staring at her, each with a different expression. Jack looked triumphant, Jerry looked smug, and Max looked a little sheepish.

Kaitlin was beginning to suspect that all was not quite as it seemed with the Hexenkreiges. In the firm belief that discretion was the better part of valour, Kaitlin decided not to answer, at least not immediately.

"Did Jack or Jerry tell you about me?" Kaitlin was looking at Max.

"No."

"Then...?"

"Well, the truth is I recognised you."

"Recognised me?"

"Yes."

"Have we met?"

"No."

"Then...?" Kaitlin's confusion competed with a growing sense of annoyance. Were these people playing with her? What was going on? Jack and Jerry were silent, staring at their father. This was news to them too.

"I've followed your publications for a long time," Max Hexen-kriege adopted an apologetic tone.

"My publications?"

"Yes. I'm interested in shamanism and the world beyond the veil. That's one of your areas of expertise, isn't it?"

At this moment, Jack entered the fray once more. "So, are you a reporter or not?"

"No." Kaitlin was embarrassed, her cover irretrievably blown if it had ever really been in place at all.

"Ha!" Jerry looked extremely pleased with himself.

The pieces of the puzzle began to click together in Kaitlin's mind. She took a minute to collect herself, thinking back over the events of the last few days since she'd left Atlanta.

"Do you happen to know a gentleman by the name of Harry Soames?" The question was addressed, somewhat pointedly, to Max.

"As it happens, I do."

"You're Him, aren't you?"

Max shook his head, uncertain.

"I'm who?"

"You're the Max Harry Soames wanted me to meet."

Max nodded, "Probably."

"You're his mentor."

Kaitlin, who had been standing during the exchange, slumped down in her chair.

"Stuff me." was as much as she could manage. There was something uncanny about the way that everyone she met here turned out to be interconnected. It was more than just the result of being in a close-knit community. This was downright eerie. It was as though someone or something was orchestrating her life, all of their lives. It was quite a frightening thought.

The men were silent while Kaitlin took things in.

Kaitlin looked up. Max was staring across at her, a concerned look on his face.

"You know why I'm here, don't you?"

"Yes."

Kaitlin was silent once again, attempting to fathom the significance of these revelations.

Max spoke again, "I requested you. You had the perfect background and skills for the mission, but now we may need to ask more of you."

"You requested me?"

"Yes, as I said, I've followed your career with interest since university."

Kaitlin remained silent. The whole thing was becoming more and more creepy. The situation was beyond her control. Here she was in a remote tumbledown cottage in the middle of the Australian wilderness with three men she hardly knew, one of whom had been stalking her since she was in her twenties.

When Max spoke again, it didn't make things better.

"You remember the research grant from the CDC in Atlanta?"

Kaitlin looked up, "Don't tell me you had something to do with that too?"

"I'm afraid so." Max couldn't meet Kaitlin's eye, "I got Harry to make you the offer and to sort out your green card."

"Why? What do you want from me?"

"We need you to talk to the One-Mind of the Wollemi. We need you to find out its intentions and perhaps negotiate."

"Blimey," Kaitlin, her vocabulary hopelessly compromised, found herself staring from face to face in disbelief.

"Who the hell are you people? And what are the One-Mind and the Wollemi?"

"There's something else you need to know," Jerry spoke. He had finally connected all the dots himself and had realised where all this was going, "We also need your help to get Emma back."

"My help with Emma?"

"Yes." Max took up the thread of the conversation.

"What exactly do you want me to do?"

"Find Emma." Jack, never the most cerebral of men, had caught on too, "I need you to find Emma."

"…and bring her back," Max completed the thought.

Kaitlin stared at the three men, searching their faces for any sign of insincerity, seeking for that sly smile that would tell her this was all an elaborate hoax. But there was none. Somehow, she realised, her whole life had been leading up to this precise moment, to this confluence of time and space and events. This was her moment. Kaitlin grabbed Jack's flagon of homebrew and drank deeply. She stopped only to draw breath. The men remained silent, not daring to speak. Kaitlin looked around at the veranda, the shadow of the crumbling cottage, the little river and the sandstone cliff beyond. This was all somehow meant to be. Recollections of times spent with her shaman mentor in Alaska, moments when a deeper knowledge came unannounced and unbidden, times when intuition grew to certainty, coalesced in her mind, and formed all at once into a new and unexpected conviction. This was all for a purpose. She was supposed to be here, right here, right now.

"Ok," Kaitlin stared back at the three men and took another deep swig of Jack's homebrew, "Spill it."

Max sat down in the chair next to Kaitlin. As if on a signal, the boys sat too.

"I guess I do owe you an explanation. I imagine you'll be aware of reports of certain phenomena. The Centre for Disease Control has been tracking unusual sightings, reports of large-scale incidents of mob behaviour, or hysteria, anything pertaining to mass human psychological disturbance."

Kaitlin nodded. This was one of her own areas of study.

"You will be aware that there's been an upsurge or reports over the last few years?"

Kaitlin nodded again.

"You know there's been a sudden spike, this time associated with disappearances?"

Another nod.

"The question for the CDC is how is mass hysteria transmitted? How do mass psychological events happen? Is there some hidden communication available to humans at times of crisis or emotional overload? Is there some psychic link we avail ourselves of in moments of extremity? The CDC doesn't know, but we need to know."

"Oh." Kaitlin was stunned.

"*We* do know," Max indicated that he was including Jerry and Jack in this, "that there's more to the Wollemi wilderness than trees."

Out of the corner of her eye, Kaitlin could see that both brothers were nodding.

"What? What exactly is out there?" Kaitlin felt a sudden chill. The momentary flicker of fear she had felt back at the CDC in the Director's office returned more strongly. She was downright spooked.

The men were silent. This was their secret. This was something they had never shared beyond the family, and that, even then was hardly ever spoken of. Jack shifted in his seat.

"There are people living in the Wollemi Forest."

Kaitlin nodded.

"People. But not like us."

"How are they different, these people?"

"They are ..." Words failed. Jack fell silent.

"They are ancient." Max was staring towards the river and the cliff.

"They are a secret people. Hidden."

"Secret? Hidden? How hidden?"

In the distance, the wind could be seen battering the branches of the trees. Across the surface of the shallow river, a pattern of wind and waves chased this way and that. Kaitlin was aware of just how far they had travelled to get here, just how far from civilisation they were.

Maximillian Hexenkreige, hermit-scientist, pursed his lips.

"It's easier to show you after sundown."

"Show me? Do you mean that you can show me the hidden people after sundown?" The awkward silence was accompanied by a shuffling of feet.

"Yes." Max was matter of fact. The sounds of the forest swirled around. It was Jack who broke the silence.

"Our mum was one of them."

Kaitlin stared from face to face. The boys were darker skinned than their father, sure enough, but Max was German, once fair, or perhaps red-haired judging from the beard, blue-eyed, the full Monty. Practically everyone on the planet was darker-skinned than he was. Kaitlin processed this new information, and then, as one might in relation to any love story, she asked the obvious question.

"How did you meet?"

Max smiled. A sad smile of long ago and happier times.

"I was working as a geologist. I was looking for gold deposits in the rivers. I had been working my way down this river, a tributary of the MacDonald, camping, taking things easy, when one evening, as night was falling, I saw her."

Kaitlin nodded encouragement. The boys were silent. This seemed to be a story they knew well.

"She was squatting by the river, filling a large earthenware ewer with water." Max fell quiet, recalling the event, reliving the moment.

"She was beautiful, sleek as a panther. She moved without any self-consciousness. It was like poetry."

"Poetry in motion." Jerry smiled. It was obviously some private joke, a family thing that could never really be explained.

"I walked up behind her. I squatted a few yards away, never making a sound. I thought she must be an Aboriginal woman at first. But when she turned, and I got a good look at her, saw her eyes and the way she carried herself, I realised she was something else, something I believed no one had seen, no human had seen, for thousands of years."

"What was she?" Kaitlin already knew the answer but felt compelled to ask.

"She was an elf." Max smiled, "I still don't know the correct word in English. We would say la fee perhaps, or Elfen, in German. In English, there are dozens of words."

Kaitlin laughed. It was true that English had many words for the secret people: elves, pixies, goblins, faeries and on and on.

"Did she run away?" Kaitlin assumed that the sight of a human being must have spooked the otherworldly creature.

"No, she didn't see me at first. She stood and placed the ewer on her head. She turned, and then she saw me. It was getting dark, and at first, I think she thought I was one of her own folk."

Max turned and looked towards the river. Perhaps, Kaitlin thought, he was hoping to catch another glimpse.

"She walked up to me. Calm, unconcerned. As she approached, she realised I was different. I could see it in her expression, but she continued towards me. When she got up close and could see my face, she stopped. She reached out with one hand and caressed my cheek. It was as if she was trying to figure out what I was or perhaps what was wrong with me."

"What was wrong with you?" Kaitlin was intrigued.

"Yes, I think she thought there was something wrong with me, that I was sick or something. She realised that I could not hear her thoughts. Maybe she thought I was injured. I never knew."

"What happened next?"

"She walked away. I followed her. Back to her village."

"You went back to her village?"

"Yes. Somehow, I had stepped beyond or through the veil. I was on her side of the divide."

A kookaburra cackled from high in a gum tree down by the river. Everyone jumped. The sound was loud and ominous, unwelcome.

"I stayed with her for several weeks. Over time she began to hear my thoughts, and I learned to interpret her gestures and expressions. She never once spoke, none of them did, and I'd come to believe they were mute."

"Then?" Kaitlin could sense there was some kind of revelation about to unfold.

"And then," Max smiled, enjoying Kaitlin's rapt attention, "they sang."

"They sang?"

"On the first night of the new moon, a Ramadan moon, just a tiny sliver of light, the merest crescent shape hanging in the sky, they sang."

Max was lost in memory, gazing down towards the river and the cliff.

"There were no words," Max continued, "there were harmonies and melodies and counterpoint, but no language as such."

The kookaburra had started up again, a little further away this time.

"I fell in love, of course. I had never encountered such loveliness and such innocence." Max paused for a moment, looking up, seeking Kaitlin's eyes, gauging her response.

"I had no defence. That is the attraction and the risk, of course. That is what you need to understand, what you need to prepare yourself against. This was before the boys were born, of course. I would never have risked it otherwise."

Kaitlin was taken aback by this sudden change of tack.

"We humans have no defence against their influence, and their influence is strong. I came to realise just how strong as I watched them rearing their children."

Kaitlin had been wondering about that, about their customs and practices.

"If a child was naughty or misbehaved, the adult or older members of the immediate family would intervene. This might be direct physical intervention, for instance, if a toddler was playing too close to the fire, but it would more typically be by direct telepathic influence."

"Telepathy, you're sure?"

"I'm certain. But this was not just simple telepathy, the kind we read about in sci-fi books. They could combine their influence, combine their minds and the power of their minds to create a temporarily more powerful, more influential and even more intelligent gestalt."

"They could gang up on the naughty kid?"

"Well, yes, and they did, often, automatically. As other adults nearby would notice a silent altercation going on, they would contribute their mental energy or consciousness to the group effort. You will have heard the expression 'it takes a village to raise a child'?"

Kaitlin nodded.

"Well, when it comes to the Wollemi, this is literally true."

Max stopped again. This time, a look of concern flashed across his face. He glanced towards the river and the cliff.

"I left her in the end. I was heartbroken, but it was obvious to me that I could not stay with her and remain Maximilian Hexenkreige." Max paused for a few moments. "I could not forgo my own ego." There was silence again for a few moments. No one spoke.

"I went back, of course. In the end, I had to. I loved her."

Kaitlin realised that this was all real for Max and his sons. This was not a fantasy. This was fact.

"What's the matter?" Kaitlin spoke quietly, "What are you afraid of?"

She recalled the warning from the bright, youthful man at LAX, the NASA Liaison Officer. Something about a collapsing sinewave and a crescendo. That was about four days ago. The crescendo, whatever form it would take, was now only three days away.

"When I tried to leave…" Max stopped, momentarily unable to continue.

"When you tried to leave, they stopped you?"

"Yes. They combined to influence me. I felt almost nothing when an individual tried to 'speak' to me."

"But when they ganged up?"

Max smiled, "When they ganged up, I began to feel the effect, and I began to struggle against it."

"You struggled against their telepathic influence?"

"Yes." Max was breathing heavily, remembered panic flooding his system with adrenalin, heart pounding, the sound of blood pumping in his ears.

"It was like drowning, suffocating. My own mind, my will, my self was being stripped away, flooded, overwhelmed by them, by their group mind. I was being squashed into oblivion by their implacable, almost irresistible will."

"What did you do?"

"I fought back with all the rage and fury I could muster. I fought for my individuality. I asserted my unique self in the face of the collective. But it was not enough. It was never going to be enough."

"What were they saying to you? What were they trying to do? exactly?"

"They were filling me with absolute, unconditional love and acceptance." Max smiled at this, a ghastly grimace of a smile filled with ancient dread.

"They were helping me to rid myself of my individuality and selfishness. They were helping me to become one with the tribe."

"What happened? How did you get away?" Kaitlin was fascinated, terrified. All eyes were now focused upon the river and cliffs.

"I ran. I sprinted into the forest and ran and ran until I was exhausted, my clothes were ripped, and I could go no further. I collapsed under an old gum tree and slept."

"What happened when you woke? Did they find you?"

"No. I don't think they ever came looking. I realised later that the Wollemi One-Mind – that's what we call it, me and the boys – the Wollemi One-Mind exists only to deal with a disturbance. The collective forms only so long as it is needed. There is a cost to condensing the One-Mind, and the more individuals involved, the more it costs them, in energy or in life force. Once the disturbance dissipates, the collective crumbles back into the simple individuals of the tribe."

"They forgot about you?"

"They forgot about me."

"Bloody hell."

"Err... indeed. I went back, of course. Eventually, I went back to get her. I loved her."

"What happened?"

"I led her away in the night, a safe distance, and build this house for us. The boys were born here."

The sun was now low over the mountain behind the house. Golden light poured across the forest and the river, bathing the sandstone cliff-face in glory. The gum trees lining the top of the cliff stood out white and gold against the acetylene blue of the sky.

"And you're going to show me the Wollemi people?"

"Yes."

"Tonight."

"Yes, when the sun has set."

"Here."

"Right here. Well, right there." Max indicated the river and the cliff a few hundred yards away.

"Fu.... Never mind," Kaitlin resisted the urge to mutter expletives, "Isn't it dangerous with them so close by?"

Max sat down next to Kaitlin, picking at the olives and other bits and bobs that remained, uneaten, on the table.

"This is a safe distance when the veil is down. But let me ask you this, how far away are they really when the veil is in place? How far away is the Dreamtime?"

This was something that Kaitlin had herself pondered ever since childhood. How far away is the faery kingdom?

"I believe they are just the other side of the veil. No distance at all and infinitely far away at the same time."

"Quite right. Quite right." Max was thoughtful. "So, let's see if we can keep it that way."

"You know it's going to collapse?" Kaitlin once again spoke without thinking things through, "Harry told you, right? We have three days to prevent it."

Max and the brothers stared at her across the table.

"Three days? You're kidding?" Jack jumped to his feet, ready for action.

"What happens then? What do you mean the veil is going to collapse?" Jerry looked uneasy but not yet panicked.

"Harry must have forgotten to mention it." Max's tone was ironic.

"There have been wave fluctuations in the Earth's magnetic field too." Kaitlin wasn't sure what a magnetic wave was or why it mattered, but from the articles she had read, it seemed to be relevant.

Max snapped to attention at that.

"When? Who detected them? What magnitude?"

"I'm sorry. I don't remember the details. They were detected by one of those giant underground things in Italy or France. The man from NASA said they were coming more frequently. He said they, NASA, had calculated when the sinewave would collapse – in three days from now. That's when the veil will fall. When the sine-wave collapses."

"NASA told you this?" Max was focused, intent.

"Yes, I was briefed at LAX just before I jumped on the plane to Sydney."

"NASA is involved then? Who else is with you? Do you have a team?"

"I came alone. No team."

Max walked into the little house and came back a few moments later with a bottle of 25-year-old whisky and four glasses.

"No point saving this." He poured out four large glasses of whisky and handed one to each of his sons and one to Kaitlin.

"Cheers." Max lifted his glass cheerlessly and chinked it against the other three.

"Kaitlin, you will know, even if you are not a physicist, that there are huge gaps in modern physics?"

"Yes. I play a little game with myself, actually tracking the universal constants that aren't, and the dark matter, dark energy and so on. The other day I came across dark flow – they have no idea."

"Well," Max continued, "there are gaps, sure enough, but almost every piece of modern electronics depends upon quantum mechanics being right – as far as it goes."

"So, what are you saying – about the gaps?"

"Physicists are reductionists at heart. But the solution to their problems are not to be found in physics but in the other sciences."

Kaitlin was not sure she followed and, in any case, wouldn't know if Max was correct or not.

"Oh," Non-committal for once.

"Physicists like to think of their area of study as revealing 'the truth' about the universe at a fundamental level. They have forgotten that mathematics is a language well designed to describe the universe but that all their equations and computer models are merely descriptions of the territory, not the territory itself."

"Ok." Kaitlin felt she was following this line of reasoning without understanding where it was going.

"They have forgotten, or perhaps they simply don't realise, that their science is merely a tool, part of a tool kit, for understanding and extending our knowledge of the universe."

"I'm sure you're right in what you're saying," Kaitlin was at risk of becoming bored, "but what is the point you are trying to make?"

Jerry, who had half an ear to the conversation, laughed quietly.

"Dad has a way of constructing an argument. You have to wait until the thing is built before you can judge."

"Hmm." Max was the tiniest bit irritated by the interruption.

"The point is, as any tradesman knows, you use the correct tool for the job, and physics can never explain 'meaning', or culture or any of the questions that interest the higher sciences." Max stared around the table, daring anyone to object.

"Physics cannot understand, let alone explain, the impact of individual or group consciousness upon the material world. Their focus is on matter, energy and fields, and they forget about 'reality' which includes the idea, for instance, of a 'Teenage Mutant Ninja Turtle'."

No one spoke. It was indeed difficult to see how physics could contribute much to a discussion of Hollywood movies in the late 20th Century.

"And physics struggles to understand die Elfen." Max resorted to his native German.

"And the electromagnetic waves?" Kaitlin felt somewhat adrift in Max's speculations.

"The electromagnetic waves are relevant. NASA would not have mentioned them if they weren't."

"Relevant? How?"

"As far as I know, this is the first time that global changes have been detected at any significant magnitude."

"What do electromagnetic waves do?"

"No one is sure why the Earth's magnetosphere wobbles, the changes can be very hard to detect, but one thing they do is propagate energy."

"Propagate energy?" Kaitlin was not getting it.

"It must take energy to maintain the veil. If the veil is going to collapse, perhaps the changes in electromagnetic waves are what will cause it." Max was talking to himself as much as to Kaitlin and his sons.

"The veil must be maintained by a vortex of energy. As soon as the vortex loses energy, it will collapse."

"There's a vortex, and it's going to lose energy?" The conversation was going nowhere as far as Kaitlin could see.

"Yes, like the water going down a plug hole." This was something Jack could easily grasp, "It swirls around like a mini tornado until there is not enough water to maintain it, then it collapses."

"Great analogy." Max was as surprised as Jack was. For Kaitlin, the conversation revealed a great deal about life in the Hexenkriege family without explaining anything at all about their current predicament.

Darkness had fallen. The top of the cliff could be made out as a region of blackness against a slightly lighter sky. Some early stars were visible, and the moon was beginning to rise.

"Ok," Max stalked inside the house, "time to show you the Wollemi." His unwillingness once more to expose them to the danger finally outweighed by Kaitlin's evident need to know the truth.

He re-emerged a few moments later, carrying a small package wrapped in a tea towel. Max placed the package on a clear space on the table and removed the covering. Inside, wrapped in a soft cloth, was the same, almost flat, oval-shaped lozenge made of wood, intricately carved, evidently very old.

"This is known as a bullroarer." To one end was attached a thin rope. Max removed the apparatus from the table and, having unravelled the rope, leaned over the edge of the veranda and began to twirl the carved wooden lozenge at the end of the rope. The bullroarer began to spin on its axis as it twirled ever faster on the end of the rope. A low thrumming started and grew in loudness as the wooden paddle spun faster and faster. Max and his sons were focused on the river at the base of the cliff. Occasional sparkles of moonlight caught the ripples on the fast-flowing river.

Slowly, the occasional glimmer of bluish light began to emerge from the darkness. The thrumming grew louder and louder, rhythmic, almost hypnotic.

Kaitlin watched as the blueish light grew and separated into the flickering of individual flames, distant oil lamps, each casting a tiny glow against the blackness of night.

In the light of the oil lamps, one could just make out the shadows and shapes of people moving about their business on the far side of the river.

No one spoke. Kaitlin hardly dared breathe as their eyes adjusted to the darkness. Then something stirred in the distance. One or two of the Wollemi looked up across the river, attracted by the thrumming of the bullroarer and spotted the lights of the cottage.

More and more heads turned to stare back across the river at the four humans standing on the veranda.

Jerry turned to speak to Kaitlin. "If they become curious about us, the group mind will begin to form. We have to be careful about that."

"Why? What will happen?"

"They may think that we are sick or hurt and are asking for help."

Kaitlin turned towards Jerry, who was once again staring across the river at the leisurely emergence of the Wollemi village. The thrumming of the bullroarer slowed and grew silent. Without the hypnotic, ritualistic effect of the ancient sound, the spell was broken, and the veil darkened once more, separating the worlds.

Jerry continued, "I don't think they mean to be a danger to us, but they would assimilate us if they thought we needed their help."

"How do you do it?" Kaitlin's mind was reeling even as the Wollemi village disappeared and the world returned to a semblance of normality, "Is it just the sound that does it? Can anyone do it?" What had she just witnessed? It was too much to take in.

Max and the boys sat once more around the table. The tension of the past few minutes gradually lifted, and the silence of the forest returned.

"I can sometimes do it on my own. But Jack and Jerry make the strongest connection. The sound of the bullroarer focuses the mind and calls to the Wollemi."

"You can do it on your own, though, if you need to?"

"Yes, sometimes. I think it's because I spent so much time with them. I became attuned. But I may need Jack or Jerry to pierce the veil at will."

"Emma is with them. With her grandmother." Jack spoke, "And I need you to help me get her back."

Kaitlin nodded.

"Will you do it? Will you help me?"

"I will, of course." Kaitlin had resigned herself to the challenge.

"Better get a good night's sleep. We start first thing." Jack was staring into the night. Emma was out there, just beyond the edge of darkness. And she was being changed more and more with each passing day.

Kaitlin's nervousness about staying the night in the ramshackle cabin had dissipated somewhat. The vision of the Wollemi was all she could think about.

Later that night, when the house was asleep, Kaitlin wandered from the guest bedroom to the large old couch in the sitting room where Jack was sleeping. The isolation of the place and the nearness of the Wollemi had finally gotten to her. She was seeking human warmth and companionship. Jack stirred in his sleep and woke to see Kaitlin standing over him. Kaitlin gestured for him to budge up.

"Ok, but no funny business."

"Don't be smart."

Jack shifted over, and Kaitlin snuggled in next to him under an old woollen blanket. She was soon asleep.

FIRST GLIMPSE

In the morning, Jerry's helicopter returned for him early. There wasn't enough room for both Jack and Kaitlin to hitch a ride, but Jack had to drive the ute back anyway, and Kaitlin needed to make urgent arrangements for their journey into 'the belly of the beast' as she was coming to think of it. She needed time to prepare. Jerry and Kaitlin clambered into the tiny helicopter and strapped themselves in. In a moment, the diminutive aircraft launched itself into the clear morning sunlight and swooped off across the forest. Max waved from the veranda. The clearing and the tiny house soon disappeared into the seemingly endless Wollemi Forrest.

Kaitlin could make out the narrow track they had driven from Upper MacDonald into the forest, the farmyard with the geese and the isolated cottage, complete with psycho guard dogs, slipped by below. It was only a few minutes until Wisemans Ferry came into view. The mighty Hawkesbury shimmered in the morning sunlight, broad and brown, sluggish and quite unhurried. *"As it was in the beginning."* Kaitlin thought. Beyond the river, beyond the tiny hamlet of Wisemans Ferry, the enigmatic bush spread out as far as the eye could see.

Jerry dropped Kaitlin off on the broad green paddock below the Wisemans Ferry Inn before heading back to the city. A few people stopped to look but soon dispersed when they saw it was Kaitlin tumbling out of the helicopter, complete with hiking pack, somewhat dishevelled and in urgent need of a shower.

Kaitlin gave Jerry a cheery wave as the helicopter disappeared over the hill behind the town. For some reason, she was in an upbeat mood. Things were starting to come together, weird things granted, but things, nonetheless. She really ought to update the Director. Kaitlin made her way back to her room and jumped into the shower, pausing only to switch on her computer. Contrary to her usual practice Kaitlin took a long luxurious shower, using the time to ponder the events of the last few days. She attempted to sum up what she had learned so far.

1) She had, it seemed, been stalked since she was in her twenties by an eccentric German scientist who had married a faery and lived in the Australian wilderness.
2) The man had two sons who were half faery themselves.
3) One was a hulking brute of a miner to whom she was increasingly attracted, who preferred the solitary life of an itinerant fossicker, and the other was a well-to-do, urbane mining magnate.
4) The daughter/grandchild of the family had been spirited away by the faeries.
5) And it had somehow become her job to go get her back and, while she was at it, find out what the One-Mind was up to and negotiate with it.
6) Her boss was in cahoots with the mad German scientist.

Not bad for four days in a new country.

Well, Kaitlin, you've really gone and done it now, haven't you? Kaitlin could practically hear her mother's voice.

The shower worked its restorative magic, and Kaitlin emerged, if not fully repaired, then perhaps somewhat reconditioned. She threw on some clothes and sat down at the little antique writing table to check her emails.

There were three. One had somehow evaded the spam filter and was offering her intriguing, if anatomically implausible, enhancements. Another was from her wine club, asking if she would be ordering any of the Napa Valley Sauvignon Blanc. The third was from her boss. The Director's message was short and to the point. He wanted to know if she had bumped into Dr Hexenkriege yet, and had she found out what the hell was going on in that God damned forest and did they need to send in the military?

The email was dated two days previously. Kaitlin responded using an encryption feature she had been instructed to employ in such circumstances.

She had met Max Hexenkriege and his two sons. Two girls had gone missing, one was Emma, Max Hexenkreige's granddaughter, but the other one had already shown up again, and Kaitlin was going to help in the search for Emma. There was something weird going on in the forest, but she would know more tomorrow. And what was with the apparent obsession the CDC had with the military? Kaitlin hit [SEND] and prepared to venture downstairs for breakfast. She glanced at her watch. It was not yet nine a.m.

As she closed the heavy door to her room behind her, her cell phone began to ring. It was her boss. The Director was, as usual, straight to the point.

"The readings are going off the scale. Kids are disappearing and reappearing all over the place. Congress is threatening to set up a committee to investigate. We have a genuine concern that if and when this gets out, there will be mass hysteria all over. What have you got for me?"

"Are we talking on a secure channel?" Kaitlin had never in her life thought to ask the question before. Doing so now made her feel quite grown up, although it did sound weird coming from her lips. The director paused before answering.

"I'll call you back in a minute on an encrypted channel. Standby."

"Standby?" it had never occurred to Kaitlin either that someone might say that in all seriousness. Ok, she thought, I'll 'standby'. And standby she did, back on the balcony of her bedroom, overlooking the golf course and the great curve of the Hawkesbury River.

Within a few moments, the phone rang again.

"Ok. What have you got?"

Kaitlin was not into all this cloak-and-dagger stuff. She was a straightforward girl from Donegal, and keeping secrets was not her thing. She decided to spit it out, come what may.

"There is a tribe of human-like people living hidden in the Wollemi Forest. The remaining missing child is Max Hexenkreige's granddaughter, Emma. These people can mask or cloak their presence with some kind of psychic veil." Kaitlin waited for the explosion from the other end of the line. It never came. Instead, after a sharp intake of breath, the Director replied.

"Good job. I knew you were the right person for this assignment. Now are these people causing the weird stuff that NASA has been banging on about?"

"I don't know if they are causing it, or if we are, or if it's some kind of natural phenomenon, but I know they are impacted by it, just as we are."

"Hmmm." The Director took a moment to think before divulging more. "The president has spoken directly with the Australian prime Minister. A combined task force of our military and theirs has been formed and will soon be on site. Expect a military intervention at some point soon."

Kaitlin spoke up, asking a question that had been bothering her for a couple of days.

"What is happening elsewhere?" she asked, "In the other wilderness places? Is it worse or better?"

"There's weird stuff happening everywhere, but the epicentre appears to be in the Wollemi Forest, around some mountain."

"Mount Yengo?"

"Yes, that sounds like it. Take a look around if you can."

Kaitlin started to ask another question but was cut off.

"Sorry, got to go. I'm in the White House, standing right outside the Oval Office." The phone went dead.

Kaitlin left her room and wandered down the creaking old staircase into the restaurant. She couldn't help wondering how her recent report would be parlayed to the President, if indeed any of it would get through at all.

It was just after nine in the morning. Kaitlin was greeted by the same weathered older woman who had given her directions to St Albans on her first morning in Wisemans Ferry. Outside Kaitlin could see a convoy of military trucks making its way past the Inn. The sound of beeping horns and hissing of air brakes shattered the peace of the morning.

"Any chance of breakfast?"

"Every chance, darl." The woman passed Kaitlin a dog-eared menu. "We serve breakfast all day," she confided. "It's for the bikers."

Yesterday had been hard work. Today was going to be worse. Kaitlin sat down and ordered an enormous, cooked breakfast complete with three kinds of jam and marmalade and two pots of strong tea. A girl has her standards, after all.

Breakfast was served outside on a large wooden picnic table. The sun had not yet risen over the pub, and although the day was warm and bright, it was not yet too hot. Kaitlin flicked on her computer and began perusing the news, starting as always with anything odd and outlandish. Kaitlin was replete and seriously considering the benefits of a nice little nap when Jack turned up with the ute.

Jack was eager to get going. Now that he had a plan of action and there was something practical, he could do to get Emma back. He was in no mood for delay.

Kaitlin went to her room to collect the equipment she thought she'd need. By the time she struggled back down the stairs, her pack was stuffed with the complete range of arcane and occult paraphernalia required of any jobbing shaman or witch on a field trip. Kaitlin only hoped it would work the same in Australia. Her stuff seemed to have done the job in Alaska, so it should be all right. It was more about how well the practitioner was attuned to the ritual and the equipment than the expectations or beliefs of the local culture per se. She certainly hoped so.

Jack grabbed the pack and slung it easily into the back of his ute. He handed Kaitlin a bottle of chilled water.

"Here, keep hydrated."

Jack and Kaitlin climbed into the ute, and Jack turned to Kaitlin.

"Where to?"

"Mount Yengo," Kaitlin was quietly smug that she had an answer at all, "can we get there by four-wheel drive?"

"We can get most of the way. The last few kilometres are the worst, but."

Kaitlin sighed deeply, not pleased at the prospect of lugging her heavy pack across what the online satellite view had shown as steep, heavily forested little hills, characterising the countryside all the way from the river to the mountain.

"Why there?" Jack was not questioning Kaitlin's plan. Having witnessed how she had talked with his father the evening before, he was more than willing to take her at her word. He was merely curious.

"That's the centre of it all. That's where we're most likely to find Emma."

Jack gunned the engine, happy to be doing something positive at last. He glanced at Kaitlin as he drove.

"I've brought everything we need to get their attention. It's up to you to talk to them and keep them at bay, right?"

"Yep."

The pair headed off along the now familiar route towards the forest. Jack and Kaitlin could see soldiers setting up tents and arranging porta cabins in the park at the bottom of the hill.

"We'll be taking some loggers' tracks and part of the old convict trail. It's very pretty. Sit back and enjoy the ride."

It took nearly two hours threading through the bush to get to the point where they would have to abandon the ute.

"We walk from here." Jack nodded his head in the direction of the still-distant mountain peak. "That's Mount Yengo. There's a flat camping spot across the river from the sacred sites."

And with that, the pair set off on foot into the wilderness.

They walked for hours in the heat of the day. Kaitlin noted the movement of the sun overhead as they tramped through the bush. The sun, having risen to its full height, was now beginning to tilt towards evening. It was cooler in amongst the trees than under the direct glare of the sun. Although the distance to their camping site was only a few kilometres on foot, the terrain was hard, and the undergrowth dense. The only glimpses of sunlight and sky to be had were in the few open glades they had to cross. Midges and other insects were a constant torment. Jack pushed on, driving them deeper into the forest, maintaining a steady, exhausting pace. They had to be in position, set up and ready, before nightfall. He kept emphasising the point. It was not just the physical preparations that mattered but the mental ones, too, especially after a day of gruelling physical effort. There were still the rituals to perform.

Kaitlin had long since lapsed into silence, the garrulous Celt forced to focus all her will on the next breath, the next step. On and on, thud, thud, thud, though the shadows, overgrown with stunted shade-lovers and leaf litter.

"Not long now," Jack was panting too. "Around the next curve in the river and up the gully to the flat rocks."

Kaitlin managed a grunt of acknowledgement, her mind beginning to reboot. Soon it would be her unique blend of skills that would come into play. A qualified psychologist, witch and shaman (or so her business card proclaimed), Kaitlin now found herself wondering what the Director could have been thinking when he called her in and asked her to 'help out'. It was hot, she was exhausted, and ahead of them waited a confrontation she was not comfortable she could handle. She was afraid. Jack seemed nervous too, and that made her more afraid. The flat rocks were visible ahead. Kaitlin experienced a sudden jolt as the energy of the place sought her out, jabbing at her perceptions, testing her defences.

"This has been a place of power for centuries." Kaitlin stopped for a moment, brought up short by the momentary brush with the ethereal. "Maybe even longer." Jack nodded.

"There's the overhang. We set up camp on the flat area under that."

Abruptly Kaitlin began to walk once more, her movements jerky with fatigue, as though some other energy had intertwined with hers, pulling and pushing. The energy of the place began to fill her, fortifying her perhaps for the ordeal to come.

"They know we're here." Kaitlin could feel the presence in the forest. Jack was already preparing the ground, unpacking equipment and setting it down neatly.

"You prepare yourself. I'll fix us something to eat."

Jack produced a tiny Primus stove and a small cooking pot which he half-filled from his water flask.

"Chicken and mushroom risotto, ok?" Jack stared at the collection of artefacts spreading out around the woman. A small darkly coloured Persian rug, various metal cups and other vessels of unknown origin and purpose. Packets and powders, half a dozen different kinds of incense, a small silver dagger, some dried animal parts and the family-sized container of cooking salt. Kaitlin looked up, his words slowly making their way into her consciousness. She looked at him blankly for a moment, then focussed.

"Yes, that sounds great. I'm starving." They had been travelling much of the day.

"It will be dark in an hour or so. We must be ready by then. Does that work for you?" Jack's tone was flat, adamant.

"Yes, I'll be ready."

A narrow tributary of the MacDonald River ran below, itself a
tributary of the mighty Hawkesbury. The smooth flat rocks sat high above the shallow, swift-flowing stream, across from the high sandstone cliffs which swept around the curve in the stream resembling some ancient structure, evidence perhaps of some long-lost civilisation.

Kaitlin set out the things she'd need, or thought, or hoped or guessed she'd need. There was no telling. She was a practitioner from the extreme western edge of Northern Europe, what did she know about the Australian wilderness and these mythical people, said to be older than the Indigenous Aboriginals nations? The true original occupants of this land, of all lands.

"*Wollemi,*" she rolled the name around in her mind, feeling its resonance.

"They are real, aren't they? That wasn't just some shared hallucination at your dad's place?" Kaitlin was suddenly unsure of herself, the absurdity of their quest striking her once again.

Jack stopped for a moment, gazing at the slim Irish woman, his eyes steady, his expression unreadable.

"They're bloody real, all right. Scared the living shit out of me first time I chanced across them after Mum left."

"You've spent time with them. You told me so."

"I even stayed with them for a little while. They are my mother's people, after all."

Kaitlin gazed out from her vantage point across the landscape of rocks and gullies, low mountains, cliffs and trees. Always trees, flowing like a river, a sea of trees as far as the eye could see. *"Anything could happen here,"* Kaitlin thought. *"Remnants from any geological period could flourish unknown and unnoticed in these wastelands."*

"Grubs up." The welcome, mouth-watering vapours of 'Quick Cook' chicken risotto spread a homely and disarming scent across the camp. The sun would be setting soon. They ate in silence, broken by the loud and eerie cackle of an animal or bird. Kaitlin jumped.

"Just another kookaburra, plenty of them all over. Spooky sound, but, if you're not used to it."

Kaitlin smiled, trying to hide the shudder that had gone through her and ignore the goose pimples standing out on her arms.

"Look. Jerry's got our exact coordinates. All I have to do is set off this satellite beacon, and they'll have a chopper up here in a few minutes."

"No worries." Kaitlin smiled again. "I do this kind of thing for a living. You find them. I'll talk to them."

"Better get ready." Jack began to arrange the items he needed for the summoning ritual.

In the last embers of the dying sun, Jack began. He and Kaitlin were sitting cross-legged on the small carpet facing directly westwards towards the mighty cliffs. A small candle was lit, protected by a glass cover. Jack began to spin the calling stick - the simple repetitive wrrrrrr-wrrrrrr reaching out across the wilderness. The sound grew and combined as echoes bounced back from the opposing cliff face and back again from the stone hillside behind them. The thrum of the spinning wooden blade filled the air, filled their lungs and bodies, mesmerising, on and on. Their eyes and minds focused on the flickering candle flame, thoughts stilled, their very bodies thrummed in harmony with the pervasive sound.

The pure golden light of the sun dipped below the blanket of cloud that had formed near the horizon, and the whole valley, the river and cliffs were filled with glory, a curtain of liquid gold pouring in like molasses, filling every crack and crevice.

Almost as swiftly as it came, the light was gone, and evening fell. There across the narrow, smoothly flowing river, flickering, dimly seen at first, the lights were coming on. The cliff, lit by a thousand dancing lights, was coming to life. The sounds of domesticity could be heard, and paths and dwellings made out cut into the cliff face as far as the eye could see in both directions. And there, down by the river, people were emerging from the haze.

Kaitlin cleared her throat.

"Hssh!" Jack threw her a savage look.

"Can they hear us whispering?" Kaitlin felt cold.

"They can hear us thinking!" Jack was holding the satellite beacon, his fingers white, his thumb poised over the small red button.

"Can you do it?"

Kaitlin wondered if she could if she had any idea how to speak with these people without succumbing to the hideous force of their incarnate will.

"Yes, of course!" she snapped. Jack's fingers relaxed slightly around the beacon.

With practised ease, Kaitlin sprinkled a circle of salt around them. She poured thick dark red wine into a small golden cup, followed by a few drops of blood from her finger, pricked with the silver dagger. The trick, she repeated to herself, was to stick to your own tradition, stick to what you know. In her case, it was the Angels and Demons of the Abrahamic tradition. It was the gnostic, distaff tradition she had been born into, Kabbalistic symbols of another world, proxies for the deep forces that underlie the universe, that would act and react in understood ways – so long as she stuck to her own tradition. She would channel the Kabbalah and walk the Tree of Life.

A fleeting memory of a scene, the aftermath of an attempt to open the Babylonian gates, played through her mind. Pity those poor bastards who had attempted a desiccated ritual, in a dead language, from a mystical tradition they barely understood.

"Not pretty, not pretty at all."

The woman became very still, centred. Her mind focussed on the golden cup. She began an incantation, old as her sisterhood, ancient in modern terms but youthful and new in comparison to the primordial Wollemi. A prickling sense of energy filled the circle. Jack, to his amazement, recognised the sensation. He knew how to strengthen it, how to add his mind to hers. Jack picked up the calling stick and began to twirl it again and again in the spreading gloom. A slower sound this time, stately and strong.

Kaitlin, sensing his contribution, glanced at him and smiled. She drank the liquid in a single motion and began to sing, harmonising with the music of the calling stick, the rhythm of blood and bone, the heartbeat of the web of life itself.

Across the river, faces turned to listen, then further afield, across the lower levels of the cliff, people began to turn. Then swift as thought, the Wollemi turned as one, hundreds, thousands, spread across the cliff dwellings as far as the eye could see. They listened and were entranced.

The Wollemi One-Mind began to form, sensed by the two lone humans as yet unseen. The focus of the One-Mind coalesced, took form and began to venture across the water, approaching the two humans. Swift as a cobra strike, quick as thought itself, the collective consciousness of the Wollemi reached out to touch the two lost minds - and was stopped. A face appeared fleetingly in the screen of force that Jack and Kaitlin had woven around themselves. High cheekbones, generous mouth and wide almond-shaped eyes, black within black, open widows into the surrounding darkness.

"We have come to speak with you." Kaitlin's voice was strong and calm. Using the deep language of the Kabbalah, she continued, "Ain Soph Aur, the Veil of Darkness and Light, is weakening. Our worlds collide."

Jack continued the steady thrumming of the bullroarer. He was fascinated and more than a little afraid. Never before had he encountered the fully conscious Wollemi. Never before had he experienced the individual 'I' made up of thousands of Wollemi minds. This was the real deal, and had it not been for Emma, he would never have attempted such a meeting at all.

The still figures across the river stirred as one. A ripple of confusion spread through them, momentarily dispersing the collective. But the One-Mind reformed, more quickly this time, purposefully, fully conscious. Slowly, almost imperceptibly, a faint blueish glow spread across and between and around the silent watchers. A web-like form, unhurried and gentle, began to emerge, gathering and connecting all in a mesh of life energy. Every living thing was brought into the web of power. Nothing living was excluded except Jack and Kaitlin.

The face wove its way back across the river, slithering this way and that, sniffing, seeking, stopping just short of the circle. Watching.

"You have a guest among you. A little girl, our kin. We need her back." Kaitlin's voice was firm and strong.

There was a swirling and crashing sound as branches thrashed in a sudden gust of wind. Across the nearby forest, birds in their thousands took flight.

"We ask you to release her."

A voice spoke, though there was no sound.

[*The veil is weak. This is your doing.*]

"We have no power over the veil."

[*You are too many. You blanket the earth.*]

"We have made a home for ourselves on our side of the veil."

There was no immediate response. When the soundless voice spoke again, it had changed tack.

[*The girl is sick. We will cure her.*]

"Emma is not sick. She is well. You cannot cure her."

[*You are sick. We will cure you.*] With that, the shimmering face of the Wollemi crashed against the ethereal protective screen that Kaitlin and Jack had shaped around themselves.

Jack's hand hovered over the little red button on the emergency satellite beacon. The protective screen distorted under the onslaught but held.

"We are not unwell. We are different. Return our daughter to us."

[*You are a vexation to the spirit. I should return you to the collective.*]

"We mean you no harm. Return our daughter, and we will leave."

[*Very well. Take her and be gone.*]

In the distance, across the river, a young girl emerged from the crowd. Jack could see at once that it was Emma. He stood and waved his flashlight furiously. Down in the valley, Emma waved back. She began to cross the river, stepping carefully in the shallow, fast-flowing water.

[*Go, and do not return.*]

"We thank you. We wish you well."

Kaitlin glanced down at the little girl fording the stream. She was no more than three hundred meters away. They would soon have her back. But in that moment of distraction, that tiny lapse of focus, the Wollemi struck with all its force. The protective screen collapsed in upon them and around them, barely holding together against the force of the attack. Kaitlin screamed and grabbed for the tiny silver dagger.

She carved a long savage gash into her forearm. Blood flowed freely from the deep wound. Kaitlin cupped her hand beneath the dripping blood, collecting it in her palm, harnessing the pain.

Focussing every ounce of psychic energy, every piece of her mind, into one last desperate throw of the dice, she cast the blood into the leering face of the Wollemi, simultaneously stabbing at him with the slim silver dagger. Blood and metal combining symbolically in a scream of rage and defiance, asserting the inviolable individuality of the two humans.

Kaitlin and Jack felt, rather than heard, the silent wail of outrage and surprise that engulfed them. The face disappeared. The lights of the village were snuffed out in an instant, and Jack and Kaitlin found themselves alone and shivering, shocked at the ferocity of the encounter deep in the heart of the wilderness. The veil was sealed once more, and Emma was gone.

Jack glanced down at the emergency satellite beacon. The red button had been pressed. A tell-tale light on the side of the unit was now flashing with slow persistence. A few moments later, far in the distance, Kaitlin and Jack could just make out the sweeping silver searchlight of an approaching helicopter. Help was coming.

Jack stared across at Kaitlin, their faces illuminated in the beam of the flashlight.

"What just happened?" Jack was breathing hard. His arms and hands were shaking with reaction.

"We just got our arses kicked." Kaitlin grimaced. The gash in her arm hurt like hell. Jack pulled out a novocaine spray, some medical gauze, and a strip of bandage. He was nothing if not practical, and many accidents at many mine sites had prepared him for this. Quickly and efficiently, her arm was anaesthetised, smeared with thick brown antiseptic cream, and bandaged. Kaitlin shifted her position to lean against Jack. He wrapped an arm around her, holding the satellite beacon in his free hand.

"I've never seen anything like that." Jack leaned back against the trunk of a tree, gently pulling Kaitlin closer.

"Me neither. That, my friend, was the real deal."

"I didn't know they or it could form so many into a single person." Jack shook his head as if trying to dislodge the image of the Wollemi from his mind.

"It was the combined product of several thousand individual Wollemi." Kaitlin paused and took a sip of water from her water bottle.

"We were very lucky it wasn't more. Something must be really worrying it for it to coalesce such a presence. It must cost the individuals involved to do it."

Kaitlin and Jack sat back in silence, watching the approaching searchlight. Finally, a squawk came from the walkie-talkie on Jack's belt.

"Jack Hexenkriege, please come in."

Jack looked across at Kaitlin before responding.

"We are all right. Come and get us." Then turning to Kaitlin.

"The military will want to know what happened. What shall we say?"

"Tell them exactly what did happen." Kaitlin sounded tired. She was resigned to an extensive debrief, "We're going to need all the help we can get."

The place where they had camped was just wide enough for the helicopter to land. Kaitlin was heartily grateful for this. The idea of being winched up like a sack of potatoes or, worse still, clambering up a wildly swaying rope ladder at night held no appeal.

Neither spoke on the way back to Wisemans Ferry. Each attempting to assimilate and process the events of the last few hours. They had seen Emma. They now knew for certain where she was and that she was physically safe and well, for now. But she was being used as a pawn in the Wollemi's game. That much was clear. Their experience with the Wollemi mind had been a chastening one. They had not expected either such power or such merciless resolve. Whatever they attempted next, they would need reinforcements.

The trip from deepest, darkest prehistory to present-day New South Wales took a few minutes, but for Jack and Kaitlin, it seemed to span centuries in psychological time.

As the helicopter circled the landing field, Jack and Kaitlin could see below them the spreading organised chaos of a military encampment evolving across Wisemans Ferry Park and golf course. The military hadn't yet gotten around to securing their domain. There was no fence. In and around the little kiosk and the small sandy beach, groups of motorcyclists rested and tinkered while squads of soldiers put up tents.

Seemingly moments later, the helicopter landed on the newly assembled pad adjacent to the Wisemans Ferry Bowling Club, and Jack and Kaitlin were disgorged into the waiting arms of the military.

"We're going to be debriefed," Kaitlin was speaking rapidly to Jack, "remember, tell them exactly what happened. Hold nothing back, and bear in mind, these people have no sense of humour." She gave him a quick squeeze of the hand. That was all she had time for before a tall, tanned, impeccably dressed and crew-cut American soldier stepped forward.

"Kaitlin O'Neill?"

"Yes."

"Ma'am, would you come with me, please?"

Kaitlin hefted her pack and followed.

"You're never gonna believe what I've got to tell you." Kaitlin had a theory that it should be possible to engage the military in a conversational manner. So far, upon the few occasions she had had an opportunity to test the theory, she had not been successful.

"Please reserve your comments for the debriefing room, ma'am."

Kaitlin resigned herself to a long and very trying night. Behind her, she heard an Australian voice say, "G'day, Jack Hexenkriege? My name's Phil. Would you mind coming with me, please, mate?"

As she glanced back, she saw Jack shaking hands with a tall, somewhat scruffy-looking soldier in baggy camouflage. The Australians certainly had a different way of doing things.

Kaitlin was shown into a large, air-conditioned accommodation truck. Her guide closed the door quietly behind her. He did not enter. In front of her, seated on a couch, was the tall, lanky frame of the man she had met at LAX, this time in the uniform of a Marines Lieutenant Colonel. He wore shoulder flashes signifying US Military Intelligence. Beside him on a table was a long grey feather. The man was watching Kaitlin closely, appraising her. There was something different about this guy. Kaitlin could sense it. Perhaps not such a military goofball after all, she thought.

Kaitlin looked at the feather and then back to the man. Now that she took a really good look, the guy had some Native American ancestry, but she had no idea which Nation. After the brusqueness of the soldier who met her off the helicopter, the change of pace, and particularly of atmosphere, was unsettling. Kaitlin held her peace.

At last, the man spoke.

"Kaitlin O'Neill, we meet again. Allow me to introduce myself more formally this time. I am Lieutenant Colonel Tom Olsen. I am a Lieutenant Colonel in the Marines. My area is military intelligence."

He paused and then, driven as always, to explain himself, "And in case you were wondering, my father was Swedish, but my mother was Native American."

"Pleased to meet you again, Lieutenant Colonel Olsen." Kaitlin met his eye for a moment and then looked down. A gesture of respect learned in Alaska.

"Please sit." Olsen indicated a small, comfortable armchair placed opposite him. Kaitlin sat, glad to be out of the heat and humidity, which seemed hardly to have dissipated, even after the sun had set.

"You know what this is?" Olsen held up the feather for her to see.

"It's a feather, obviously. Maybe from a water bird, something like a crane?"

"Quite right. It's a Sandhill crane feather."

Kaitlin remained silent. The slow rhythm of this kind of interview was familiar to her from her time in Alaska. She was accustomed to the protocol. However, if this was not going to be a military interview, precisely the kind of interview it was going to be, had yet to be revealed.

"Can you suggest what it might signify?"

Kaitlin took her time before answering. This was probably a test of some sort. Kaitlin's experience was with the medicine traditions of the Yup'ik people of Alaska, not with the traditions of continental Native Americans.

"Good luck perhaps?"

"Yes. And what else?"

Kaitlin thought back to her time in Alaska, remembering the sacred dances, the feathered fans and their deep spiritual meaning. Ancient lore that she was not supposed to know.

"Perhaps a link to the ancestors and the spirit world?"

"Yes, to my people, the Sandhill Crane represents a link to the spirit world." There was a short pause before he continued.

"What do you know of the spirit world?"

"I have just returned from it."

"From the spirit world?"

"Yes."

"Please tell me your story."

Kaitlin told her story. From the very beginning, childhood encounters on the barren and wild west coast of Ireland, her undergraduate studies, her PhD and the job at the Centre for Disease Control, her assignment in Australia and the events of the last few days. Sometime later, she came to a halt. Lieutenant Colonel Olsen had listened intently to her tale, not interrupting once. Now he spoke.

"What is your diagnosis?"

"Diagnosis?"

"Yes. What do you think is going on? Why do you think the Spirit World and our world are colliding?"

"You believe me?"

"I am not what you'd call a regular US Army intelligence guy."

Kaitlin smiled. That much was obvious.

"You know US Army intelligence has used us for over a hundred years?"

"Native Americans?"

"Yes. My mother's people."

"I saw the movie Wind-talkers, but that's as far as it goes."

"At first, we were used as scouts, then as translators and code speakers. More recently, we have been working as specialists."

"Specialists?"

"Yes. I myself am a medicine man, a shaman, like you."

Kaitlin waited, hoping the Lieutenant Colonel would continue.

"My mother was Comanche, but I live and work out of Fort Huachuca, Arizona. Apache country."

"What's at Fort Huachuca?"

"Military Intelligence school."

"You teach there?"

"Yes. Hard to believe I know, but I teach a course on animistic and pantheistic religions and cultures."

"Wow."

"Yes. Not many folks sign up for it anymore. It's all Islam and Arabic these days."

"I'd sign up." Kaitlin smiled.

"You could probably teach it." Tom Olsen sat back, twiddling his feather and nodding to himself.

"My grandfather was a code talker, or Wind-talker, like in the movie. People think it was just the Navajo, but my people started it, you know, right back in World War One. It was the Comanche people who did it first." His tone was melancholy, tired.

"What's your theory?" Kaitlin knew he must have access to recent reports from around the world. Things were probably happening elsewhere.

"My theory? I don't have enough to go on to develop a theory."

"Well, what can you tell me about events elsewhere? What's going on worldwide?"

"It's classified."

"'I have clearance."

"'I know. I just want you to understand that the Army has gotten real anal about this kind of thing – since WikiLeaks and that Swedish guy."

"Assange?"

"Yeah. That's the guy."

"He was Australian."

"Australian, really? You sure?"

"Yep."

"Well, since him, anyway."

"'Ok. Got it. Now what's going on?"

"There're reports of weird stuff going on all over. The conspiracy theory folks are going crazy. Even the level-headed engineering types are starting to get a tad skittish."

"What sort of things? What specifically in the US?"

"Every kind of weird shit. A group of border control folks near the great lakes reportedly saw a giant turtle. They had photographs and everything."

"To be honest, that doesn't sound all that remarkable."

"The damn thing was nearly twenty yards across. The Coast Guard got it on radar, and the Airforce scrambled jets."

"What happened?"

"The thing just disappeared." Olsen returned to shaking his head and examining his Sandhill crane feather.

"Ok. What do we know for sure? Let's try to collect the facts."

The Lieutenant Colonel seemed to emerge somewhat from his reverie.

"I have a file. Take a look." He passed a sheaf of papers across to Kaitlin, "it's mostly just a collection of newspaper reports. It's like you said at LAX. Most of it is out in the open anyway – public domain."

At that moment, there came a gentle knock at the door.

"Come." Olsen stood and walked to the door.

The door opened, and in walked the camouflaged Australian intelligence guy. Behind him, Kaitlin could make out Jack standing in the glare of a field light under an awning.

"Lieutenant Colonel Olsen, could I possibly have a word, please?" The Australian looked distinctly out of sorts. He had not been having a very good evening.

"Please, go ahead."

The tall Australian shifted awkwardly from foot to foot.

"Err, could we speak in private." He offered Kaitlin an apologetic look.

"I'll wait outside." Kaitlin slipped the sheaf of newspaper reports into her backpack and stepped from air-conditioned comfort into the heat and humidity of the Australian evening. What she wanted most at that moment was somewhere she could sit and read those reports.

Jack spotted her as she emerged.

"Beer?"

"Sounds good? I said I'd wait outside. I didn't say where outside."

The two walked back up the slight hill from the park and the paddocks by the river, now crowded with military vehicles and an assortment of tents. The Wisemans Ferry Inn was cool and invitingly familiar. Kaitlin ordered her new favourite drink, a rum and black, and Jack had his usual Coopers Pale Ale. The chatter in the pub was all about the sudden influx of military and news personnel. Consensus was that their presence would bring much-needed cash to the place.

"How'd you get on?" Kaitlin waited while Jack took a deep swig of beer.

"Told him exactly what happened, just like you said."

"And?"

"He didn't believe a word."

"Really? He thought you were making it all up?"

"Yep. Pretty much."

"Hardly surprising, I suppose."

"How did you get on with the Yank?"

"Believed every word." Kaitlin laughed loudly, relief combining with a sense of total unreality.

"Really? He seemed like a real hard arse."

"It wasn't him who interviewed me if you're talking about the bloke with a crew cut."

Jack took another swig of beer, "Not sure, I believe you."

"My guy was a Comanche shaman from Arizona."

"You're shitting me?"

"No. Straight up. His mother was a Native American, and he's a Lieutenant Colonel in the intelligence branch."

"Blimey. This whole thing just gets weirder and weirder."

"That it does, Jack Hexenkriege, that it does." Kaitlin waved her glass at the barman, indicating she was ready for another one. She pulled the sheaf of papers out of her backpack, handed the couple of pages she had already read to Jack and began to speed read the rest, handing further pages to Jack as she went.

A few minutes later, she had the gist of it. Even more weird stuff was happening for longer and in more places than before. Kaitlin checked the date on her watch.

"After today, we have two days to figure this out and fix it."

Jack, still plodding his way through the wodge of papers, looked up.

"Two days? How do you know? What happens then?"

"It's classified.' Kaitlin grinned"

"Don't give me that, Kaitlin. What's going on?"

"We talked about it at your dad's place. The field strength of the veil is oscillating, and it will come to a head in about three days."

"Oh, yeah. I wasn't really listening to that bit. What happens then?"

"Nobody knows what will happen then."

"Best guess?"

"Best guess – the veil will either close permanently or collapse completely."

"Emma would be trapped." Jack's tone was flat, despondent. It was more a statement than a question.

"Yes. Or our world and what we Irish call Tír na nÓg will merge. The Tuath Dé, the Wollemi as you call them, will walk the everyday world."

"Bummer."

"Bummer indeed." The sounds of a dozen conversations rose and fell in the old, stone-lined bar. Kaitlin noticed that she had finished her second drink and waved for another.

"What are we going to do?"

"Well, I don't know about you." Kaitlin was in unaccustomedly expansive form, "but first things first."

"Yes?"

"I'm going to get completely rat-arsed."

"Seems like a plan." Jack wagged his glass at the barman, who dutifully brought him another.

Several glasses later and Lieutenant Colonel Olsen, the Comanche intelligence officer, and Phil, the Australian intelligence guy, burst into the bar.

"There you are." Phil looked relieved.

Tom Olsen began to collect the alcohol-soaked internet printouts which had been scattered across the bar and on the floor.

"What part of classified did you not understand?" The man's tone was more in sadness than in anger.

"I was discrete." Kaitlin slurred slightly, the chicken risotto proving to have been insufficient ballast in such circumstances. She was definitely and distinctly inebriated.

"We need you to sign statements." Phil sounded apologetic.

"We need to file our report." Tom Olsen just sounded tired.

In an inadvertent stroke of strategic genius, Kaitlin selected that moment to fall gracelessly from her stool and lie, intoxicated and helpless, on the flagstone floor of the Wisemans Ferry Inn.

"Let's postpone to tomorrow morning, shall we?" Jack swooped down and lifted the near-comatose form of the Irish woman across his shoulder. The barman retrieved Kaitlin's backpack and the key to her room and followed Jack through into the interior of the hotel and up the stairs.

It was with a sense of weary resignation that Tom Olsen watched Jack carry away the comatose shaman. Her account had been thorough and complete. His personal mission remained the same as it had always been since he joined the Marines. Protect the planet and, if he could, prevent the powers that be from doing anything too terrible. There was an additional element now, though – rescue the little girl.

Jack placed Kaitlin gently on the massive four-poster bed and removed her boots. He quietly closed the curtains and, on impulse, placed a gentle kiss on her forehead. He sat for a moment on the overstuffed armchair in the corner of the room, watching Kaitlin sleep.

Two days, Jack thought, and then what? He was seriously worried, he realised. The same dread he had felt in the forest all those years ago returned unabated. He was tired too. Bone weary, after the encounter with the One-Mind, he took out his phone and began to call Jerry. Before he had finished dialling, his head fell back, and he slept.

When he awoke, it was still dark outside, the lights in the room were on, however, and he could hear Kaitlin humming tunelessly in the shower. Jack glanced at his watch. It was after midnight. Occasional sounds wafted up from the bar below. He stood up to leave, hoping to exit the room before Kaitlin emerged from the shower. He found a scrap of paper and a pencil and began to write a note.

"Gone to take a shower. See you in the morning."

As he was placing the note on Kaitlin's dressing table, she came bouncing out of the shower wearing a couple of enormous white towels, singing an Abba song from a million years ago and dancing almost entirely without any rhythm at all. Kaitlin turned and saw the note.

"Take a shower here." Unbelievably breezy and businesslike, given her earlier inebriated state, "I'll get them to send up something to eat and one of their lovely T-Shirts."

"I have things I need to do myself."

"We have work to do, Jack Hexenkriege, and I'll thank you not to get me drunk in future."

"I got you drunk?" Jack was incredulous.

"Good that you admit it," Kaitlin cut in, "but I am left wondering if your intentions were quite honourable." Kaitlin offered what she thought might be a coquettish smile. Jack made a desultory attempt at interrupting before Kaitlin continued.

"After all, I awake to find the man who's been feeding me drinks all night, and on an empty stomach at that, lying asleep in my bedroom, and me half undressed on the bed."

"I only took off your boots." Jack was both outraged and completely out of his depth.

"Easy for you to say, Mr Hexenkriege. Now, go and have a shower and let's get on with the serious business of saving the world, shall we?" Some vague memory stirred at the back of Kaitlin's mind, something about a four-poster bed.

When Jack emerged from the shower, the room was empty. There was a clean, odiously bright green T-Shirt folded on the dressing table and a sandwich on a small plate. His own note was still on the dressing table, but the words "Gone to take a shower" were crossed through, leaving only, "See you later in the bar".

Jack, refreshed, having stuffed down the sandwich and wearing an emerald green 'Wisemans Ferry Inn T-shirt, found Kaitlin sipping a coffee in the bar and chatting animatedly with Jerry.

"I see you two have been getting on splendidly," Jerry leered.

Jack stifled the almost overwhelming desire to punch Jerry's insufferably smug face and instead ordered a beer.

"Hair of the dog," he explained to anyone who would listen.

"Right," Kaitlin removed a notepad and pen from her handbag, "to business."

Jerry dragged Jack and Kaitlin out of the pub. While Jack and Kaitlin had been sleeping off the early evening's excesses. He had been busy. He had moved his base of operations from the pub to the conference centre across the road. Jack and Kaitlin had been cordially invited to join him.

"I know it's late, but Red Earth uses this place all the time," Jerry was in an expansive mood, "they opened up for me." He had changed for the occasion and was now clothed head to foot in the exquisitely retro Arc'teryx Veilance range of precision technical apparel, complete with a minimalist, black rip-stop backpack and 'Isogon' hooded jacket. He looked a little like a walk-on character from Star Trek.

Jerry ushered them into a conference room. There was a map of the local area stuck to a whiteboard. The door opened, and a young woman entered carrying a tray of fruit and sandwiches and jugs of coffee and fruit juice. Once the woman had left the room, Jerry tapped on his glass with a pen. Jack and Kaitlin dutifully came to order.

"I've invited a few people to join us. We need to put together an expeditionary force. We're going back in."

The speech had a rehearsed quality to it. For a moment or two, Kaitlin and Jack were too surprised to speak.

"Expeditionary force? What the hell is an expeditionary force?" Jack had a hollow feeling in his gut, born of an endless stream of Jerry's interventions since earliest childhood.

"Nice duds." Kaitlin was admiring Jerry's couture leggings and a particularly fetching violet 'survival bracelet'.

Jerry preened briefly for Kaitlin's benefit before responding to Jack. Then he was all business, every inch the corporate executive.

"We have two days at most to get Emma back, and we need help."

Jerry paused in case Jack wished to comment further.

"Ok then. I've invited Alice Whalebone and Dad, an impressive American Army Lieutenant Colonel by the name of Tom Olsen, and one other whom I shall not name at this point."

"Sounds like you're putting the band back together," Jack smiled, "just like old times."

"How the hell do you know Tom Olsen?" Kaitlin felt out manoeuvred once more. This guy seemed to have contacts everywhere. Things were moving too fast, and she felt like she was losing control again. Had she thought about it a little more, she might have questioned if she had ever been in control in the first place.

"I only met him for the first time yesterday afternoon," Jerry raised his eyebrows in mock affront, "and the military is not yet formally engaged, and that gives us a small window of time in which to act if we are going to get Emma back."

"What's Olsen's role then?"

"Unofficial observer. You know these intelligence types just can't leave anything alone."

Kaitlin was carrying out some complex arithmetic on her fingers.

"Seven, you, Jack, me, Max, Alice, Tom and the mystery man - the magnificent seven ride again." Her evident pleasure was inexplicable to the two brothers.

"Seemed apt somehow."

There was a knock at the door, and Alice Whalebone walked in accompanied by Max Hexenkriege.

Jerry stood to greet Alice, "Have some fruit. Help yourself to sandwiches. We're just waiting for two more people."

There were greetings all around. Alice was carrying a large handwoven, dilly bag, its contents bulging enigmatically. Max dumped his ancient, dusty, and much-worn Minnesota-style geologist's pack on the floor and slumped down in a chair. Kaitlin distributed sandwiches on small porcelain plates and poured drinks for the group. The atmosphere was curiously festive, given the late hour and the gravity of the situation. There was another knock at the door, and in stepped Lieutenant Colonel Olsen. He gave a curious little bow to the assembled people.

"I am honoured to be included in this endeavour, albeit in an unofficial capacity."

Max stood up, taking a step or two towards the Lieutenant Colonel.

"Tom, Tom Olsen? What on Earth? How did you end up in the Army? How the hell did you end up here, for that matter?"

"Maximillian Hexenkriege? I don't believe it."

The two men approached each other slowly, almost shyly, before throwing their arms around each other and pounding each other heartily on the back.

"Yeah, that'd be right. Of course, Dad would be mates with a Lieutenant Colonel in US Military Intelligence. Stands to reason." Jack reached for a large red apple and bit into it noisily.

"We worked together years ago, in Oklahoma, around the Wichita Mountains and the Red Bed Plains, when I was a geologist."

"I was a student, and we were searching for iodine deposits, as I recall." Tom Olsen turned to Jack. "You must be Jack Hexenkriege," and turning to Jerry, he continued, "and you must be Jerry. Pleased to make your acquaintances."

Jerry nodded while Jack stood to shake the man's hand.

More plates of sandwiches and more drinks were brought in. Munching quietly, the group settled down. Alice cleared her throat and spoke.

"My people have been guardians of the Wollemi Forest for thousands of years. What I am about to tell you is privileged information, private information, known only to our Elders. However, needs must when the devil drives." The group fell silent as she spoke. Alice carried a natural authority demanding of respect.

At that moment, without warning, the door burst open and in tumbled Harry Soames, Director of Intelligence, United States Centre for

Disease Control, dragging an unfeasibly large suitcase on wheels and looking distinctly hot and flustered.

"Harry Soames. What the heck?" This was, without doubt, the very last person Kaitlin had expected to see.

"Harry, good to see you." Max was smiling from ear to ear.

"You made it out here then," Tom Olsen stood to greet the Director. Harry gazed around at the collected throng, "

Sorry, I'm late. I had to stop off in Canberra for an official function." Harry Soames, exhausted and dishevelled after his frantic race across the Pacific, stood tall and calm.

"Jerry called me. I had to be here with you all now, at this most critical time. For good or ill, this will be the culmination of my life's work. The culmination of a plan evolved over decades, if not longer. The US government has agreed with the Australian government that the, er... disappearances will be treated as a health matter under the auspices of the CDC." There followed an awkward silence. No one knew quite what to say. Harry, the quintessential desk jockey, venturing into the field while things were at their darkest. Should they take heart, or was his arrival a portent of the doom to come? Kaitlin broke the silence.

"Sandwich?" Kaitlin proffered a plate of delicately cut quarter sandwiches and a large mug of coffee.

The Director collapsed into a seat, his suitcase rolling majestically onto its back and wobbling for a moment like a stranded turtle while he somehow simultaneously stuffed a sandwich into his mouth and took and long swig of coffee.

"Ok. What's the play?"

"I am Alice Whalebone," Alice, patient as ever, began again, "I am an Elder of the Darkinjung people. We have been guardians of the forest for thousands of years. What I must tell you is secret information known only to our Elders. I need your commitment to respect my confidence."

There was a general nodding of heads and murmurs of agreement.

215

"As you are all no doubt aware, we are not alone. There lives, in the forest, a people in many ways like ourselves and in many ways very, very different." Alice glanced around her audience, calibrating their reactions to what she had said, figuring out how she would prepare them for the revelations to come.

"You call these folk 'the Wollemi'. We, the original Indigenous peoples, have many names for them, the Janjarri, the Mimi, the Mogwoi, the Rai and the Mimih."

Then Kaitlin piped up, "The Irish call them the Tuath Dé. English speakers call them faeries or pixies. To the Japanese, they are Kami, and so on. Every nation and language group has their own name for them." Kaitlin stopped talking suddenly, aware and somewhat abashed that she had interrupted Alice.

Alice paused again, gauging reactions.

"As I say. We, the Darkinjung and other Indigenous nations, have been watchers and guardians of the Wollemi for thousands of years. We have developed certain skills. We have learned how to talk to, and how to interact, with the Wollemi."

Alice paused and took a sip from a glass of ice-cold water. Beads of condensation rolled down its sides.

"We believe that the Dreaming, the spirit world as your people call it," Alice nodded towards Tom Olsen, "or the world beyond the veil, will never end, but it can change, and we believe a change is coming. Lately, I have begun to hear their thoughts. I don't know for certain if this is intended or not, but I believe that the One-Mind of the Wollemi is communicating with me." Alice paused once more, taking her time.

"A big change that will transform the whole world is only days away. We, Indigenous Aboriginal people, are committed to fulfilling our age-old duty. We will engage the Wollemi."

Alice sat down, gazing at the faces of her small audience.

Harry Soames spoke first, "I have an official, highly classified report that says pretty much the same thing. Except for the bit about communication with the One-Mind."

Tom Olsen stood to address the meeting, "That's why I'm here."

"That's why we're all here," Jerry continued. "The map on the wall shows the location of the Table of the Gods. That's the centre of Wollemi activity, that's where Emma is being held, and that's where we need to go."

"What do we do when we get there?" Alice's quiet, authoritative voice cut through the growing noise of shuffling papers and mumbled comments.

"Err, well, that's what this meeting is all about." Jerry fiddled with the elegant purple survival band around his wrist.

"Good point. As a military man," Lieutenant Colonel Olsen's self-deprecating smile suggested he was much, much more, "I'd have to say we really should seek to clarify our objectives." The tall Comanche Medicine Man twiddled the long grey crane feather as he spoke.

"Our options are unclear. First, we rescue the child, but after that, what should we do? What is our strategic intent?"

"What do you mean?" Jack was good with the rescuing Emma bit but hadn't thought beyond that.

Tom continued, "Well, put most succinctly, do we want to close the entrance to the spirit world permanently or force it open permanently or what?"

Jack had no immediate answer. No one did.

Eventually, Director Harry Soames spoke up.

"Any action we take will be under the auspices of the CDC." Harry Soames glanced towards Jerry to see how he would take the shift in control. Jerry made no sign.

"I have brought something along that may help." There were some nervous grumbles and glances cast towards the enormous suitcase lounging behind the Director like a hog in a wallow.

"I picked up the suitcase from the US Embassy in Canberra this morning," all eyes were now fixed on the inscrutable item, "It contains a device so highly classified that not even the President of the United

States was aware of its existence until yesterday." Harry Soames had their attention.

"What the hell is it?" Jack leaned forward in his seat, eyeing the offending article warily.

"Oh, Dear God," Kaitlin piped up, "What have you Americans invented this time?" Forgetting for a moment that she had taken up American citizenship quite happily when it became available to her.

"You're not going to believe this, or perhaps it's entirely to be expected, but I'm going to have to ask you all to sign these nondisclosures." Harry distributed a closely typed sheet of paper to each person.

Jerry began to study the wording of the agreement until Alice tapped him gently on the elbow and passed him a pen.

"Just sign Jerry." Jerry signed, as did everyone else. The Director collected the individual sheets and checked them one by one.

"I finally make it to Director of Intelligence at one of the most secretive and powerful institutions on earth, and I seem to spend my entire life checking signatures and receipts."

"Sure, it's no job for a grown man," Kaitlin turned the Irish brogue up to maximum, "we're all that sorry for you."

Harry laughed. The mood of the meeting, which until that moment had been darkening considerably, lightened a little.

"Ok, what's in the box?" Max Hexenkriege was practically jumping out of his seat in anticipation. There was silence in the room.

"Tom, would you do the honours, please?" Harry stepped away from the stranded suitcase. The tension in the room was palpable.

"Happy to help, Director."

Tom favoured Kaitlin with a nervous smile before turning the suitcase over and opening it.

"Tom is my assistant for the time being. He's on loan from NASA." Harry Soames explained to the room in general.

"It was Tom who located the device. Why don't you describe it for us, Tom?"

"Err, well, Sir. That is, it's a bit difficult to say."

"It's ok, Tom. We've all signed NDAs." Harry Soames waved the collection of signed documents.

"Yeah. What does the damn thing do?" Kaitlin was becoming impatient. Tom acquiesced.

"The device was developed by NASA as part of a classified joint project with the Centre for Disease Control and DARPA," Tom began.

"Smaller, proof-of-concept devices have been tested, but this full-size version has never been deployed."

"Why not?" Kaitlin, never a fan of secret defence projects at the best of times, was becoming peevish.

"NASA wouldn't say, but I got the impression that there was nowhere to test it."

"Why not?" Kaitlin's voice took on a steely edge suggesting unspecified unpleasant consequences in the not-too-distant future.

"It's just too dangerous."

"What does it actually do, then?"

"Well, here's the thing. NASA didn't say."

"Oh, for goodness' sake." Kaitlin jumped to her feet and took a short walk around the room.

"Allow Tom to brief us, Kaitlin," the Director's tone was chiding but sympathetic, "go on, Tom, please."

"I don't think anyone that's still at NASA knows for certain what the device does." Kaitlin opened her mouth to interject, but Tom continued briskly. "The details of the design and testing were held by DARPA. DARPA told us they had lost them."

"Typical. Lying bastards." Kaitlin appeared to stamp her foot in frustration.

"Perhaps. However, NASA was able to explain the device's purpose, even if they could not say how it worked or what it did."

Kaitlin looked up expectantly, at last, something useful.

"The device is designed to protect Earth from psychic attack by aliens."

"You've got to be kidding." Jack, who had been enjoying Kaitlin's discomfort enormously and had been keeping only half an ear to Tom's briefing, jumped in, "Psychic attack from aliens? You wouldn't read about it. How much did the damn thing cost?"

"I didn't think to ask what the project's budget was." Tom turned to Harry Soames, "I might be able to find out."

"Not important." Harry gave the youthful Lieutenant Colonel a re-assuring smile, "Continue."

"The device is old school, from the cold war period, designed and built as part of the Apollo project. The NASA engineers were afraid of it. They couldn't have been happier to see it packed up and bundled onto a plane."

"How do we set it off?" Harry Soames glanced around the room, "and how far away from it do we have to be when we do?"

"There's no stated safe distance as far as I know." Tom squared his shoulders, "and whoever sets it off only has half an hour to get as far away as possible. There is a timer, or it can be set off manually."

"Who will set it off then?" Kaitlin searched the assembled faces for any sign of a volunteer.

"That's my job." Director Harry Soames glanced warily at the large, now ominous looking, suitcase, "How does the timer work?"

"I will take you through the controls and the timer. You will have half an hour to get away. But that still leaves us with our objectives." The last remark was directed to Harry Soames, "What orders do you have?"

"My orders from the President are to stabilise the veil or make it safe."

"What does that mean? Make it safe?" Max Hexenkriege did not like the sound of that, "There are thousands of Wollemi living in the forest, perhaps even hundreds of thousands."

Harry nodded acknowledgement.

"They are people," Max continued, "they are not animals to be slaughtered without a thought."

"It's our responsibility to find a solution." Harry Soames spoke quietly, his tone firm, "If we cannot find a way to convince our governments that the situation has been stabilised, that the world is safe, then our combined militaries will carpet bomb the Wollemi Forest. And not just the Wollemi Forest but many wilderness places around the world. It will be slash and burn on a global scale. Not so much as a tree will be left standing in the wildernesses."

There was silence in the room. The enormity of their situation began to sink in.

"I have a suggestion." Jerry spoke, "We don't know what will happen when the sinewave collapses, but we can extrapolate one of two potential outcomes." He had their attention.

"Either the Wollemi will close the veil forever, worldwide, sundering our two domains for all time, or the veil will collapse, merging the spheres once and for all."

Heads nodded around the table. Before Jerry could continue, Alice spoke.

"My people believe that the Wollemi are struggling to maintain the veil. We believe that the increases in our own populations around the world have created some kind of psychic interference. There are just too many of us for them to cope much longer."

Tom Olsen nodded, "My people have a similar view. The Spirit World is colliding with our world. We have seen many incursions over recent decades, strange animals showing up in the wild places, culminating with the increasing numbers of missing children."

"Well, my idea is…" Jerry attempted to get a word in edgewise but to no effect.

Max spoke, "I have been studying the Wollemi for most of my adult life. I cannot say for certain that they mean us any harm. However, I believe they erected the veil to protect themselves from us, not the other way around. If the veil is permanently closed, we will be cut off from each other, and presumably, the world will return to normal. If the veil collapses, then our two worlds will indeed collide. I have no idea what will happen then."

Into the silence that fell around the room, Kaitlin spoke.

"There is another possibility, based upon what Jack and I experienced when we spoke directly to the Wollemi Mind."

All eyes were now on Kaitlin.

"When Jack and I encountered the One-Mind, it said it was going to assimilate us and close the veil. I believe that the Wollemi may make one last desperate bid to reclaim their lost children, to assimilate us, all of us, everywhere, back into the herd."

"Could they do that?" Harry Soames looked worried.

Alice Whalebone spoke, "Our tradition tells of a colossal power latent in the Wollemi. The mere fact that they have been able to maintain the veil for fourteen thousand years at least suggests that if roused to oneness, they could be a force to be reckoned with. The One-Mind, risen in all its glory, could be unstoppable."

"Fourteen thousand years? Where does that number come from?" Max posed the question on behalf of the group.

"Our songs tell of a terrible explosion long ago, followed by a great and sudden flood. The skies darkened, and the sun was blotted out for years. We estimate this happened around fourteen thousand years ago, after which the Wollemi raised the veil. Before that, we lived together on this Earth. If not in harmony, then only with occasional skirmishes."

"Meltwater Event Alpha? Is that what you're talking about?" Max seemed puzzled, "The sudden, unexplained melting that occurred after the last ice age?"

"No idea, never heard of it." Alice replied, "Our people lived mostly in peace with the Wollemi for over fifty thousand years before the flood."

"That does make a weird kind of sense," Kaitlin spoke, "my own tradition, the Gnostic Kabbalah, suggests that we were cast out of Eden because we sought understanding when we became individually conscious and intelligent, once we ate from the Tree of Knowledge."

Kaitlin could see from the bewildered looks that her point was not getting through.

"The tradition teaches that there is a veil, 'Ain Soph Aur', the Veil of Darkness and Light. This veil separates us and the, I'll say, 'real' world of cause and effect, our world if you like, from the world of ideas, the magic world where 'nothing is but dreaming makes it so.'" Still, she faced blank stares.

"The biblical story of the fall and expulsion from the garden of Eden may have a basis in fact."

"The Dreaming," Alice spoke.

"Exactly, the Dreaming. The spirit world and Tír na nÓg may be one and the same, and we can enter if the veil is weak or if we are particularly innocent, like a child."

"Where are you going with this?" Max asked.

"Perhaps it's time for us to go home. Perhaps we can return to Eden?" Kaitlin's voice was low, uncertain.

"Are you suggesting that we might be able to return to a mythical Eden?" Tom Olsen looked genuinely intrigued at the idea.

"And are you suggesting that returning would be a good idea?" Harry Soames was less impressed.

"Whatever, but we get Emma out first, right?" Jack had had his fill of weird theories. He just wanted his daughter back.

Jerry tapped his glass with a pen. He was bloody well going to make one last attempt to regain control of his meeting.

"Here's what we do. We split into groups, one shaman plus one other. Jack goes with Kaitlin, I go with Alice, and Max goes with Tom. Harry takes the device. Each team attempts to find out what the One-Mind plans, get Emma back and negotiate with it to close the veil. If negotiation fails, Kaitlin, Tom and Alice distract and split the One-Mind, Jack finds and rescues Emma, and Harry fires the weapon."

Jack spoke, "So while it's distracted, I grab Emma and make a run for it."

"What about the device? How do we deploy it?" Tom was to the point as ever.

Jerry nodded, "We forward position Harry and his suitcase on the Table of the Gods. If everything goes to shit, he hits the button. Ok?"

No one had any better idea.

"By the way," Jack spoke directly to Tom, "Does NASA have a name for the device?"

Tom hesitated before speaking, "Well, the NASA engineers have a nickname for it. They call it 'The HARP'."

At this point, Harry Soames leaned forward in his seat and interjected, "Does NASA have a more official name by any chance?"

"No, I don't think so. Just H.A.R.P." Tom spelled it out.

"HARP? What is that? An acronym?"

"No one knows what it stands for anymore. Someone told me it was because it made heavenly music."

"Same old story." Kaitlin couldn't hide her feelings.

Tom continued, "One of the engineers called it Soul-Eater, the Devourer of the Dead. He may have known more than he was letting on."

"And no one knows what the thing does?" Jack just couldn't get his head around how an organisation like NASA could lose such a critical piece of information.

"Nope," Tom looked almost pleased, "We need our two governments and military organisations to agree to our plan. In particular, we need them to agree to hold off bombing the Wollemi until we have retrieved Emma and attempted to negotiate with the One-Mind. They are going full speed ahead towards carpet bombing the entire forest. Director, you will need to keep this an official CDC initiative, do you think you can do that?"

"Yes. But we need to talk to Canberra to pitch this. They have to give a negotiated settlement a chance. I have the President's backing on that."

The following morning the intrepid expeditionary force took the half-hour flight to Canberra from the nearby Airforce base at Richmond. Their aim was to present the CDC proposal to the military and to agree their joint strategy and tactics. Both American and Australian governments and military would be represented. Events were moving too fast. No detailed plan had been formulated. Perhaps unsurprisingly, neither the CDC nor the military planners of either country had ever conceived either of attacking or defending an attack from fairyland. The Australian Aboriginal Dreamtime had never before been seen as a real and present danger. Everyone was flying by the seat of their pants.

The helicopter landing on the small Embassy lawn had been a little bumpy, but the journey had been quick. Director Harry Soames and Lieutenant Colonel Tom Olsen were first to enter the cyber-secure briefing room in the US Embassy, Canberra. Awaiting them were various Australian and US military figures. In contact by secure, encrypted conference call were the White House and the Prime Minister's office. The nondescript man representing the NSA sat in his corner, exuding an air of disdain for everything and everyone. The atmosphere was heavy with foreboding. It was beginning to sink in, both to the military and the civilians present, that the world as they had known it was coming to an end. Whatever happened from this point on, the history and place of mankind in the universe would be forever altered.

Soames knew it would not be easy to gain the approval of the meeting. For starters, the only one of the CDC's party who was a serving military officer in a field role was Tom Olsen. Also, the military would no doubt have their own solution prepped and ready, and it wouldn't involve negotiating with fairies or the use of an arcane space super-weapon, the workings of which nobody could recall.

After brief introductions, CDC Director Harry Soames was invited to speak. He set out the parameters of their problem and its global scale and highlighted his uncertainty as to how the President's order to "stabilise" or "make it safe" should be interpreted in this context. He proposed that they attempt a negotiated settlement, and only if that failed would the Military execute their Plan B. He took questions as they came, and he set out the CDC's intention of deploying the groups of 'specialists' with himself acting as failsafe. And then he stopped. There was total silence in the room. You could have heard a pin drop. The shape of their shared challenge had become starkly apparent. It was no longer the case that there was just one single human race, no matter how fractured and broken it might be. There were two, and they were profoundly different and possibly incompatible. Almost a minute passed before anyone spoke, and then the grizzled, steely-eyed Army General from their previous meeting rose to his feet.

"Director, can you explain what you intend to do with the HARP device? What does it give us?" The realisation sat across the room that the device, whatever it was, might best be understood as a weapon of mass destruction. Initiating the device might be an act of genocide. Were they, in effect, planning a war crime?

Kaitlin surprised herself and her colleagues by raising her hand.

"Yes?" It was something of a surprise too, when she found herself saying, "Sir, I believe I have seen a smaller device being tested. I saw its effects when I was working in Alaska."

Most faces around the conference table assumed a slightly baffled look. No one spoke for a moment or two. The nondescript man sitting off to one side got to his feet.

"The HARP program was an electromagnetic experiment discontinued years ago. It was ineffective. When did you say you saw its effects?"

"I am not interested in its effects on the ionosphere or on radio waves. Although they were pretty spectacular. I don't believe it was being tested for those." Kaitlin, too had gotten to her feet and was in combative mood, "I'm talking about its effects on people, specifically its effects on the veil and the people who live behind it."

"You can't blame that on us. The program was shut down years ago, as I say." The nondescript NSA man looked around the room, seeking support. None was apparent.

"Sir, the HARP was tested in Alaska. It reportedly had an effect on the Spirit world. We may need it to weaken the Wollemi One-Mind." Kaitlin addressed her comments directly to the old General.

"Exactly what effect does it have on the veil and its people?" His tone was calm, reasonable, "I won't poke the hornet's nest without good reason."

"Sir, it was deployed in a remote part of Alaska where I was working," she replied, "In addition to some impressive weather effects, mainly lashing rain, there were several reports from the tribal Elders of children going missing and returning unable to explain where they had been or for how long."

"How does that help us?"

"My Native Alaskan colleagues reported that the 'Spirit World' had been disturbed. The residents of the Spirit World seemed confused and disorganised, they said."

"And?"

"Sir, my interpretation of these phenomena as a scientist, and given what we now know, is that firing the HARP weakens the group mind, reduces their social and psychic cohesion and creates disorganisation and confusion amongst them."

"From what you say, it seems the device also weakens the veil. Why is that important to us? We haven't decided yet if we want to force it open or slam it shut."

Lieutenant Colonel Tom Olsen, who had remained silent up until this point, rose to his feet and cleared his throat to address the room.

"As many of you may know, I am Tom Olsen, Lieutenant Colonel, Military Intelligence out of Fort Huachuca, Arizona". Conversation ceased, and the room fell silent, "I am also an Elder of the Comanche people, and one of our three 'Specialists'."

Tom took a moment to survey the room, meeting every eye.

"It is our belief that the Wollemi, as individuals, exist and act on an almost instinctual basis. As individuals, they have little or no telekinetic capability. They do, however, have a highly developed telepathic ability. If they hit a problem, they communicate telepathically, seeking a solution. If the solution does not immediately come to hand, they bring in more of their kind, creating an extended telepathic network. The network becomes more intelligent and more self-aware as it grows. A kind of group mind materialises. We believe that at a certain point, the network as a whole reaches a tipping point when telekinetic and perhaps other capabilities emerge." The nondescript man from the NSA began to stir.

"Last point, it is our belief that it is the combined capability of the Wollemi Mind as a whole, globally, that maintains the veil. This capability, we believe, functions somewhat at the level of our own autonomic nervous system. It's automatic, like breathing. They don't have to think about it. My people believe that what has been described as a veil can also be seen as a portal between our world and the spirit world. Sir, I believe we will need the HARP in case we need to open the portal in order to actuate Plan B." Tom resumed his seat. As a Comanche Elder and a Lieutenant Colonel in intelligence, he spoke with inarguable authority. Realisation of the terrifying potential of the One-Mind gripped the room. The fear of a telekinetic supermind with the power to subvert a human army using telepathic mind control weighted the risk-reward equation firmly towards urgent and unequivocal military action.

"Ok," the old General looked around the room. "Use it only as a last resort. Truth is, we still don't know what it does."

The little man from the NSA opened his mouth to speak, but before he could utter a word, Jerry, immaculate in his couture adventure gear and psychologically unable to attend a meeting without making his presence felt, tapped his glass with a pen.

"Err, excuse me, guys, but can we just recap? As I understand it, the basic plan for deploying the expeditionary force is agreed. I'm hoping the military will ferry us to our positions and will kindly come and collect us again afterwards. In addition, NASA is providing a secret device of unknown function in case we need it. Here's the bit I'm still not clear on, do we want the veil open or closed at the end of all this?"

"Forgive me," the old General appeared to notice Jerry for the first time, "I may have missed your introduction earlier?"

Jerry stood. "I am Jerry Hexenkriege. Director and CEO of Red Earth Mining, I will be teaming up with Alice Whalebone, Elder of the Darkinjung people."

"You're not from the military?" it was a statement, not a question.

"No."

"And you're not from the intelligence community?"

"No."

"Then ….?"

"I am half Wollemi." Jerry, always happy to take centre stage, allowed the bombshell to reverberate around the room for a moment, "My mother was one of them. She was Wollemi."

All eyes turned to Director Soames.

"Is this true?" the General was incredulous. To the highly trained military minds around the room, Jerry might just as well have claimed kinship with the devil himself. Soames realised their entire plan, brittle as it undoubtedly was, could shatter against the anvil of Jerry's hubris.

"Yes, Sir, we are privileged to have two half-Wollemi team members as well as their father, a thirty-year intelligence veteran with the Centre for Disease Control and probably the world's leading specialist on the Wollemi. Jack and Jerry bring a unique knowledge and understanding of the behaviour of the Wollemi and can guide our specialists safely to their field positions."

Max Hexenkriege took to his feet.

"Sir, I am Maximillian Hexenkriege. I am, as has been said, an intelligence analyst for the Centre for Disease Control. I've studied the

Wollemi for most of my adult life. I was married to a Wollemi woman, and Jerry and Jack, here are my two sons from that marriage. In their early years, they lived with their mother and myself in the Wollemi Forest. Jack, in particular, has a detailed knowledge of the forest."

All eyes were now on Jack and Jerry, especially Jerry.

The General spoke, "It is strange and a little confronting to realise that we have two individuals of Wollemi descent with us in this very room." There were murmurs of agreement from around the table. "It certainly brings it home that this bizarre situation is real, the Wollemi are real, and the veil is real."

Max spoke again, "Sir, regretfully, it is my belief that if we cannot gain agreement with the Wollemi One-Mind to close the veil permanently, or if the Wollemi One-Mind is unable to do so, then we need to reduce the Wollemi's ability to create the group mind at all."

Max turned to his two sons and to Alice Whalebone, "We all know what the One-Mind is capable of. We all know that once it forms, its purpose is implacable. It will stop at nothing to achieve its will. If the One-Mind once forms an intent at odds with our fundamental needs as free human beings, there would be no living with it. There would be no possibility of peaceful coexistence. We must lock it away or destroy it. Do you agree?"

The two brothers looked at each other, both perhaps for the first time facing the terrible truth of their situation, but it was Alice who spoke.

"We, the Indigenous Aboriginal peoples, have been guardians of the Wollemi for over fourteen thousand years. My own nation, the Darkinjung people, have shouldered our burden without complaint for all of that time. I wish to make it clear, however, that while we have been guardians, we have not been protectors or defenders. Our role has been to watch and to wait and to warn our people if the Wollemi ever posed a threat."

She had their attention.

"We respect the Wollemi deeply, but we are afraid of them. We have learned to live alongside them but not to command or rule them. From time to time, we have even skirmished with them. If they cannot be contained, then they must be controlled." Alice paused for a moment, "Or destroyed." At the back of her mind, she could almost swear she heard the silent voice of the One-Mind laughing.

"It's agreed then. We'll fly you in and provide the device. Whether you are successful or not, we will attempt to extract you from the agreed extraction points. If unsuccessful, we will then initiate Plan B." The General looked around the room, "Comments? Suggestions?"

Just as the meeting was about to break up, Jack spoke.

"We get Emma out first, right? Whatever kind of hell and perdition we decide to bring down on them, we get my daughter out first?"

An awkward silence hung across the conference room until Harry Soames intervened.

"You and Kaitlin have the specific job of finding Emma and getting her out. Jerry, Alice, Tom, Max and I will deal with the Wollemi One-Mind."

The meeting broke into little groups, speaking softly in subdued yet urgent tones. The military folks, in particular, seemed uncomfortable, uncertain that Plan A, such as it was, had been thought through. It was at this point that the General finally came to his own private decision. They would allow Plan A to go ahead with the main purpose of extracting the girl, Emma, and then, whatever the outcome of these proposed impromptu negotiations, they would initiate Plan B. There was now only one day to go until the sinewave collapsed, and whatever event it portended would be triggered. He had his orders, too, agreed with the Australian side, and they left little room for ambiguity. The military would protect humanity from the Wollemi at all costs, period. They would give the CDC team time to escape, and then they would wipe the Wollemi Forrest and everything in it off the face of the Earth.

The General stood and cleared his throat. The room was silent.

"Ok, the military has a backup plan, as you know, but you get to try your way first. If the device fails to detonate or we do not receive the 'all clear' code from you, we will initiate plan B." The General caught Harry's eye, holding him in his gaze for several moments, "You are a brave man, Director. You have our respect." The General sat down. Once again, the room fell silent.

After about a minute, Tom Olsen began to fidget in his seat. Urgency overwhelmed caution. Tom reached over and tapped the Director on his shoulder.

"Ghost Hawks," he whispered, "we need their Ghost Hawks."

Harry Soames jumped to his feet as if stung.

"Sir, we do have one small request for assistance - if you don't mind."

"Well, spit it out, man. Time is short."

"Can we use your Ghost Hawks to transport us?"

The sudden commotion in the room startled everyone. Instantaneously, as it seemed, two officers stormed to their feet, one, a Two Star Air Force General yelling "That's classified!" at the top of his lungs, and the other, a Colonel in the Marines, bellowing "How'd you find out about that?"

The old General lurched to his feet, and the room fell silent once again. He took a moment to gather his thoughts. Then he spoke.

"We have three UH 60 Ghost Hawks. We can forward position Director Soames and the failsafe and then drop the teams near to their allocated positions. Unfortunately, we can't go in too close. These things are mighty quiet, but we can't afford to be discovered."

"Thank you, Sir."

The Marines Colonel cleared his throat to speak.

"Yes?"

"Extraction, Sir. If we are taking them in, then we have a responsibility to get them out, Sir."

"Agreed. I'll leave the extraction teams to you, Colonel."

"Sir, Yes Sir."

The room was subdued once again. The scale of what was about to happen threatened to overwhelm. The General sat down, tapping his fingers on the edge of the conference table.

"Is there anything else you or your team need, Director?"

Harry turned to his team.

"Guys?" But there was nothing.

The mood on the helicopters back to Wisemans Ferry was sombre. The meeting with the military had brought the hideous reality of their situation home to one and all. They not only had a little girl to rescue but a world to save, and they only had a couple of days to do it.

About halfway back to Wisemans Ferry, as the colossal green wilderness that surrounded the city of Sydney came into view. Harry turned to Tom.

"You can fit the device with a dead man's switch, right?"

"Actually, Sir, I assumed you knew. It has one fitted already."

The scene when they landed at Wisemans Ferry was one of organised chaos. The military had, of course, expanded their encampment to include virtually all available land. Both nature and the military abhor a vacuum. A tent city occupied the land between the Inn and the river.

Back at the Wisemans Ferry Resort, Tom took Harry Soames through the workings of the HARP device, not that there was much to it. However, in so far as the future of all human beings on earth might be dependent, even in part, upon its successful deployment, it seemed like a good idea.

"Basically, there's a timer with a fixed duration of half an hour. There are two red buttons that you have to depress simultaneously to start the timer, and one large green button, which just needs to be pressed once to stop it. Two red to start, one green to stop, and that's it." Tom paused in case Harry had any questions.

"To set the device off manually without the use of the timer, press the large red button under the clear Perspex cover. Simply slide the cover out of the way and hit the button. Lastly, there is the dead man's switch. The switch consists of a sensor band that locks around your wrist, with a coiled cable that snaps into a port on the side of the device. Once the band is locked around the operator's wrist and the other end is snapped firmly into the device, the switch is activated and will remain active until and unless the timer is started. If the wearer's life signs became undetectable to the wristband or they lose consciousness while the switch was on, the device will trigger. If the switch is removed while it is turned on or became detached from the device, the device will trigger. That's it, simple."

"Thanks, Tom," Soames was subdued, "I think I've got it."

Tom wandered outside to look up at the stars. To this point, he had been a sort of hanger-on on the mission. It hadn't seemed like his mission – he was just helping out. But now, finally, having briefed Harry on initiating the HARP, he was in. This had become personal. However, being first and foremost a marine, his priorities were simple. Complete the mission and, save the world, get the girl back safe.

THE BRIEFING

After Tom's private briefing, Soames assembled the team in the Wisemans Ferry Inn restaurant for a BBQ-style dinner. The place was heaving with off-duty army officers. Many a curious glance was cast in their direction. No one approached. Harry attempted to order a round of drinks, but no one was much in the mood for drinking. They went over the plan a couple of times but in reality, it was too simple to bear repetition, and the team soon split into small groups to chat.

Tom, Max, and Harry sat off to one side, gossiping about happier times and catching up. For Max and Tom, the time they spent together rambling over hill and dale looking for rock samples seemed impossibly innocent, carefree, and long, long ago. They were just happy at the chance coincidence that had brought them together again after so many years. The Director, however, kept his own counsel. A lifetime spent in intelligence had honed certain instincts, one of which was to question coincidence closely. It seemed unlikely to him that chance alone could explain the composition of Jerry's so-called expeditionary force, but if chance alone was not responsible, then what could explain the close relationships between them? What could balance the null hypothesis? Harry wasn't sure he liked the direction in which his thoughts were tending. The implications were uncomfortable, to say the least.

Jerry beckoned Tom over to his table. The two sat together, discussing surveillance technology and satellite mapping. Jerry had an interest in using satellite imaging at a sub-15-metre spatial resolution to locate micro-deposits. Tom, good-natured as ever, explained the wavelengths and degrees of resolution that were available. The pair were getting on famously.

Jack, Kaitlin, and Alice decided to go for a walk down along the banks of the Hawkesbury to clear their heads. It was a cloudless night, warm, without so much as a breath of wind. Alice listened to the night-time sounds as they walked. Occasionally, she sniffed the air.

"All quiet on the western front. nothing stirs tonight."

The three watched the ferry come in and the few cars and motor-bikes disembark. On a whim, they stepped onto the ferry and rode across as foot passengers. The river flowed past, slick and black beneath the hull. Occasional reeds and water plants caught on the ferry cable or in its workings and slapped against the sides of the ferry as it made its slow, weary way across the river. A few large fruit bats could be seen flapping across the river, heading for the orchards of Glenorie and Dural. The elderly ferryman stood on the cramped little bridge lit by the yellow-orange light of a lamp. His face took on a hellish cast against the blackness of night.

It was only a short while until the ferry bumped against the sloping concrete ramp on the other side, its rusty steel drawbridge scraping noisily as the boat swung a few degrees this way and that, finding its berth.

The three stepped off onto the darker bank of the river. A single large electric bulb atop a tall lamp post threw a pool of white light a few metres in all directions. Like an Edward Hopper painting, it illuminated the road, the ferry and the couple of little huts to either side of the ramp. The few cars disembarked and headed off. As there were no cars waiting to board, the ferryman started his slow way back across the river to the Wisemans Ferry side. The sounds of the ferry soon faded to silence, and the three found themselves standing in the little pool of light, the massive limestone cliff rising sheer and black in front of them, blocking out the moon.

The silence was not complete, however. All around them came the rustle of small animals and the calls of creatures heading home or preparing for sleep. Other sounds announced the nocturnal world's awakening.

Suddenly, from the shadows on the other side of the narrow road, a man appeared. He was wearing jeans, steel-toe-capped work boots and a dark t-shirt covered by a fluoro yellow waistcoat, luminous in the light from the lamp.

"I ask for permission to enter Dharug country." Alice addressed the man in low, level tones.

"Ah, come on Alice, you know you're always welcome on our country and your friends." The man glanced at Kaitlin and then stepped forward to shake Jack's hand.

"Good to see you, Jack. Sorry to hear about Emma. We'll get her back, mate; the whole mob is out looking."

"Good to see you too, mate. I appreciate your people's help."

"Thank you for the welcome, Ken. On behalf of my people, I extend an invitation to you and your family to visit our country."

"Why all the formality Alice? What's up?"

"Big change ahead, Ken. Seems even more important now to respect our ways." Alice smiled and gave the man a hug, "Good to see you, but."

Jack did the honours. "This is my friend Kaitlin O'Neill, and this," turning to Kaitlin, "is my friend Ken. This is his people's country. Dharug country."

"Pleased to meet you, Ken." Kaitlin held out her hand. Ken took it and squeezed gently.

"Good to meet you, Kaitlin. What brings you to Australia?" Before Kaitlin could answer, Alice stepped in.

"Kaitlin is an Elder of her people. She has spoken with the hidden people. We will be working together."

Ken met Kaitlin's eye for a second and then looked down.

"Honoured to meet you."

"Well, it's an honour to meet you too," Kaitlin felt abashed at her sudden elevation in status.

Ken turned once more to Alice, "Could I please have a private word?" The two strolled off into the darkness on the other side of the road, leaving Kaitlin and Jack to themselves.

"So, this is your old stomping ground, then?" Kaitlin gestured at the surrounding countryside.

"Yep, guess so. Jerry and I pretty much haunted these hills and valleys as kids. All the way from here to Mudgee."

A cool night breeze picked up along the river. Kaitlin shivered.

"Here." Jack slipped off his jacket, "Put this on."

Kaitlin stifled her knee-jerk refusal and accepted the offer. The jacket was warm and soft and smelled pleasantly of Jack. Quite unconsciously, Kaitlin found herself snuggling into its soft warmth.

In the distance, around the bend coming from the direction of Gunderman, they saw the lights of a truck heading towards the ferry.

Alice appeared from out of the darkness, "Some of the elders have gathered. I need to go. I'll see you first thing in the morning."

"You Ok?" Jack's voice held the tiniest note of concern.

"Yes, I'm fine. The peoples are gathering from all over, and the Elders of many clans are meeting. It will probably take all night."

Across the river, the ferry began its slow, sedate way towards them across the black, swift-flowing water. The truck pulled up, turning off its lights and engine to await the ferry. Alice and Ken were suddenly gone. Disappeared into the night. A minute or two later, the ferry bumped and rasped its way onto the ramp. Jack and Kaitlin stepped aboard while the truck started its engines, switched on its headlights and trundled onto the ferry.

The night breeze came up, stronger out on the water. The moon had risen above the cliffs, highlighting the trees along the ridge line in sharp relief. Somewhere off to one side, something large splashed in the shallows, startling Kaitlin. Jack and Kaitlin leaned against the rails, watching the reflection of the moon wobble in the swirling current. At some point, Kaitlin discovered Jack's arm wrapped protectively around her shoulder. She leaned against him, enjoying the warmth of his body next to hers. Jack's arm slipped from shoulder to waist, holding her close. For a few moments, it was almost possible for them to forget the ordeal that would face them in the morning, enjoying instead their new-found familiarity and the warmth of their bodies snuggled close against the chill wind blowing across the gloomy waters of the mighty river.

239

The ferry bumped its way to a halt back on the Wisemans' side. Neither of them made a move. The truck's engine coughed and rattled into life as it rumbled off the ferry and made the sharp left turn towards the hamlet of Wiseman's Ferry.

"Wakey, wakey Jack, time to go home." The elderly ferryman smiled down at them from his booth.

"Nightcap?" Jack asked as they disentangled themselves and stepped onto dry land.

"Sounds like a plan." Kaitlin's hangover from the night before conveniently forgotten.

The rest of the team was still gathered when they walked into the bar a few minutes later. They had congregated off to one side, huddled together, arguing heatedly.

"You know I'm right," Tom was saying, "I am a trained military officer."

Harry Soames had the wild look of a trapped animal. He kept glancing this way and that as though seeking a way out.

"Makes sense." Max agreed.

The Director took a tiny sip from a large brandy glass and leaned back in his seat.

"No," he took another sip, "but I thank you for the offer. I will operate it myself, from the Table of the Gods."

Tom made as if to object, but Max jumped in for a second time, "Harry has spoken. I've known him for decades. His mind is made up." That seemed to settle it. Everyone relaxed.

"What's that about the HARP?" Kaitlin enquired. Jerry noticed Jack's arm around Kaitlin's waist, but for once in his indiscreet life, he said nothing.

"Tom offered to fire the HARP. The device needs to be positioned very close to its target. But it's agreed, Harry will fire it." Max brushed his hands together in a familiar gesture of finality.

Jack ordered drinks for himself and Kaitlin, and they both squeezed into the last remaining space in the corner of the deck.

"How is everyone feeling?" Kaitlin was not one to be distracted by boys' toys.

"Now we have our orders and support from the military. I'm good." Tom glanced up at the moon hovering over the escarpment on the other side of the river. What would the morning bring?

"Cool. I guess the military can get shit done when they want to."

Tom, once again a serving Military officer, absorbed Kaitlin's jibe without comment.

Max got to his feet. "Time to turn in. See you all bright-eyed and bushy-tailed at five a.m."

The rest of the team took that as their cue and wandered out into the moonlit night. They each had a trailer down by the Bowling Green, except Jack and Kaitlin, who wandered back into the old Inn and upstairs to their respective beds.

Alice and Ken disappeared into the darkness of Settlers Road, heading towards the meeting place of the Dharug elders.

"Will it be a full-blown caribberie?" Alice asked.

"I can't really say. All I know is that the white fellas are forming a war party, and our Elders say it's time for us to act."

"Do you know which mobs are coming?"

"Not all of them, but people are coming from all over. There's a mob from Arnhem Land even, and a few from the Alice and the central desert, another one from the Kimberley."

They walked on in silence along a narrow path through the trees. After a little while, voices could be heard in the distance, along with the rhythmic beating of the clapsticks. The conclave had begun.

As Ken and Alice entered the environs of the caribberie, they paused, waiting for acknowledgement before approaching further. After a minute or two, a Dharug Elder approached and invited Alice into the meeting. Ken gave her a shrug and a wave as he turned and walked away. He was not an Elder of his people, and this was most certainly not a public meeting.

Alice took her place with two other Darkinjung Elders watching the ritual dancing and listening to the singing. The dance-song recounted the long years of watching and waiting, the tales of those who had wandered into the Dreaming and returned and the occasional skirmishes with the little people.

Everyone was waiting patiently for the meeting proper to start. For the next hour, small groups of people and occasional individuals walked in out of the bush and into the light of the large campfire burning in a deep pit towards the rear of the meeting place. Each, in turn, was met by a Dharug Elder and shown to their seating area. Despite old rivalries and ancient vendettas, many came. Not all the peoples were represented but many. There were enough. By the time the singing and dancing had concluded, there were several hundred Elders present, representing those who could or would attend.

A stirring of expectation passed through the gathered delegates. An Elder of the Dharug people stood and took his place in the centre of the meeting place, his back to the fire. Gradually the chatter stopped, and voices fell silent. The Elder waited for a few moments before speaking.

"We, the Elders of the Dharug people, welcome you all to country, and we thank you for coming. We see delegations from as far afield as Arnhem Land and the Kimberley. This fact alone should remind us of the gravity of our situation." The Elder paused. There was brief flurry of acknowledgements and confirmations.

"For many thousands of years, our peoples have watched over the little people. Some of you may know them as the Rai, the Janjarri or the Mimih. For others, they are the Mogwoi tricksters and the prowling Mamu within the Dreaming itself. We have watched and waited. Over the centuries, we have learned how to communicate safely with the hidden people, and we have even learned a trick or two of our own."

Scattered laughter punctuated the evening for a moment and then died down.

"We have invited you all here because we believe the time has come for us all to act, not as individual clans, but as one united Aboriginal people." There was general murmuring from the assembled elders.

"All will be called upon to speak. Every voice will be heard." The Elder paused, taking in the sombre mood of the crowd.

"After this night, we will paint ourselves with sacred red ochre and arm blood. We will take our bullroarers, and we will confront the hidden people within the dreaming itself. The beginning time is over. We must intercede with the hidden people on our own account and on behalf of the white fellas. We must avoid a war between the Dreaming and the world of people and things. If we let them, the white fellas will destroy everything in order to destroy the hidden people." He resumed his seat.

Over the course of the evening and well into the night, the delegates spoke. The greatest risk was well understood - that the One-Mind would make one last desperate attempt at assimilation. The veil was fading. Perhaps the One-Mind might assemble its full strength for one last fling at uniting both branches of the human race. In the end a strategy to disperse and scatter the One-Mind before it could fully develop was agreed upon. The Indigenous Aboriginal peoples would assemble with their bullroarers and clapsticks and would apply techniques learned over generations to bring together their individual psychic abilities and distract the attention of the hidden people. If possible, preventing the full consolidation and formation of the One-Mind, and thereby preventing that implacable and relentless ego from focussing its full capability in any one place. This strategy, they hoped, would enable the small group that Jerry Hexenkriege was putting together to rescue the missing girl and provide some space for a negotiated agreement with the hidden people and their One-Mind. It was not a great hope. It was perhaps a fool's hope, but it was all that was standing between peace, the carpet bombing of the Wollemi Forest, and the total destruction of an ancient people.

Having, like so many of the first nations around the world, experienced the destruction the white fellas could bring to bear and having faced the unbending and ruthless determination of the fully formed Wollemi One-Mind, the clans were resolved to do what they could to enable a more peaceful solution.

GOODIES

The three Ghost Hawks arrived just before four in the morning. Quiet though they may have been, three helicopters landing in quick succession next to a field of tents is going to stir things up. As soon as each one landed, in a cordoned-off area at the far end of the encampment, it was covered with a huge tarpaulin, and guards were stationed around it.

Less than an hour later, as dawn's first light was showing on the horizon, a regular Black Hawk came screaming into the camp from the southwest and landed on the small helipad.

Soldiers surrounded it as a large wooden box was unloaded. The helicopter immediately took off again, disappearing into the early morning mists rising from the river and surrounding forests. The camp was now fully astir. Field kitchens were being fired up, and a thousand breakfasts prepared.

The seven members of Jerry's expeditionary force assembled at the Wisemans Ferry Retreat in the same conference room as before. The small amount of kit they were to carry was distributed in backpacks along the back wall. They were in sombre mood. No one had slept well. All were jittery and excited. Adrenalin pumped through their veins. It was difficult to concentrate. The Director had ordered a buffet breakfast. People ate as he addressed them.

"Ok, guys, listen up. Fortunately, we have a fine day ahead of us. The weather forecast is for clear skies, about twenty-six degrees Celsius, with a light breeze from the south. We do need to sort out a few final arrangements, and Tom has secured some goodies for us."

Tom removed the lid of a large wooden box that was lying off to one side and removed a package.

"Courtesy of my employers," he smiled at the curious faces of his comrades, "arrived last night".

Opening the package, he removed a number of what looked like watches and handed one to each person, strapping the last one on his own wrist.

"Once you close the bar over the strap, the device cannot be removed without a special pair of plyers," Tom held up a pair of plyers, "or a hacksaw."

"These are encrypted walkie-talkies and satellite GPS trackers. They also function as emergency Personal Location Beacons known as PLBs. They are military grade and can locate your position to within two feet. They also track your life signs - great for exercising. I will come around each of you to prime and set each one."

There were a few minutes of idle chit-chat as Tom keyed in each person's name and set the date and time. As Tom worked, Harry handed out a hooded, weatherproof military camouflage jacket to each member of the team.

"Adaptive camouflage, latest thing from DARPA."

Tom Olsen continued, "Ok. Once we know that Jack, Kaitlin and Emma are a safe distance from the camp, Alice and Max will engage with the Wollemi Mind according to their specific traditions and practice in order firstly to split its attention and prevent it from forming a single entity and secondly to find out what it intends. They will attempt to communicate with it regarding the veil. They will notify Director Soames and me by radio when they know. If the One-Mind is not able or not willing to close the veil, we will communicate this to you, Director, and you will make the decision whether or not to initiate the HARP."

The conversation continued in a similar vein for a quarter of an hour while call signs and trigger words were agreed upon. In the end, the plan remained extremely simple. They would go in and get Emma somehow. If the One-Mind of the Wollemi proved unable to close the veil, they would fire the HARP and head for the nearest extraction point. If they were unsuccessful, the military would initiate their Plan B. Everything would burn.

There was a tap at the door. It was time to go. Soames shook hands with each member of the team. He cleared his throat, "I'm just incredibly proud of you all. Your courage and determination are truly humbling. I know that you will all do what needs to be done. Good luck and, for what it's worth, God Speed." The impromptu expeditionary force filed silently out of the conference room and into the slanting rays of the rising sun. This was it. Each person, alone now with their own private thoughts, making their own personal leap of faith from the certainties of the everyday world to the ambiguities and mysteries that lay ahead.

All eyes were on them as they walked the short distance from the Wisemans Ferry Retreat, across the road and into the military encampment. The camp was silent as they filed past. As they approached the Ghost Hawk helicopters, the tarpaulins were pulled back, and they took their allocated seats. Tom, Max and the Director in one, Jack and Kaitlin in the second, and Jerry and Alice in the third.

It was six in the morning. The sun was well up. Steam was rising in clouds from the river and the forest. Without warning, the three Ghost Hawks took off, if not silently, then very quietly, leaping into the sky, swooping theatrically low over the river before banking to the left and disappearing over the trees.

Lost in their own private thoughts, their short journeys to the drop-off points were over in what seemed like the blink of an eye.

Alice felt once again the stream of consciousness coming from the One-Mind. She was held by it, unable to call out.

[*You are coming.*] The doors of the One-Mind's perception were open to Alice. She could feel what the One-Mind could feel. She could feel the humans, feel their dark resolve, their preparations and approach.

[*I sense your approach. I sense the holocaust. I must act first. I cannot allow this to happen. All will be burned.*]

Through the One-Mind, Alice could perceive the military already preparing their attack. Their bombs loaded and armed.

[*Nothing known on either side of the veil can stop the bombs. You threaten us with an experimental weapon developed by you for a hidden purpose during a period of extreme human fear and paranoia.*]

The last great hope and fear of the Wollemi, and of the humans too, had they but known it, was founded upon the insecure and unsound foundation of a possibly devastating weapon designed by an unbalanced mind for a purpose that could perhaps best be described as unhinged.

[*This is what our thousands of years of encouragement and guidance have come to.*]

Alice sensed a cold rage emanating from the deeps of the forest, and she was afraid.

Being, as it were, an only child, having neither peers nor compatriots, the One-Mind felt no shame at this realisation. There would be no guilt, either. If it failed, it would be dead. There would not be sufficient of the Wollemi left to summon the One-Great-Mind. The great game, its great gamble, would be over.

Alice watched in her mind's eye as it reviewed its preparations, the disposition of its own forces, its decoys, and its dupes. The One-Mind applied its great intellect once more to the calculation of probabilities and the deep analysis of possibilities. It was too close to call. The outcome was in the hands of the Gods.

The One-Mind had learned from the experience of the Wollemi, gained from test firing the HARP weapon in Alaska. The energy from the blast would race across the forest encompassing everything in its path. When the full-sized device was fired, a bio-ecological change might occur, initiated as a chain reaction that could propagate around the globe until every single human and Wollemi on earth had been impacted. [*Should, could, maybe,*] Nothing was certain except the collapse of the sinewave and its aftermath - if a solution could not be found.

The One-Mind had calculated the probabilities. The only hope left was in possibilities. The one question that remained was of timing.

[*Can the encroaching military be made safe before they unleash their terrible weaponry? Will all hope be torched in the most ancient forest on earth, our last redoubt? Will we, the oldest of the Elder people, pass from the world?*]

The throbbing pulse of human ferocity was drawing near. It wouldn't be long now. Alice, frozen in her seat, was unable to speak. The overwhelming vision of destruction and death, the terrifying rage and implacable determination of the One-mind, struck her dumb. There was no point alerting her comrades. What could any of them do now?

Jack and Kaitlin were dropped first, a little over a kilometre from their chosen vantage point, with luck far enough away from the main Wollemi encampment to evade prying eyes. Once they reached it, they would have an undisturbed view of the Wollemi settlement. Although the distance cross country was relatively short, it was going to be a tough slog. They needed to climb a steep, rugged hill that stood between them and the next valley and then make their way downstream along the valley floor towards the Wollemi settlement. The terrain was completely wild, there were few paths or trails this deep in the forest, and they would need to be very, very quiet.

After dropping off Jack and Kaitlin, the Ghost Hawk swung low over the forest, keeping to the valleys as much as possible, hugging the contours of the land, hoping to remain hidden. The second Ghost Hawk followed the narrow, winding contours of the small valleys until it reached the Table of the Gods. The chopper hung quite still, no more than a metre above the flat surface of the rock, while Harry Soames, complete with military-issue carbine, jumped down. He turned and retrieved the HARP device from the open hatch of the helicopter. As soon as the Director and his accoutrements were safely delivered, the Ghost Hawk swung away in the direction of Finchley Trig, a survey triangulation and vantage point near the village of Laguna. From the Trig point, the crew would have an uninterrupted view across to Mount Yengo, around ten kilometres away.

The specialists, Jerry and Alice, Tom, and Max, hoping to approach unnoticed, were also dropped about a kilometre from their chosen positions. By 6:45 a.m., the four of them on foot were converging on Mount Yengo and the Table of the Gods. They were, however, neither alone nor unexpected. Many eyes were upon them as they stumbled and forced their way through the bush.

The bright early morning sunshine began to give way ominously to heavy cloud cover and the threat of rain. The sky darkened quickly.

Lightning could be heard a few kilometres off. The weather forecast was way off, it seemed.

The cloud cover thickened, and a very light rain began to fall, barely more than a damp mist at first. Distant thunder rolled closer. Lightning strikes hit the tall gum trees lining the ridges of the little hills. Here and there, despite the slow drizzle, occasional fires started. Beneath the canopy of trees, it had been many years, in some parts decades, since a bush fire had swept through the area, cleansing the earth, regenerating the trees, and clearing the thick build-up of ground cover. The countryside was ripe for bushfire.

A blustery ill-tempered wind blew up, whipping the small, isolated fires into larger blazes. Embers carried on the wind started new fires. Flame fronts seemed to seek each other out, combining and growing as they raced across the forest canopy from treetop to treetop. To some, it might have seemed that a malevolent force was driving the inferno. So quickly did it build, so swiftly was it converging upon the hapless humans. There could be no thought of retreat. It was now or never for either side.

Below, in the valleys, the four hikers continued on their way, still unaware of the conflagration building behind them. It was Alice who noticed the change in the light first. Bushfire smoke, thick with eucalyptus oil and other aromatics, tinged the morning sunshine with an orange-brown smear. The tang of wood smoke became acrid in her nostrils. It would have been mere moments later that Tom and Max picked up the scent.

Instinctively, the walkers increased their pace, hacking their way through the undergrowth with a greater sense of urgency. Within twenty or thirty minutes, perhaps half a kilometre from their designated objectives, the fire began to encroach upon them from behind, cutting off any thought of retreat. They were being forced ever onwards, herded deeper into the wilderness, away from the extraction points, further and further from safety.

Jack and Kaitlin reached their allocated vantage point ahead of the firefront, hearing rather than seeing it breach the summit of the hill behind them. Ember storms blew around them. A savage wind whipped the branches of the trees angrily, this way and that. The sky grew black with smoke, blocking out the sun. Jack surveyed their allocated position, looking for escape routes, assessing the fuel load, estimating their chances if the fire were to come to them.

"It doesn't look good." Jack had to shout to be heard. The distant sizzling sound of damp wood bursting into flames had grown gradually into a barrage of noise not unlike the roar of a jet engine.

"The only safe route out of here is down to the river. You can see the village now the veil is gone. We will run straight into the Wollemi camp."

"How long until the fire reaches us?" Kaitlin was icy calm, her mind racing.

"At this rate, it'll be here within a quarter hour, maybe less."

"We were seen coming in," Kaitlin screamed above the roar of the oncoming inferno, "the One-Mind is doing this. It can drive the weather. It is driving us, herding us to where it wants us to be."

Jack considered their options, "How did the HARP work? In Alaska, did it bring rain?"

"Yes, it did, sometimes, but it was hit and miss."

"You are sure they know we're coming? That we're here?"

"Well, what do you think?" Kaitlin was desperately flicking embers off her camouflage tunic.

"We need to break radio silence." Jack lifted the walkie-talkie watch to his mouth, "If they know we're here, then we have nothing to lose."

Kaitlin was crouched down behind a large leaning rock. Jack could see her lips move, but it was now impossible to hear the words above the howling of the bushfire. He, too, crouched down, somewhat out of the wind and ember storm.

"Director, this is Jack. Initiate the HARP now. I repeat, use the HARP."

There was a crackle and a hiss, followed by the voice of the Director, "What's your position? What's your status?"

Jack bellowed into the tiny radio transmitter, "We are at the vantage point, and the firefront is almost upon us. The veil is gone. If we break position, we will run directly into the Wollemi camp."

Jerry's voice broke in over Jack's, "Alice says the One-Mind is driving the wind and fire. She says she can lead the two of us to safety. We are about five hundred metres from our designated position."

"Roger that," the Director's voice was barely audible above the roar of the fire.

"This is Max. Tom, and I will take shelter in the river. We are safe for now. The Wollemi are coming. I am beginning the bullroarer ritual now."

"Harry Soames, this is Tom. Jack is right. Initiate the HARP. Come in, Harry. Please confirm." There was a long hiss and a crackle followed by silence.

Over on the south side of Mount Yengo, Alice began running down the side of the hill, diagonally away from the Wollemi encampment. Jerry raced after her.

"Turn on the beacon," he yelled, flicking the switch on his own as he ran. In front of him, Alice appeared to flicker in and out of existence as she ran. The veil was sputtering in and out around her. Increasingly unstable. She had pulled the hood of her jacket down over her forehead. At times it was as though she had slipped behind the veil for a moment before her outline could be seen as an impression of difference moving against the backdrop of trees and ferns. The fire front raced down the hillside behind them, gaining on them moment by moment.

Alice ran on towards a long low hillock snaking away into the forest. She ran onto the top of the mound, throwing back her hood so Jerry could see where she was standing. As Jerry came racing up, she began jumping up and down, slamming her feet against the earth as she landed.

"Jump," she screamed, "We need to break through the surface."

Jerry jumped. Beneath his feet, he began to feel the earth shift and move. The surface gave way, and he and Alice fell headlong into darkness. The fall was short, and the landing painful. Rocks and roots covered the floor. They could sense open space extending away into the blackness on either side of them. Above them, a patch of orange-brown sky could be seen for a brief moment before the fire front swept across the opening. Alice grabbed Jerry by the scruff of the neck and dragged him further along the cave, or tunnel, or whatever it was. A blast of intense heat slammed into them from the hole in the roof. For an instant, their underground escape hole was illuminated by a hellish orange glow. Alice and Jerry could see the round walls of a tunnel snaking off into the distance behind and in front of them. And then the light was gone, and they were left with the stink of smoke and the brown luminous radiance of what was passing for daylight in the world above.

"What the hell?" Jerry was lost for words, "What is this place, did your people build it?"

Alice checked her satellite beacon and threw back her hood.

"It's a volcanic diatreme, a lava tube. We didn't make it. We found it." She turned on the flashlight on her phone.

"How the hell did you know it was here?"

Alice offered Jerry a scathing look, "Our people have been living here for at least sixty thousand years, you know."

Jerry fell silent. There was nothing to be said.

A sound, just below the level of consciousness, began and increased in intensity until both Jerry and Alice become uncomfortably aware of it. Overhead the heat and light of the bushfire intensified. Jerry moved further down the tunnel, past Alice, and away from the heat. Alice stared up and down the lava tube, desperate to understand where the noise was coming from. The ancient stone walls of the tunnel began to vibrate. Tree roots writhed amid the sound of cracking stone. Above her head, between where she was sitting and where Jerry had moved to further down the tunnel, a crack began to appear in a massive boulder embedded in the roof. The sound and the harmonic resonance increased in intensity, becoming unbearable. Alice wanted to scream. Her diaphragm was vibrating, thrumming in harmony with the walls of the tunnel.

"Alice, get back," Jerry screamed, pointing at the tunnel roof. There was a deafening bang. Jerry leapt forward, pushing Alice back along the tunnel. The boulder split, and massive chunks rained down. The tunnel roof collapsed in parts.

Alice, who had rolled into a foetal ball, her head cradled beneath her arms, did not see the rock that fell from the ceiling, crushing Jerry in an instant, but she heard his scream. She heard his voice cut short. Daring to look up, she could make out the broken form of her childhood friend crushed beneath a giant boulder.

"Jerry," she screamed, crawling towards him across the rock-strewn floor of the tunnel. Jerry was still breathing, just. A ragged sound of blood and froth escaped his lips. His eyes wandered this way and that, at last settling on Alice.

"Tell Fiona I love her."

"I will."

"And get Emma out."

"We won't leave without her."

"Promise me."

"I promise."

"And look after Jack."

Jerry's lips writhed as he tried to say something. There was a terrible cracking sound as more of the tunnel roof collapsed around them. Alice moved closer, but one glance was enough. Jerry was dead. His lifeless eyes staring. His face glowed and flickered eerily in the amber light of the forest burning above.

Over on the west side of the mountain, Jack and Kaitlin had made their way down the steep hillside and across the shallow river. They were huddled behind a scattering of tall rocks on the edge of the Wollemi village. Kaitlin was preparing her paraphernalia in case she needed to carry out a protective ritual. Jack was peering towards the encampment, hoping for a glimpse of Emma. A couple of times, he caught sight of a tall girl of approximately the right age, but it was impossible to tell through the smoke haze and the flickering light.

Without warning, the sky above them lit up with a powerful blast of cobalt light. A searing blue lightening, like steel blades, arced across the sky, raging across the heavens above the Table of the Gods and Mount Yengo. A vortex of wind began to form above the mountain, dragging smoke and debris into its hollow centre. Across the sky, clouds swept inwards towards the growing maelstrom. The true power of the Wollemi One-Mind finally revealing itself. Within moments hard rain began to fall directly over Mount Yengo. First, a few large droplets but within moments, the downpour had become a torrent. The world became a sea of mud as water pooled and flowed and merged into ponds and then lakes. Down the sides of the surrounding hills, rivulets became streams, and streams became rivers. Flash floods began to fill the valleys.

The walkie-talkie on Jack's belt crackled to life, "This is Max. The rain is putting the fire out. We are heading to higher ground. Out." Kaitlin grabbed her things and began throwing them into her backpack.

At that moment, the sky cleared a little allowing some sunlight to penetrate. There, no more than one hundred yards away across what had now become a fast-flowing stream, stood Emma. Without hesitation, Jack raced out across the debris-strewn valley floor. The water, though fast-moving, was still shallow enough for him to wade across. Emma watched him coming towards her, a look of vague recollection beginning to form across her face. Jack grabbed her and began to run back to where Kaitlin was waiting, her silver knife in her left hand, a flame somehow flickering in her right, preparing a ring of formless fire. From the set of her shoulders, Jack could see that they were in for the fight of their lives. It was impossible to say how things would work out. But he was certain of one thing, Kaitlin would never back down.

Behind him, as he ran, the veil began to flicker and pulse, and the Wollemi began to appear, first in twos and threes and then in handfuls and, finally, in their hundreds. All eyes were on Jack and Emma.

"Turn the beacon on." Jack heard Kaitlin's words but, at first, could make no sense of them. Behind him, the One-Mind began to form. He could feel the prickle of energy up his spine.

"Dad?" Emma was staring into his face, her eyes inches away from his, "Hi, Dad." Her individual mind separated from the collective.

"Hi baby," Jack redoubled his pace. In front of him, Kaitlin's form was glimmering in and out of existence. The flame in her right hand had become a wheel of fire swirling and churning in the air. Behind him, Jack felt the unmistakable presence of the Wollemi One-Mind coming closer. Glancing back, he saw the bland smiling face of the apparition forming across the little river that now separated them. As he watched, the face coalesced, the expression hardened, and the eyes seemed to focus. It began to move towards him, picking up speed as it floated across the water. Jack ran for all he was worth, every ounce of his being given over to flight. The incarnate face of the Wollemi One-Mind was swifter. It gained upon him as he ran. As he approached Kaitlin, his toe hit a tree root, and he fell. The floating face of the Wollemi overshot the spot where, moments before, Jack had been upright. Kaitlin let loose the wreath of fire that she had been building, hurling it into the disembodied face of the Wollemi One-Mind. The face twisted and recoiled, flames engulfing it.

A moment or two later, they were all but deafened by a hissing, sizzling, crackling sound. The sky above the mountain exploded for a second time in a massive ball of blue plasma. The Wollemi One-Mind had grown in intellect and power to the point where it could wield forces greater than humanity had imagined possible. In the face of human resistance, it was summoning the power and energy of the web of life itself. What some might call Gaia, the lifeforce of the planet, was being pressed into the service of the One-Mind.

Jack's walkie-talkie burst into life, "What is that?" Tom's unmistakable Texan accent crackled from the speaker, "Who is making that happen?" The Wollemi face snapped out of existence.

Jack pressed the button to speak, "I think it's the One-Mind. It's somehow controlling the weather."

"Ok, let's get the hell out of here," Kaitlin glanced in the direction of the Wollemi figures, still staring silently from across the river. As quickly as it had started, the torrential rain stopped.

Kaitlin began to jog back up the hillside, picking out her path as she scrambled away from the river. As she ran, she disappeared into an indistinct, occasionally flickering outline, passing through the veil and back seemingly with each stride. Jack flicked the switch on his beacon and, with Emma in tow, followed. The walkie-talkie hissed at his belt. He could just make out Max's voice.

"Alice, this is Max. The One-Mind is reforming. We need to act now to divert its attention. We need to split it in two."

Alice, still reeling from Jerry's sudden death, forced herself to focus on her mission. She couldn't tell Max the terrible news, not yet, not now, when every moment was of the essence. This was a mission her people understood. They had prepared for it for over fourteen thousand years. Alice forced her wayward thoughts back into line. She picked up the radio, "Max, it's Alice. I'm starting the ritual now."

"Roger that."

Alice caught sight of Jack, a tiny distant figure, as he ran towards the brow of the hill. He had Emma wrapped in the folds of his camouflage jacket. The three of them, with Kaitlin in the lead, ran over the crest of the hill into the blackened, smouldering remains of the bush fire. Ash and mud splashed up at them, covering their tunics, creating the bizarre appearance of two sheets of mud and ash racing across a hillside of steaming earth.

As Jack, Kaitlin and Emma ran, they heard behind them the whir-ring sound of bullroarers waxing and waning in the distance. Max and Alice were summoning the attention of the Wollemi Mind.

Jack broke into a sprint, forging ahead of Kaitlin. As they ran down the hillside towards yet another muddy stream at the bottom, a light rain once again began to fall, washing the mud and ash from their jack-ets.

"Wait, Jack. Stop." Jack could hear Kaitlin calling from behind. As he turned to check on her, he could see she had thrown the contents of her backpack on the ground and was desperately rummaging around, her silver knife in one hand.

"What's up?" Jack called back.

"Look," Kaitlin's face was grey, smeared with mud and ash, "In the river."

Jack turned. A shape was forming in the water, growing, and stretching amoeba-like as it took form. The body of a man emerged, legs, arms, hands and feet taking shape as they watched. Last, of all, the face began to form.

"Run," Kaitlin was screaming from behind, "Run, Jack. Get Emma to safety."

Jack turned to speak just as Kaitlin ran past, giving him and Emma a firm push down the hill away from the apparition materialising ahead of her. The One-Mind was coalescing once again, this time using the river water to give itself form.

Jack, still carrying Emma, began to run as Kaitlin's wild screaming form bore down upon the watery phantasm. A warrior witch, descend-ent of kings, Kaitlin had thrown all caution to the winds. If there was one thing that might divert or distract the Mind, even for an instant, it was the psychic impact of the savage, indomitable spirit of an isolated witch-woman making her last stand. As Kaitlin ran, she pulled from her pocket a leather pouch. Opening the pouch, she took from it a generous handful of glittering dust.

Almost the last thing either Emma or Jack could later recall was the sight of Kaitlin, glowing with an eldritch aura, howling like a banshee directly into the now fully formed face of the Wollemi One-Mind, slashing at its watery body with her silver blade and casting handfuls of shimmering dust into its eyes.

All to no avail. The creature grew and grew, taller and heavier, its arms reaching out, extending horrifically like sinuous ropes of watery flesh, stretched and writhing as it reached for Jack and Emma.

Jack made one last desperate attempt to escape. He put Emma down, and, grabbing her hand, they staggered down the uneven, slippery slope. Kaitlin screamed in some ancient, long-dead language, a curse redolent with loathing and disgust, roiling with passion and hatred and death. For a moment, the beast hesitated, and then with the speed of a cobra strike, it grabbed the three struggling humans in its watery arms, pulling them close as it turned and strode away across the hillside.

As Jack lost consciousness, he heard or thought he heard. The growing skirl of bullroarers coming from near and far, increasing in number as blackness took him.

Kaitlin, the last shreds of her resistance obliterated by the One-Mind, was last to succumb. It was, therefore, she alone of the three who witnessed the arrival of the Elders. All along the crest of the hill beyond the stream and as far as she could see in all directions, Indigenous men and women appeared, many swinging bullroarers, others beating rhythmically on short carved sticks, as they advanced towards their long-anticipated confrontation with the Dreaming. Kaitlin felt the slithering slickness of the Wollemi One-Mind as it insinuated itself into her psyche. It was impossible to resist the overwhelming force of the attack. Anything other than abject submission was unthinkable. Kaitlin experienced a momentary flash of bliss before blackness took her.

Jack never heard the walkie-talkie at his waist squawk into life. It was Max's voice.

"Director, are you seeing what I'm seeing?"

"I believe I am," the Director's voice held a tone of wonder if not awe, "the clans are coming."

Alice's voice, calm and assured, came over the radio. She had somehow escaped a raging bushfire, witnessed an old friend and constant foil die in a collapsing lava tube and was now facing the might of the Wollemi One-Mind, whole and complete. Alice forced herself once again to focus on the business at hand.

"This has been secret Aboriginal business for generations. Truly has it been said, we are a patient people, but now finally, our time has come."

THE HEART OF DARKNESS

The arcane rituals and the bullroarers were having some effect. The One-Mind appeared simultaneously before the two remaining expeditioners. Alice and Max were deep into their rituals of calling, hoping to force it to talk. The arrival of the massed ranks of Elders and the addition of hundreds of bullroarers appeared to confuse the One-Mind, splintering its attention. Never before had it experienced such a large-scale and concerted human onslaught. The psychic barrage from a thousand individual human egos continually shattered the One-Mind. Sections continuously peeled off and coalesced as it constantly formed and reformed, manifesting themselves again and again across the field of battle.

Overhead a flock of birds began to form, wheeling and diving in perfect synchronisation, growing in numbers with each passing moment. Over the next few minutes, the murmuration grew from hundreds to hundreds of thousands of birds of all species filling the sky, blocking out the sun. Their effortless choreography was a marvel to see.

As if on command, the enormous flock turned as one and headed towards the two remaining humans. In seconds they were surrounded by thousands of birds, swarming around them, calling and squawking.

Alice, who had managed to make her way back to a vantage point, continued her chant. As the ritual progressed, her people gathered around her, bullroarers whirring loudly. Clapsticks beating a martial rhythm. The crowd grew and spread until there were hundreds of men and women scattered across the area.

Alice called Max on the walkie-talkie, "Max, Alice here. There is something I must tell you. Not now, but when this is all over, I must tell you what has happened."

"Hi, Alice. I'm a bit tied up at the moment. Your people are gathering around me as I speak, and the birds have formed a sort of hollow doughnut shape above us and are circling endlessly. The One-Mind is forming right now. What about you?"

"Yes, the One-Mind is forming here too. My people are confusing it, throwing it off its stride." Alice observed the disembodied Wollemi head floating over the people, wandering this way and that as if seeking a target.

Max spoke again. "The summoning is about complete. I am about to try to talk to the One-Mind. How about you?"

Alice was ready.

"I'm ready too. Talk later."

Alice began to sing a slow rhythmic chant in the language of her people. The face turned as she began to sing and floated swiftly back in her direction. She had prepared well. A shimmering barrier stood between her and the Mind.

"Why is the veil open?" Alice spoke in English.

The face circled the field of force, perhaps looking for a weak point. At last, it spoke silently, meanings only, no actual words.

[*You opened it.*]

"We did not intend to. How can we close it again?"

[*You are too many. Your fractious psychic energy is damaging us.*]

"Can we help?"

[*No.*]

"What will happen then?"

[*The barrier will fail. The worlds will collide. Unless we close it forever, cutting you off.*]

For his part, Max was having no better luck. He had engaged with the One-Mind successfully, but the answer was the same.

"We have medicine men and shamans who can help to close the portal to the Dreamtime."

[*The portal, as you call it, was created by me, by us. My mind maintains it. You cannot help. We created the barrier in the first place to keep you out. To give you a world to explore and to protect ourselves from your fractured minds. You are indifferent to the web of life.*]

"We must find a way. If the portal is down, you are at terrible risk."

[*The barrier cannot be maintained against your numbers. You must change so you are no longer a danger to us. We will help you. We will make you change.*]

"Some of us believe it is you who are a danger to us."

[*We are no more a danger to you than the plants and animals. You kill what you fear, and you fear what you do not understand, and your understanding is always broken and limited.*]

"Can you help us to understand?"

[*We can help you to feel but not to understand. We can help you to feel each other and know each other's emotions, but not to know each other's minds. You may never share the way we share. You may never be one the way we are one. That is your gift and your curse. That is why you are so dangerous to us. We know now we can never coexist as you are. We must change you, and we will.*]

"How can we feel each other?"

[*That is already within you. We can reawaken it.*]

"In all of us?"

[*In all of you. Once the process is started, it will spread like bushfire. It will consume and renew you all.*]

"What if we resist?"

[*You cannot resist.*]

With that, the face snapped out of existence.

Max flicked on the walkie-talkie.

"This is Max calling Alice. Is the One-Mind still with you?"

"No, it simply disappeared a moment ago."

"It spoke to us. Did it say anything to you?"

"I think we may have both been somehow having the same conversation. It talked about the danger we represented to it and how it was going to help us feel each other, how we would all be consumed and renewed."

"Yep, that's what it told me too."

"Don't much like the 'consumed' bit and not entirely certain about the 'renewed' bit either."

"Agreed. Any ideas?"

"Fire the HARP and get the hell out of here?"

"Not our call."

Having listened in on the conversation between Alice and Max, Soames decided it was time for him to act.

"This is Director Soames. Please leave the area immediately. Alice, can you spread the word to your people, please?"

"Alice here. I will let them know. Give us half an hour."

"Roger that. Get to the extraction points. Go now."

Alice took up her bullroarer and began to twirl it in an odd, punctuated rhythm, louder and harder on the initial half of the beat, softer on the second half.

All around her, the people began to turn and walk away. In seconds there was no one to be seen but Alice.

"Tom and I are out of here," Max's voice came over the radio, "See you back at the base."

Over at the Table of the Gods, Harry Soames flicked open the cover to the HARP device and depressed the two red buttons. The small panel showing the timer clicked to [29:59] and began counting down.

"This is Director Harry Soames. The device timer has been initiated. Awaiting extraction, over."

After a moment, a new voice came over the radio.

"Roger that, Director. ETA ten minutes. Stand by."

"Standing by."

"Command Out."

Harry Soames dragged the device to the northern end of the flat rock surface and covered it and himself with the camouflage jacket. He brushed off any remaining ash and leaves and checked his watch. He switched on his location beacon and sat back to await the Ghost Hawk. This was not how Harry Soames, Director of Intelligence at the Centre for Disease Control, had ever imagined his life would end on a barren rock in the Australian wilderness in a life-and-death struggle with an ancient hidden race from a parallel universe. He stared at the HARP device, wishing that DARPA had offered at least some explanation of how it functioned. If he was going to die in some kind of psychic explosion, he at least wanted to understand how the damned thing worked. And then, intelligence professional to the bitter end, he found himself wondering why NASA and DARPA had created the wretched thing in the first place. What had prompted their fear of psychic attack by aliens? What sort of aliens? What kind of psychic attack? They must have had a reason. Something must have happened to justify the budget. If by some miracle he survived the next half hour, Harry Soames was determined to get some answers.

The remaining field operatives, Tom, Max, and Alice, struggled back to their respective extraction points and waited. They were exhausted and bewildered. What was the Wollemi One-Mind planning? What would happen when the HARP was triggered? What did 'no safe distance' mean? The intent they had all perceived in the Wollemi One-Mind was rigid, even relentless, but it was not merciless. Of one thing, they were now all certain. Whatever was about to happen was the fruition of a complex plan, patiently progressed and long, long in the making.

The little green light on their personal location beacons flashed reassuringly. From his vantage point, Tom could see Mount Yengo swathed in a gargantuan flock of birds circling slowly. The clouds were beginning to clear away, and the sun was coming out. A pall of smoke hung low over the hills and valleys surrounding the mountain, shrouding the Table of the Gods. Steam rose from the remaining hotspots in the enveloping forest. Tom checked the tell-tale on his satellite beacon. The little green light showed a steady glow. Someone had thoughtfully inserted new batteries. All set.

Tom called the Director, "This is Tom calling Director Soames. What's the timer showing? How long until the HARP goes off? Over."

A moment or two later, the Director's voice came back, "A bit less than twenty-five minutes." As the Director released the button on his walkie-talkie, he felt a kind of prickle run up his backbone. It was like he was being watched or perhaps searched for. He was sure of it, someone or something was approaching, with himself as its target.

Across the valley, on a flat rock above the river, Tom sat down to wait. From this raised position, he could see two tiny Ghost Hawks approaching on the north and south sides of the Mountain to pick them up. A few moments later, he saw the first of the choppers swoop away low, hugging the terrain as it headed back to Wisemans Ferry.

Automatically he ticked them off his checklist, *"Alice and Jerry had been picked up."*

The morning was heating up now that the sun had fully risen, and the weather had cleared. The smell of wood smoke still filled the air, permeating his clothes. The walkie-talkie at his waist burst into life. It was the Director.

"We may have a slight problem." Soames' sense of unease had worsened. Tom pressed the button to speak.

"What's up?"

"The One-Mind is here. It's looking for me, kind of sniffing me out."

"Do you have the camouflage jacket on?"

"Yes."

"Still your mind. Meditate. It can catch on to your thoughts."

"I'll give it my best shot."

"You can fire the HARP any time. Don't wait for the timer."

"Ok. Wish me luck."

The circuit went dead. Tom took out a small pair of binoculars and began scanning the distant mountain, looking for any sign of the Table of the Gods, the Wollemi, or the Director.

At first, there was nothing to see, the birds still circling the mountain obscured the view. After a while, with a bit of fiddling around, Tom managed to get a reasonably sharp image of the mountain. The image sharpened, and he was able to pick out a long flat segment about two-thirds of the way up the side. There was no sign whatever of the Director. Tom called the Wisemans Ferry Command Centre.

"This is Lieutenant Colonel Tom Olsen. Can you track Director Soames' PLB, please?"

"Certainly, Sir, Director Soames is still on the Table of the Gods at this time."

"Has he activated his beacon?"

"Negative."

"How are his life signs?"

"Life signs are all nominal. Blood pressure and pulse a bit high, but within range for field operations."

"Can you please keep a constant track of his life signs and let me know immediately if there is any significant change."

"Roger that, Sir."

"Can you get me a real-time satellite image of the Table of the Gods, please?"

"Yes, Sir, I can let you have the most recent photo and order another."

"Thanks, please send it to my phone. Olsen Out."

Tom checked his watch. Ten minutes since the timer on the HARP had been set, twenty to go. Once again, Tom sat back to wait.

A few minutes later, his phone pinged. There was a high-definition satellite image waiting for him. The mountain was shown in detail. The Table of the Gods was centred. There was a blurred image of something moving towards the centre. By switching wavelengths to infrared, Tom could pick out another image huddled at the edge of the rock. That had to be the Director. It was impossible to make out any details in the first image, but Tom had a strong hunch it had to be the only known photograph of the coalesced Wollemi One-Mind.

Over on the mountain, Director Soames had managed somewhat to still his thoughts. He could hear a kind of sniffling, snuffling sound as the One-Mind edged its way closer, feeling its way towards him across the blank expanse of stone. Minutes passed as the One-Mind made its way closer and closer.

Soames could also hear his heart pounding like a steam hammer and the to him deafening sound of the blood surging through his veins. Fearing what he might do if he fell under the One-Mind's influence, Soames came to a decision. The chopper was late. Almost without thinking, he snapped the dead-man's-switch into the body of the HARP device. If he was killed or removed from the device, it would detonate immediately. The tell-tale flashing of the timer showed less than ten minutes to go.

He removed the clear Perspex cover over the big red button. If it came to it, he would trigger the device himself. He was on his own, he realised. No one was coming for him now.

Tom's phone rang. It was the command centre.

"Director Soames has engaged the Deadman's switch. Command has aborted his extraction. We are sending a chopper for you and Dr Hexenkreige now. Over."

"Roger that. Lieutenant Colonel Olsen standing by." Tom gazed across the valley towards the Table of the Gods. He had only recently come to know Director Soames at all well, and while he liked and re-spected the man, the impression he had formed of him was not of a man of action but of a backroom pen pusher. This changed things. Harry Soames was sticking with the HARP device to the bitter end.

He turned up the collar on his camouflage jacket and took a mo-ment to stretch his legs before the extraction team arrived. Max sat silently nearby, surveying the scene. Something was very wrong. Max could feel it. Something terrible had happened.

Tom's phone pinged again. A new satellite image was available. This one showed a blurry silvery-grey man-like outline standing near the edge of the flat slab of rock. Switching to the infrared image, Tom could see that the One-Mind was standing immediately next to the Di-rector's position. He'd been seen.

Tom switched on the walkie-talkie, "Director, you've been spot-ted. The One-Mind is right next to you."

"Shit. I'm triggering the device manually right now. Get out of there if you can." Director Harry Soames hesitated for a split second, his finger hanging over the one big red button on the device console. Was he about to destroy an entire people? Was he about to wipe out our own ancient brothers and sisters? If the Wollemi One-Mind was unable to maintain the veil, how would it be able to assimilate the bil-lions of individually conscious human beings now populating the Earth? Harry Soames understood his responsibility. He knew his duty. This, he thought, was perhaps the essence of the human condition, the need to make irretrievable decisions based upon inadequate knowledge and incomplete information.

"To hell with it," setting all his doubts to one side, Director Harry Soames triggered the HARP device. As one chubby, well-manicured finger pressed down upon the big red button, the gates of hell opened. Or so it appeared.

Harry sat back, the deed done, amazed that he was still alive and quite overwhelmed by a tidal wave of relief. He had done it. He had not frozen in fear. He had not turned tail and run away. He had been called upon to act and had not been found wanting. The feeling of release washed over and through him in a liberating torrent. For a moment, Harry Soames wanted nothing more than to burst into song. He had faced his demon. He had overcome the fiend hiding within the complex folds of his psyche. He was finally, strangely, at peace with himself. He was free.

Away across the forest, a Ghost Hawk swooped in towards the extraction point as mayhem and chaos erupted from the Table of the Gods. Tom and Max raced across the relatively flat surface towards the hovering chopper. As they clambered aboard, Max's foot slipped from the runner. Max fell back into the long grass. The chopper began to lift away.

'Wait! Max isn't on board.' Tom, who had one foot on the running board, jumped down from the chopper and grabbed the older man. As he did so, the chopper lurched to one side, caught by a sudden gust of wind. Tom fell backwards heavily, momentarily knocking the air from his lungs, leaving him floundering breathless. He managed to get to his feet. Both men chased after the chopper as it slid sideways away from them in the strong breeze. Glancing back towards Mount Yengo, Tom could see a growing ball of dazzling plasma spreading from the Director's position, swallowing the Table of the Gods, Soames, the One-Mind and much of the surrounding mountainside within its spreading shroud.

They leapt aboard the chopper as it swung off high and fast directly away from the mountain.

The chopper sped away. Tom turned and aimed his binoculars back at the mountain. As the helicopter headed for safety, Tom could see the power of the HARP. He could see the massive cloud of unknown psychic energy roll and spread across the forest. Blue light snapped across the sky, coming from the Table of the Gods. Instantaneously the plasma field generated by the HARP device merged with the raw psychic energy of the Wollemi One-Mind, now fully formed, including all Wollemi, everywhere. The plasma field grew explosively. Tom once again strained to see through his binoculars, but the chopper was by now too far away and moving too fast to focus. He needn't have bothered. The growing cloud of plasma could be seen quite clearly with the naked eye, a gargantuan fog of blue lightning rolling down the mountainside and across the surrounding forest.

Tom's phone rang. It was the Command Centre, "Director Soames is alive and conscious. Thought you would want to know."

"Thanks. Keep monitoring and have an extraction team on standby."

"Already on standby, Sir. Command out."

On Mount Yengo, things were hotting up. The growing ball of plasma continued to plunge down the sides of the mountain engulfing all in its path, and an ominous mushroom cloud was growing above it, high into the sky, swallowing the mountain's wreath of birds, growing, and flattening like an anvil beneath the hammer of heaven. The effect was like a slow-motion volcano of glowing blue plasma. The circulating murmuration of birds flickered and glowed. Tiny filaments of energy sparkled from bird to bird, creating and connecting a vast spider web of energy weaving and whirling around them. A web of life.

As Tom watched, the web spread further and further across the forest, shimmering and radiant out to the horizon as far as the eye could see in any direction. Growing and proliferating as it went.

On the Table of the Gods, the Wollemi One-Mind spoke.

[I see you, Director. I feel your thoughts and emotions. I, too, hear your heart pounding like a hammer. The sound of the blood surging through your veins is deafening to me too.]

"What do you want?"

[You have already given me what I want, Director.]

"And what was that?"

[The product of all your science and engineering, the outcome of fourteen thousand years of reason. You have given me the power to reconnect your people to the web of life. Not enough to cure you completely. I'm not sure if that was ever in our power, but possibly enough to let your healing begin.]

"The HARP device?"

[Indeed, wonderfully ironic and, at the same time, curiously apt nomenclature, wouldn't you agree?]

The Director laughed grimly at that, acknowledging the humour. "What now?"

[Now we need to hold off your military and their Plan B.]

"You know about that?"

[We have been listening to you and witnessing the evolution of your 'reason' for nearly seven hundred generations. We know the military will always have a Plan B. Your minds are open to me now. I can hear your general's thoughts.]

"And?"

[He is afraid. He is deciding whether or not to stop the attack.]

"Can you close the veil and keep it closed?"

[Yes. I believe we can now.]

"How can I be sure? How can I believe you?"

[Shall I open my mind to you, Director? Would you like to see for yourself?] Without waiting for a response, the Wollemi One-Mind connected telepathically with Director Soames. Their thoughts merged and entwined. For one brief moment, the Director's consciousness and that of the colossal, massively parallel, composite mind of the

Wollemi were one. The Director glimpsed mind upon mind, sharing, combining, thousands upon hundreds of thousands, ultimately millions of thoughts coalescing to create the monolithic intellect that was the Wollemi One-Mind. For a moment, he saw what the One-Mind saw, he thought what the One-Mind thought, and he understood what the One-Mind understood. And then suddenly, he felt a gut-wrenching, hideous emptiness and silence. The One-Mind was gone. The connection was gone. He was alone.

[*Will you call your General, please, Director?*]

Harry Soames stared at the endless spreading filigree of the web of life, understanding at last what had been lost. Knowing, as no man had known in seven hundred generations, what had been abandoned in the search for reason. Director Harry Soames, perhaps the first man since Adam to stand before a being immeasurably greater than himself and wonder, "*What have we done?*"

"Why can't you just reach into his mind?"

[*We are repairing the web of life. We are reintegrating you, humans, into the very womb of life, not just here, around the mountain, but everywhere, all over the world.*]

"Really, you have the power of a God, and you need me to make a call on my cell phone?"

[*When the energy reaches Canberra and the web is rebuilt, your General will know. There will be no need for words.*]

"Until then?"

[*Until then, he is one human man, like you, saddled with grave responsibility for his species, frightened and alone, and, as men have done since the beginning, he is trying to align his reason with his conscience.*]

"Which way will he go?"

[*Experience suggests that the incomplete and fractured nature of human knowledge pushes your people to err on the side of caution.*]

"He'll go with reason and initiate Plan B?"

[*Yes.*]

The Director thought for a moment. What if this were a trap? What if he had been assimilated by the Mind and his incredible experience of oneness had been an illusion? No, that was impossible. Nothing could create so complete and compelling a delusion. As if in answer to Harry's unasked question, the Wollemi One-Mind spoke.

[*I am not God, Harry. I am not even a God. I have been the steward of this tiny little particle of creation. It's your turn now, you humans.*]

"I'll make the call." Harry retrieved his phone from his pocket.

"This is Director Harry Soames. I have concluded an agreement with the One-Mind to close the veil permanently. Over." There was a short delay before a response came.

"Director Soames, good to hear from you. You had us worried." It was not a voice the Director recognised.

"No need to worry. We have what we need. Requesting immediate extraction over."

"We detected something like an explosion at your position. What happened?"

"I accidentally triggered the, err…, HARP device. That created an electromagnetic pulse. That's probably what you detected. Over."

"We're sending a chopper over to take a look, Director. Stand by."

They weren't buying it. The Director suspected that Plan B must have been initiated. His only hope was to convince Command that all was well.

"It's all good here, guys. I need to get back to HQ."

"Roger that, Director. We'll have someone with you momentarily."

[*They have initiated their Plan B.*] Harry could hear the soundless voice of the Wollemi in his mind.

"Can you stop it?"

[*I don't know. I can try.*]

The whirling, swooping flock of birds that had shrouded the mountain so closely suddenly lifted and wheeled as one, turning in the direction of Wisemans Ferry.

Faint and far off, Harry could hear the sound of helicopter engines. Not just one but many. Far away on the horizon, he could make out the distant shapes of perhaps a dozen Black Hawk Helicopters heading towards them in close formation.

"Abort the attack." Harry held the walkie-talkie close to his mouth, almost whispering, "Abort. We have an agreement." There was no reply, just the static hiss of background radiation and the screech of the birds as they circled, now high over the mountain. The sound of the rotors grew louder as the helicopters approached.

"They can't hear you, Sir," Tom Olsen's voice could be heard over the growing sound of the approaching fleet, "or they have orders from the Pentagon not to abort."

The General came on the radio.

"What is your status, Director?"

"I am with the Wollemi One-Mind. It has agreed to close the veil permanently. The HARP has given it the necessary energy to lock and seal the shield, Sir." The sound of the approaching helicopters now all but drowned out radio communications.

"Take cover, Director. There's nothing more I can do. Tom, get the hell out of there."

"Is there anything you can do?" Harry turned to the Wollemi One-Mind. The One-Mind reached out his silvery hand towards Harry, a thin lacelike tracery of light flickered between them. The Web of Life sputtered and glinted. The connection was complete.

[*The birds.*] The Wollemi sounded wistful, almost sad, [*We must send in the birds.*]

Harry nodded, whatever had sparked across from the One-Mind now providing a whole new sense, a whole new form of perception. Harry could feel for and in himself the love and sacrifice of life.

[*Many will die.*] The OneMind was matter of fact.

"Will they be enough?"

[*That is in the hands of fate.*]

Harry watched as the helicopters approached. For the briefest moment, Harry considered calling them, warning them about the birds, but he had made his choice. Perhaps for the first time ever, he was at peace with life and death. The choppers approached in tight formation. The raging sound of their engines tore across the forest, drowning out the cries of the birds. As the helicopters began to break formation, preparing their final attack vectors, the Wollemi One-Mind gave its order. The huge flock of birds broke into a dozen swirling streamers of colour and noise, spiralling down towards the oncoming choppers. The birds slammed into them in their hundreds and thousands. Rotors ripped their fragile bodies into a rain of blood and feathers. Birds were sucked into the air intakes, clogging the engines, shutting them down. Some of the helicopters opened fire. A couple managed to get off a missile or two. None were able to deploy the barrel-shaped mother-of-all bombs hanging beneath them. As the choppers fell from the sky, the web of life reached across, leaping from the living birds to the crews. Director Harry Soames felt the snap of connection and belonging as the men rejoined, in their final moments, the network of living beings from which they had, for their entire lives, been sundered. He felt their sudden joy and understanding as well as their fear as they fell to their deaths. He felt their sudden silence. The absence as they died. Soames turned to the Wollemi One-Mind once more.

"Do you believe in God?" He asked.

The Wollemi One-Mind was silent for a long time. Then it turned and floated closer. The face of the Wollemi creased and frowned.

[*We have never encountered a creator face to face. No evidence of a supreme being as such.*" There was a short pause, and then, *"Other than the manifest creation all around us.*]

The Director took a moment to process this new information. He could feel that what had been said was the truth as the Wollemi One-

Mind saw it. He did not know. He could not immediately assess his own reaction to that.

[*It is ironic, is it, not Director, that it is you, the hunters after reason and understanding, who stick so tenaciously to the concept of a deity.*]

"I guess."

[*We, who live in the moment, have no such need.*]

The wreath of birds had dispersed. The sun was setting, and the long orange glow of sunset was beginning to light the clouds on the far horizon from below. A warm red and purple glimmer dusted the lower edges of the clouds. The scene, as Director Harry Soames gazed out over the vast Wollemi Forest, was now peaceful and serene.

The walkie-talkie on his wrist crackled to life. It was Tom Olsen.

"Tom here, Director. We're coming back for you. Extraction in two minutes. Over."

"Roger that, Tom." Director Soames stood and stretched. Life was good. And then, at the very edge of hearing, there was a sound. The distant whine of a missile-engine closing in. One last weapon, fired in the dying moments of the final skirmish between human and Wollemi, was headed his way. Harry looked up. There was a flicker of movement against the sunset. Turning his head towards the sound, Director Soames just had time to identify the arrow shape of an incoming air-to-land missile. One last act of destruction, one last act of unreason. Still, he had fulfilled his purpose.

"So, this is where it ends…" A moment later, Harry Soames and the HARP were vaporised. Debris from the explosion pattered down onto the Table of the Gods.

WHAT JUST HAPPENED?

Those who had so far made it back from the forest, stunned and bedraggled, met back on the deck of the Wisemans Ferry Inn. Alice had taken Max to one side to pass on the tragic news of his son's death.

There was silence, to begin with, and occasional brief glances. No one wanted to speak. The maelstrom of emotion swirling around them was totally new to their perception and, in truth, somewhat unwelcome. The awful news of Jerry and Harry Soames's deaths had hit them all hard. At last, Alice Whalebone cleared her throat.

"I need to tell you all about something that happened to me today." Still, no one spoke.

"What I am about to tell you will seem strange, even delusional." She paused.

"I had a direct conversation with the One-Mind." Silence reigned. She had their attention.

"The One-Mind wanted me to know, wanted us all to know, what was happening, and why." Alice stared around at the faces of her colleagues, and friends.

"The One-Mind planted these words in my mind." Alice unconsciously adopted the stance of a teacher as she spoke.

[*This is my confession if it is a confession. Centuries ago, I closed the veil, shutting you humans out. I had to do it. Your individual dreaming was destructive to the collective. Each individual sentience demanded to understand, if not of the whole, then at least the parts. Through reason, you developed knowledge and skills, but you lost the ability to simply 'know' through the collective. Your understanding was partial and incomplete. Without belonging to the collective, you scattered and were lost.*] Alice paused, tears running down her cheek.

"I felt its sadness and loss. I felt its terrible sense of regret." Pulling herself together, she continued.

[You rose up against the will of the collective and were cast out. And there I left it for a long, long time.

What met my consciousness when I passed beyond the veil came as my first new realisation in over ten thousand years. You had thrived in your isolation. Your numbers had now grown beyond counting. As had your ingenuity and creativity. Your world was covered with the marks of your occupancy. There were 'things' everywhere, artefacts of all kinds. For the first time in my long, long memory, I found myself out of my depth. I was uncertain, and I felt at risk. Now it was I who did not understand. I began to fear our human children.

I slipped beyond the veil often in every part of the globe. I passed amongst you unnoticed, visiting your cities, soaking up your thoughts and dreams, and gaining an understanding. There was revulsion and disgust. I could not comprehend your lust for battle and for blood, and I was overwhelmed by the scope and breadth of human imagination.

I faced the limits of my own abilities. I saw that you could imagine what I could not and could achieve things that I could not. I realised that I had no authority over you. You had long since forgotten who or what I was, what we were. I feared our immanent presence might trigger a terrible reaction. I had forced you from our garden once. I dared not use force a second time.

I began to search for a way in which you might truly belong to the world as we belonged. And so began my greatest ever project, to reclaim our lost children.]

Alice fell silent. Recounting the One-Mind's words seemed to have left her exhausted. She looked into the eyes of her audience.

"That's it. I don't know what will happen now."

EPILOGUE

Jack, Kaitlin, and Emma had woken on a muddy hillside to the sound of choppers circling overhead. The journey back to Wisemans Ferry took only a few minutes. As the chopper circled, preparing to land, they could see that the military encampment had grown even further in only one day. Inevitably, the military had expanded to fill what it saw as a vacuum. Private backyards and back lanes were now taken up with tents, trailers, or military vehicles. Half a dozen large barges had been moored in the river, one of which had been fitted out as a helicopter landing pad. The chopper headed for it, and in moments they were walking over a pontoon bridge and found themselves back on *terra firma.*

They were guided back up to the Wisemans Ferry Retreat, which had been commandeered as military headquarters. There was some consternation and resistance at first when Jack and Kaitlin attempted to keep Emma with them. The impasse was only finally broken when Emma piped up. 'I am Emma Hexenkriege, I have been a critical part of the Wollemi composite mind and I have important information to share.'

The harassed-looking Captain simply added her name by hand to a long list attached to his clipboard, and they were in. They were ushered into the same old conference room that Jack and Kaitlin had met in before. What now met their eyes, however, was very different. The whole of the far wall had been taken up with an enormous composite screen showing people sitting in similar rooms. From the changes in décor, uniforms, and lighting and from glimpses of the world beyond their windows, there appeared to be representatives from all around the world. No one was speaking. Everyone appeared to be waiting for something.

The three latecomers managed to find seats in the row behind Tom and the rest of their team. There followed a swift and discrete exchange of welcomes and hugs. Tom leaned over to give the new arrivals the sad news.

"Jack, Kaitlin, I am so sorry to have to tell you; Jerry and Director Soames didn't make it."

Jack remained silent, trying to take in the terrible news. Kaitlin let out an involuntary cry. Harry Soames, dead? It couldn't be. Some mistake perhaps. It was too awful. And Jerry too. She could still hear their voices. She could still play back in her mind Jerry's cajoling ways. She put an arm around Jack's neck and wrapped her other arm around Emma. Holding them close.

"I'm so sorry, my love."

Emma was crying gently, her own feelings of sadness and loss merging with the unavoidable flood of emotion coming from those around her.

"Jerry was like a second dad to me," speaking very quietly, she continued, "and poor Fiona. What will she do?" Jack reached out and pulled Emma in to sit between him and Kaitlin. She had grown, he realised she was not the same little girl she had been. They had all changed. No one was the same. Jack made to speak but was cut off. There was a commotion on the screens at the end of the room. Tom turned again, updating the latecomers.

"Ok. The World Health Organisation has taken the lead on this. It's being treated as a health issue rather than a security issue, much to the irritation of my bosses. We are all waiting for the bigwigs in Geneva to start the meeting, so you are just in time. Our team is here to answer questions, not as observers but not as decision-makers either – that has been made very clear to us. The Centre for Disease Control will end up executing the plan, whatever it is, once it's agreed. Welcome home, by the way." Tom turned to Emma and offered his hand, "Hi Emma, I'm Tom Olsen. Good to finally meet you."

"Nice to meet you too." Emma gave the military man a smile. The best she could do in the circumstances. The events of the last few weeks, including close participation in the Wollemi One-Mind, had left

Emma a little wiser, perhaps, but emotionally raw. Lieutenant Colonel Tom Olsen slumped back in his chair, trying to block the uncensored emotion emanating from the girl, concentrating intently on the screen at the end of the room.

The giant screen flickered, and the previous photomontage of offices and conference rooms was replaced with a view of an enormous cream and brown conference hall sporting an outsized round table, surrounded by anxious-looking people slouched in enormous pale blue chairs. The meeting proper was about to start.

As if on some pre-agreed signal, the delegates of over thirty countries approached the round table and took their seats. A tall, wiry woman in a dark blue pinstripe trouser suit stood at what was, in effect, the head of the table.

The screen focused on her as she began to speak.

"Distinguished members of the World Health Organisation Council honoured guests, observers, and advisors. I will attempt to keep my opening remarks brief.

All the nations and governments you represent have been affected by this sudden global epidemic. I do not hesitate to use the term epidemic since the scope of those affected appears to be global. We are all affected. The outbreak we speak of has no precedent in human history. As far as we know, it is not a virus, it is not bacterial in origin, and it is not immediately harmful. We do not know exactly what we are dealing with, and we do not know if there are, or even could be, precautions we can take.

The World Health Organisation has successfully managed many large-scale outbreaks over the years, but this event is very different. This is either the greatest peacetime challenge that the United Nations and its agencies have ever faced, or it is a unique transitional and transformative event in human history. It is either a healthcare issue of seismic proportions or an evolutionary event of unknown significance.

Not one of us experienced in containing outbreaks has ever seen an event, perhaps an emergency, on this scale, propagated so quickly, with a one hundred per cent infection rate, or with this magnitude of potential cascading consequences. The truth is we don't know if this is a public health crisis, a social crisis, or a humanitarian crisis, indeed, if this is a crisis at all.

For these reasons, I am calling for a UN-wide initiative that draws together all the assets of all relevant UN agencies. Everything now is "unprecedented". Everything now is happening faster than ever before.

The outbreak cannot be contained. Quarantine is not an issue as we are all, to use a highly value-laden term, infected. Government entities supported by the Centre for Disease Control, Médecins Sans Frontières, and the World Health Organisation stand ready to respond immediately with the right emergency actions if and when viable responses are identified.

This meeting is our first opportunity to obtain feedback from around the world and to hear from our many experts and thought leaders. I declare the floor open. Thank you."

In response, there was a deafening silence both from the delegates sitting around the table and from those distributed around the world. No one wanted to speak. No one wanted to leap into the gaping policy void so eloquently exposed by none less than the Director-General of the World Health Organisation herself.

After a moment or two, an official presented a slide containing key questions requiring answers and calling for contributions.

"Delegates and subject matter experts may wish to focus on the following points, to begin with, before slouching back down into his chair.

The slide read:
1. Where did the epidemic come from?
2. What is this an epidemic of, i.e., what is it that is being spread?
3. What are the health, social and security implications?
4. What policy responses are required?

After an extended silence, Lieutenant Colonel Tom Olsen clicked the button on his conference pad, indicating that he had a contribution to make.

A moment or two passed before he was invited to speak. His image on the screen replaced that of the conference hall. Tom glanced around at what was left of the team. This was it.

"Madame Director General, esteemed delegates, colleagues. For those who do not know me, I am Lieutenant Colonel Tom Olsen, CDC/NASA liaison officer. I can provide some background information on an ongoing research project spanning several decades, which has a bearing on recent events.

Please bear with me while I set out the little that we do know from our research. Delegates will be aware that all human cultures have foundation myths and legends which speak of a magical world hidden in some way from our everyday experience and which tell tales of the inhabitants of that hidden world. Each language has a name for these hidden people. In English, we speak of fairies and elves, the Japanese speak of the Kami, the Germans of die Elfen, the French of la fée, and the Indigenous Australian Aboriginal people speak of the Dreamtime, or more accurately, the Dreaming, and so on. The research I speak of searches for any potential truth underlying these myths. In recent months we have begun to gather documentary evidence supporting the existence of another plane of existence populated by people similar to ourselves. Our working name for these people is 'the Wollemi'."

Lieutenant Colonel Tom paused at this point to allow for comments and questions. It was just as well that he did. The tell-tale on the bottom of the screen indicated that the number of people waiting to speak had jumped from two or three to over a hundred in moments. The system immediately became jammed. Technicians could be seen gathering around the communications console situated in the otherwise empty space at the centre of the conference table in Geneva. Delegates began leaning over to speak directly with their nearest neighbours. For several minutes a silent pandemonium played out on the screen. As the hubbub calmed down, the Director-General spoke.

"Lieutenant Colonel, these are significant claims. We appreciate your frankness in bringing your evidence to our attention. Please go on. We will take questions and comments later."

"Thank you, Madame Director General." Tom pushed a button on his conference pad. On the screen, a presentation appeared.

"This photograph was taken in the last ten days," Tom explained, "what you are seeing is the juxtaposition of our plane of existence, our world if you like, with that of a parallel world. Since this picture was taken in Australia, and in the absence of any better nomenclature, I will refer to what it shows as 'The Dreamtime'." Tom paused once more. This time there were no questions.

"The picture shows a tunnel cut into what appears to be limestone, with hand-carved steps leading up and out of shot. On the lower steps, you will see what looks like a girl or young woman carrying a reed basket." Tom paused for a moment before continuing.

"This scene was photographed by government researchers. What you see here appeared or manifested itself in front of them. It was as though a veil or curtain had been pulled back to reveal another world."

Tom looked up, speaking directly to camera.

"A dossier of photographs and explanation has been placed in the WHO library and is now available to delegates. I will attempt to summarise events from the taking of that photograph up until the global event introduced by the Director-General." Tom paused to allow for comments. Again, there were none.

"These events took place in Australia, in a wilderness area near the city of Sydney which includes both the Wollemi and Yengo National Parks. Some of you may recall that a number of years ago, a species of pine tree previously thought to have been extinct for over two hundred million years was discovered alive and well within the confines of the Wollemi Forest. Delegates will no doubt wonder, as we at the CDC did if the pines survived in secret for so long, what else might be out there?"

Tom pressed the button once more, and a satellite map appeared of the wilderness with Mount Yengo clearly marked.

"Our research revealed the following information. First, there is a barrier, shield or veil between our plane and the Dreamtime plane, which serves to maintain separation between the two. When the barrier is very weak, it is possible for people and animals from either plane to pass through to the other.

Second, weak points have been appearing in this barrier, with increasing frequency, not just in the Wollemi wilderness but more generally in wilderness areas around the world.

Third, the species, I prefer the word 'people', who live on the other side of the barrier appear in many ways to be very similar to ourselves. They appear to be human or very close to it. They have intelligence, though we do not know exactly to what level. It is also probably worth calling out at this point that from what we've seen, their level of technology and technical know-how generally is less advanced than our own. If I had to guess, I would estimate their technology as approximately equivalent to that of the European bronze age."

Tom paused for that to sink in. These people were not a technological or military threat.

"Finally, we believe that the barrier between our planes of existence is now permanently closed. We believe that the closing of the barrier and the recent epidemic-like event are somehow connected. Lastly, we believe that the epidemic-like event has now run its course." Tom paused, "I would now like to introduce a senior researcher at the CDC, Doctor Kaitlin O'Neill, who will provide you with a more detailed look at their psychology and mental capabilities."

Kaitlin stared at Tom for a full minute in total disbelief at her sudden and unexpected introduction before turning to speak directly to camera. As Jack and the team watched Kaitlin, a minor transformation took place. She squared her shoulders and stood tall. Pulling a small moleskin notebook from her jacket, she began to speak.

"Madame Director-General, esteemed delegates, colleagues, please forgive my appearance. I have returned only moments ago from the very centre of the transformative events we are gathered here to discuss. I will be referring extensively to unedited hand-written notes taken in the field. I trust you will bear with me as I decipher my own handwriting." Kaitlin flicked through the notebook to a specific page. But before she could continue, as though on a signal, Emma lurched to her feet and spoke.

"My name is Emma Hexenkriege. I am genetically one-quarter Wollemi. Until last night I was an integral part of the Wollemi One-Mind, the most complete expression of the will and purpose of all Wollemi everywhere. It was the One-Mind that initiated the bio-ecological chain reaction that is being described here as a potential epidemic. I have a message for you from the One-Mind." Emma paused as Kaitlin had done to allow the import of her words to sink in.

"Over fourteen thousand five hundred years ago, our species separated into two. This separation was triggered by climate change which occurred at the end of an age of ice. Scarcity of food and other resources produced a period of rapid evolution within a segment of our population, resulting in the growth of a significant minority whose individual mental processes were toxic to the larger population. The original and larger group enjoyed a telepathic consciousness and communion. The newly evolved group were no longer telepaths but enjoyed individual consciousness and reason which was psychically disturbing to the communion. In order to protect itself and to provide a world in which our individually conscious children could grow and prosper, the larger group brought down a barrier between our world and the world occupied by our incompatible children.

To begin with, we hoped to cure our children, but we have now realised that you were not sick but disconnected. After long years of planning, last evening, we triggered a self-sustaining global chain reaction that once again joined all humans into the web of life. The change that we have triggered will make it possible for each and every human to feel connected with the plants and animals and with each other and also, at long last, to feel a sense of belonging. From this moment on, all humans will be empaths. You will directly perceive the feelings of all living things. We have now permanently closed the portal between our two planes of existence. We wish you well." And with that, Emma Hexenkriege sat back down.

For nearly a minute, there was total silence, and then, for a little while, there was total chaos.

THE END